THE STREET RAT'S GUIDE
TO SPELLS AND ROYALTY

L.R. Weltmann

Our Corner Publishing

To request permissions, contact Our Corner Publishing at info@ourcornerpublishing.com

First Edition

Design by Matcha Mochi | matchamochidesign@gmail.com
Cover Art by LR Weltmann

979-8-9863336-4-9

www.ourcornerpublishing.com
www.lydiaweltmann.com

TABLE OF CONTENTS

CHAPTER 1

This was the apple's fault.

I flailed my way to the river surface with a large gasp, bruised apple clutched in my right hand. I stood a better chance at swimming with both hands, but no way was I letting go of the apple now. It was the fruit's fault I was in this mess.

Okay, technically, stealing the apple might have started the chase, leading to the guards cornering me on the bridge. Which led to me jumping off the bridge to escape.

Admittedly, not my best plan. I regretted the choice the second I sank into the icy river and remembered two very important things.

One: It was March and the river was freezing.

Two: I didn't know how to swim.

Getting arrested didn't sound so bad anymore.

If there'd been no apple, I wouldn't have stolen it. Therefore, this was the apple's fault.

It was going to taste delicious when I finally had a chance to eat it.

"Get back here you filthy street rat!" The guards on the bridge shouted. Guards might mean safety and protection for everyone else, but they meant danger to street rats and other scum like me. If no one important would miss you, being arrested was code for 'Ship them off to the King's Airforce where they'll never be heard from again.' I needed to get back on land if I didn't want them to corner me.

Ha. As if I could control where I went in the water. It was all I could do to keep my head above the surface. Walls on the riverbank kept the waters from flooding the streets when it rained, but it also kept dumb people like me from easily drifting to safety. All the gears and bits I kept in my pockets didn't help, not to mention the wrench dangling from my belt.

New priority: Don't drown. Even if they did pull me out of the river and take me to the guardhouse, I could probably escape before they got there. I'd done it before.

Or, if I could maneuver myself through the water, I could reach the waterwheel coming up. Similar wheels lined river, powering many of the city's factories.

It was a dumb plan. Jade would skin me alive if she knew what I was about to do. But with all the other stupid stuff I'd done that day alone, what difference would one more make?

"Please let this work," I muttered, praying to some deity I didn't believe in.

The waterwheel turned lazily. It was easy enough to grab one of the spokes and let it pull me along a few feet. It was much harder to hold on when the spoke started rising into the air.

I jammed the apple in my mouth to free up my other hand and hooked my feet onto whatever holds I could find.

"Hey, what do you think you're doing?" one of the guards yelled.

I spared a moment to raise my middle finger at them. That was all the time I had, because now the real challenge began. I had to climb on top of the water wheel, while it was moving, and then figure out a way down.

One of the benefits of this water wheel was that the attached cotton factory came right up to the river, so the guards had no direct access to me.

That was the only benefit.

The wheel continued to turn. I struggled to keep my grip and keep climbing. My boots slipped off the bar and I dangled from my hands, barely holding on when the rotation dunked me into the water.

I almost lost the apple.

King's bloody beard. I hated water.

I wasn't sure how I managed to get on top. Most, if not all, of my effort was pure spite.

Staying on the wheel? That was more of a challenge than getting up there had been. I had to hold onto the sides and continuously crawl, and I had to pray I didn't slip. Nothing was dry.

"Where are you going to go now, Ace?" a guard yelled. He peered around the corner of the factory. Another guard leaned around the front corner. This one in particular had been chasing me for years, but I didn't know when he'd learned my name.

I shook my head, both at myself and at the guards. I was an idiot for more than one reason, but the guards weren't much better. They'd been chasing me around this city for almost a decade, and they still thought they'd cornered me. I'd been willing to jump off a bridge, despite not knowing how to swim, and I wasn't out of tricks yet.

I couldn't go down, and they'd blocked either side. The only place left was up.

The window about five feet above the wheel was easy enough to jump to. My fingers hooked onto the ledge, and I braced my feet against the wall.

With a lot of cursing and aching muscles, I grabbed onto the top ledge of the window and rested my feet on the bottom ledge. A careful leap, and now I dangled from the edge of the roof. Hauling myself onto the shingles with trembling arms, I finally had a chance to take a victory bite of my prize.

9

The apple tasted like the river, which was disappointing. But I ate it anyway, because I had not done all that work for nothing.

I ate as I walked, crossing the top of the roof like a tightrope. The barest breeze went right through my river drenched clothes, and I shivered.

I jumped to another roof, and then up to another, dodging around crooked chimneys and their steam clouds. A few streets over, the clock tower jutted into the skyline, and I used it to orient myself. I finished the apple, core and all, and tossed the stem to the ground below.

With both hands free, my progress picked up considerably. Just in time, too, because the guards had finally unmoored their steamcycles.

Small and agile, steamcycles were only big enough for one or two passengers. Unlike steamcars, riders had to straddle the engine in steamcycles and risk burning their calves on the copper pipes connected to the pistons mounted on the back half. Without the extra weight of a full cab, steamcycles could fly faster and higher.

Four steamcycles popped up over the roofs, the guards crouched low over the steering wheels, goggles lowered from their dark blue caps to cover their eyes.

Like this, they would catch me easily. I couldn't outrun steamcycles over the rooftops.

So, I dropped back down to the ground, using a restaurant's hanging sign to swing safely to the cobblestone.

A few people screamed at my sudden appearance. One recognized my bright red hair and made a grab for me, but I ducked and sprinted down the street. I passed a newsboy and plucked the boy's cap right off his head, setting it on my own in one smooth motion. That would hide my cursed hair, at least. I was far less noticeable when people couldn't see the unusual color.

The damp clothes gave me away for a while, but I knew the streets better than the guards ever would. I charged up the steps outside the hatmaker's shop onto Rowan Boulevard, weaved through a crowd listening to a Chimer yell about revolution, and slipped into the alley between the best baker in town and the meanest butcher.

The clock in the central square chimed seven times.

I rounded the corner out of the alley and collided with someone, sending us both to the ground.

"You clumsy oaf!" the man yelled.

"Sorry, sir," I said. I jumped to my feet and helped the older man up. Better to play the apologetic kid than make the man even angrier. "Late for dinner, Ma's probably worried sick, you know."

"That doesn't excuse you," the man snapped. He had a narrow face and arched brows, and his clothes looked personally tailored. Black boots shone on the cobblestones, neatly laced, and his coat sleeves ended perfectly at his wrists.

I helped myself to the man's pockets while brushing him off, slipping a heavy wallet under my stained shirt.

"I'll be more careful, sir," I promised.

"See that you do," the man said, glaring.

I picked up his top hat. Bronze goggles sat around the base. He must use steamcars a lot to be willing to spring for such a nice set. I held out the hat for him.

The man hesitated before taking it, staring at me with narrowed eyes.

"Um…sir?" I prompted. The man didn't know I had pickpocketed him, did he? That was always awkward. Plus, I didn't know if I was up for another chase through the city.

The man reached his hand out. Instead of taking his own hat, he grabbed the newsboy cap I had just stolen. "I knew it."

"Hey! Give that back!" I may have only had the hat for five minutes, but I was rather attached to it already.

"You're coming with me," the man said, trying to grab my arm.

11

I danced out of the way. "Not a chance in hell." Still holding his top hat, I bolted. The man could keep the newsboy cap. This hat and the goggles would pay for a weeks' worth of meals. Not to mention whatever was in the wallet I'd nabbed. I might even be able to afford my own decent coat for once.

A hand grabbed my shoulder. "You're not getting away so easily, not this time."

This time? I'd never met this man in my life. I'd remember running into someone this wealthy.

"You've got the wrong guy," I told him, twisting out of his grasp.

"Oh no, you're definitely the one," he said.

He reached for me again.

A fox jumped down from a windowsill, landing perfectly on the gentleman and knocking him into the street.

"Nice save, Sel!" I cheered, already running away.

Sel bounded after me and overtook me, leading me around a corner. I knew he would lead me to safety. He always did, ever since I shared a meat pie with him as a kid.

I didn't know where Sel lived most of the time, but he always appeared when I needed help. His fur was a strange mossy green color, and a gold collar hung around his neck. Some rich person probably didn't keep a close eye on him one day, and now Sel roamed the city as a free fox.

In a way, he was a street rat just like me.

CHAPTER 2

My magic lesson ended with me in a bush.

"Jack!"

"Your Highness!"

The first person had been my mother, the queen and my spellcasting tutor. The second had been my personal guard, Lucas. Both voices were muffled by the dense shrubbery around me.

"Here!" I yelled back. Moving on my own did little good. I was half in the bush, legs flailing wildly in the open air. A branch poked my back, and another scratched my cheek. Something tore when I wiggled, and I sighed. Mother would not be happy if I'd ruined another pair of pants.

Hands wrapped around my ankles. "Don't worry, your Highness, I've got you," Lucas said.

"Wait a moment," Mother said.

The leaves rustled and shifted around me, creating a gap Lucas could drag me out of. When I was back on the ground, Mother released her spell and the branches shifted back to their natural state. There was no evidence I'd just been part of the hedge that surrounded the garden. We were in the center of a small maze of hedges and flower beds, one of the most private spots on the palace grounds, and therefore ideal for learning secret magic.

Mother appeared in front of me, hands on my face, on my shoulders, over my front. "Are you alright? Where are you hurt?"

Lucas and my mother's two guards were close at hand, but they relaxed when they saw no injuries.

"I'm fine," I laughed, pushing her hands away. "Just scratches, I promise."

"You don't feel dizzy? No aftereffects from the spell going wrong?" she questioned. Her eyes scrunched in doubt, and she cocked her head. Her red hair stayed perfectly around her face, not a strand out of place.

"Nothing," I promised. The spell hadn't gone that wrong. I just… overshot my target, a little. Instead of transporting to the edge of the clearing, I'd ended up in the surrounding hedge. I doublechecked my pocket watch, brushing off some dirt from the palladium plating and flipping open the case. There was only one hand, pointing to the three. A typical position for the end of my magic lessons.

Mother breathed a sigh of relief and her shoulders sagged. She was a worrier. The slightest hint of danger to me had her overreacting.

"Maybe we should push back your trip tomorrow, just in case," she said.

"What?" Now I felt sick to my stomach. Snapping the watch cover shut, I shoved it back in my pocket. "No, I'm fine, please don't do that." I'd been looking forward to going to town for weeks.

"Your Majesty," Lucas intervened, putting a hand on my shoulder. Lucas was almost a full head taller than me, and about as thick as a wall. He was also a man of few words, and he didn't have to say anything else to get his point across to my mother.

She twisted the ring on the index finger of her right hand. It felt like she twisted my own insides with it. "I'm doing it again, I know."

Her paranoia was understandable. I used to have a twin brother, but he'd been stolen from our nursery when we were infants. She never recovered from it.

It was why she learned magic, despite the dangers. It was a

14

secret ability passed down through our family, but my ancestors hadn't learned much beyond the basics of protecting the Kingdom for centuries. Not since the Exodus.

"Very well. You can still go," she allowed. She continued twisting the silver ring, and her mouth twisted in a frown.

I sighed in relief. "Thank you."

She half smiled for a brief moment, and then her gaze wandered to the tops of the hedges. "I think we're done for tonight. Get some rest. You don't want to fall asleep tomorrow."

I nodded. "Yes, of course."

Lucas and I headed out of the Royal Gardens. I looked back at my mother's face, still staring off into the distance.

I frowned, knowing exactly what was going through her head. I'd scared her tonight. It didn't matter that it had been only a few moments. That was all it could take for me to be ripped away from her forever, as she liked to remind me.

"She'll be fine," Lucas said.

"I hope so." I ran a hand through my black hair, straightening it as best I could without a mirror.

I'd taken after my father in terms of looks. His skin was several shades browner than my mother's pale hue, and his hair was pitch black. My skin was somewhere in the middle of them, but my hair was all my father. My eyes, though, were the same grayish-blue almond shape as my mother's.

I often wondered what my brother would have looked like. They told me he had mom's red hair, but no one could accurately predict who he'd have taken after. Would he have the same hooked nose as dad? Or would his slope more like mom's?

"Your Highness?" Lucas asked.

I came out of my daydream to find we were already in my sitting room. I must have been standing here for a while; the lamps already glowed brightly. "Sorry, Lucas. Just thinking, is all. You can go as soon as the night guards are here."

He nodded, and I retreated into the bedroom. I yanked off layers of clothes as I went, tossing my tie over the bedside clock and throwing my ruined jacket to the foot of my bed. It missed and landed on the floor, and I toed off my shoes to join it. One went too far and hit the copper pipes lining the baseboards of the room. I walked to my window while unbuttoning the top of my shirt and pushed the wired glass open. My rooms overlooked the eastern courtyard, where guards practiced their drills and trained new recruits.

The sun was almost gone, but I could still make out my mother's figure walking the outer perimeter of the courtyard. She paused at certain intervals, placing her hand on the stone wall that surrounded the entire palace.

I knew she'd be checking the barrier tonight.

The barrier was a magical shield protecting the palace from outside magic. It did nothing against typical human attacks, and it was powerless to stop magic that was already inside the perimeter. The original spell had been laid into the very foundations of the palace when it was built, using runes and spellwork that had been forgotten over the centuries. Only the basic upkeep was passed down through my family now. Mother had taught me how to manage it years ago.

It really only needed to be checked once a year. Mother checked it at least once a month, if not more. She had been as long as I could remember. Dad said she used to barely ever check it, and he'd often had to remind her in the early days of their marriage. Her frequent checks now were a method of coping after my brother was taken, especially since the man responsible was never caught. My brother was never found, either, so my mother never stopped.

His kidnapping had prompted her and my father to learn more about our family magic, because his kidnapper had used it to steal him away, and they'd sworn they would be ready to face him again, only that day never came.

She moved on from the courtyard, and I crossed my arms over

16

the window sill and let the night air wash over me. I didn't know if she ever honestly expected that man to come back, or if this had simply turned into a nervous tick, like twisting her ring.

I viciously hoped that man was as dead as my brother probably was.

CHAPTER 3

Did I wake up because it was cold or because there was rain leaking through our roof? The answer would be neither.

I woke up because sweet, angelic Damon pounced on me.

A knee in the stomach will really get your blood going in the morning.

Damon was the youngest member of my little family. I found him wandering the streets about two years ago, when he was five or six. He hadn't known where he'd come from or who his parents were, and I couldn't help but bring him back to Base.

'Base' was what the four of us called our little abandoned house. It had seen a bad fire about ten years ago, and the owners left and never came back. I'd just met Malik and we'd been looking for a place to sleep out of the rain when we found it. We'd only meant to stay the night, but we kept coming back, and now it was ours.

Half the house was collapsed, and there were holes in the remaining roof. All the glass windows were broken, and smoke had stained most of the walls and ceilings. We used the broken wood from the collapsed half of the house to build fires, but we kept a dedicated pile as a makeshift wall between the room we lived in and the open air next to it. Anything valuable in the house had been taken after the fire, and we'd burned or thrown out most of the rest

18

of it.

For the most part, we lived in the old kitchen and dining room. In warmer months, we spread out between the rooms more, but in the winter we all slept in a big pile next to the iron stove in the kitchen. The backdoor was in the kitchen, too, and that was usually the door we used to avoid attention. People on the street knew we lived here, of course, but as long as we avoided them and kept out of their way, they were content to stay out of ours.

It wasn't the grandest home by any stretch of the imagination, but I couldn't imagine myself being happy anywhere else.

"Come on, let's go!" Damon said. "I'm spending the day with you today!"

I pushed him off and rolled onto my side, teaching myself how to breathe again. "Who said I was dragging you around today?"

"I woke up and you're still here!" he smiled at me.

I groaned and buried my head in the blankets.

"Go away," I muttered. Whatever time it was, it was too early for this.

He shook my shoulder. "Come on, please!"

This was why I normally woke up before him and escaped before he was aware of the world. But every now and then I either slept in or he woke up early, and this madness happened. Since Malik hadn't yelled at us yet, that meant he was gone already.

I heard Jade giggling and lifted my head to glare at her. She was the oldest of our family at sixteen, and the only one who'd run away from home. Her skirts were dirty and the hems frayed, but she usually stayed out of trouble. Unlike me, she actually tried to work for her meals, picking up quick jobs selling papers or delivering mail. Usually, she brought Damon with her to keep him out of trouble, too.

Malik, the last member of the four of us, was around fifteen like me, and he tended to get in as much, if not more, trouble. He liked thrilling chases through the city more than I did, and he liked to do them by stealing steamcars.

We didn't let Damon go with him very often.

"It's been a while since he went with you," she said, crossing her arms and leaning against the doorway. "Just let him come."

I made the mistake of glancing at the child in question. His blue eyes opened impossibly wide, and his lower lip trembled.

I was a slave to that look.

"Alright, fine, just get off me."

Damon cheered and his weight disappeared. Breathing became much easier.

I sat up and yawned, stretching my arms above my head. I felt grosser than usual, like half of the river still clung to me. Funny how jumping into water did nothing to make me feel clean.

I retied my boots. They were still damp and I pulled a face. I'd have to try and get back early tonight so I could leave them in front of the stove.

Damon all but dragged me out after that. He had far too much energy in the mornings.

"Where are we going to get breakfast?" he asked, slipping into the back alleys between the houses.

I trailed behind, still scrubbing sleep from my eyes. My wrench bounced against my thigh with every step. I hardly ever used it, but you never knew when you would need to smash a window or borrow a steamcar. "Where do you want to get breakfast?"

"Can we go to Sal's?"

I pulled a face. "He hates me." That wasn't saying much; most people in this city did.

"That's why it's funny when you get something anyway!" Damon giggled.

"He does make the best faces when I steal sausage right out from under him…"

Damon gave me those big eyes again, and I caved. Sal the Grouchy Sausage Man it was.

Since I had a decent amount of money thanks to the wallet I stole, breakfast was uneventful. I had to show Sal the cash before he believed me, and he glared the whole time, but Damon and I walked away with two steaming sausages apiece.

We wandered around the city while we ate. Paperboys shouted headlines on the corners, shoving papers in people's faces. They fought to be heard over the hum of the steamcars. Most street steamcars were louder and heavier than what the guards used, especially the older models.

"Now what?" Damon asked, wiping sausage grease off his chin.

I finished off my last bite. "Now, I think it's time you learned the gentle art of pick-pocketing." Malik would have been the better teacher; people rarely let me get close enough to practice. He was invisible on the streets, and could make out with wallets and pocket watches before the owners even knew he was there. I usually had to do the accidental bump trick, which was only successful half the time.

Malik didn't have the patience for teaching though, so Damon would have to deal with me.

"Really? You're gonna teach me?" Damon asked, eyes wide and sparkling.

I got the feeling dealing with me wasn't a letdown for him.

We found a quiet alley and I tore off one of the buttons on my jacket. For the rest of the morning, he practiced bumping into me and trying to sneak it out of my pocket. Even for a beginner, he was terrible at it. The few times he managed to even get the button out of my pocket, I felt his hand in there and would confront him, and the guilty look on his face gave him away every time.

By noon we were both pretty frustrated.

"I'll have Malik give you some tips tonight," I said, rubbing my forehead.

Damon pouted and crossed his arms. "Can we go to Old Harry's?"

I checked the time on the clock tower. "I don't know, it's kind of far. We might not make it back by nightfall at this point." Old Harry was an inventor outside of town. He'd been nice to me as a kid, and I visited once in a while, usually by myself.

"Please?" Damon begged, giving me that face.

"Alright, we'll try."

He skipped along beside me when we walked back out onto the main roads.

An icy wind blew through us and I hunched into my jacket more. The sky was cloudy, too, so there wasn't much warmth to be found. Hopefully it wasn't about to rain. It would be just my luck if it started to downpour when we were halfway there.

We never made it that far. A guard grabbed both of us by the back of our collars and dragged us backwards. "Well, well, well, what have we here?" the guard asked. His dark green jacket was neatly pressed and the gold buttons shone. Either he was brand new, or he was the type with a stick up his ass.

Judging by the gray in his hair and the creases on his face, my guess was the second one.

"Let go!" I snarled, twisting and taking a swing at him. He let me hit him in the stomach, his grip only tightening.

"We didn't do anything!" Damon joined in.

"Ha!" the guard barked. He shook me. "His hair speaks for itself, you rotten thieves."

Damn my hair. Why did I have to be one of like three people with this cursed hair color?

I punched him again, slammed my heel on his foot, slugged him across the face, and even kneed him in the groin, but he didn't release us.

"Ace," Damon warned, voice low and scared. "More guards are

22

coming."

I whipped my head around. Down the street, two guards rushed towards us. "King's beard." If I was lucky, they'd throw me in jail. More than likely, I'd be shipped out to the King's Airforce.

Damon would never be that lucky. He was too young and small to be any good to the king. They would place him in the orphanage, a fate worse than whatever waited for us in the Airforce.

Panic made my blood run cold and my stomach dropped to my feet. I would never let that happen. I would never let him go through what I did in that terrible place.

The guard holding us grinned. "Looks like your luck finally ran out." He pushed us forward.

Did they even know what fate they were actually sentencing him to?

Anger replaced my panic, warming up my frozen blood. I stepped forward, slipped out of my coat, and then turned and slammed my fist into the guard's face.

He reeled back and loosened his grip on Damon just enough that Damon could run for it.

And we ran.

Damon stayed on my heels while I led him down every back alley I could find. There was no sign of the guards chasing us, but I didn't stop until we were on the other side of the city. Then we collapsed and struggled to catch our breath.

King's beard, that had been too close. I couldn't believe I let a guard get that close to him.

"You okay?" I asked.

He offered me a smile and nodded. "I wasn't worried."

Well. That made one of us. The kid put way too much trust in me sometimes.

I ruffled his hair and shook my head. "Let's get some water, yeah?" Along the way, I'd keep my eye out for a good cap.

We turned back towards the main road. A black shadow jumped from the ground to the wall and then slipped around the corner, out of sight.

I froze. Blinked.

Damon tilted his head and called it weird.

I yanked him back towards me. "Let's go the other way."

He tilted his head. "It was just a shadow, wasn't it?"

"Probably." A really weird shadow. It gave me a bad feeling in the pit of my stomach, though. A chill ran down my spine. "We'll just… go around."

He gave me a funny look and then shrugged. For him, that was the end of it.

I kept looking back every few steps. Nothing moved when I was watching, but some shadows looked darker than I thought they should have. How could I prove that though? I sounded crazy in my own head.

"Are you okay?" Damon asked.

"Course I am," I said.

"We're safe now, right?"

"Completely safe." I could only hope I was right.

We didn't run into anything before the well, and I dropped the bucket in while looking around. Damon kept glancing about, chewing on his lip. My worry made him worry, and I hated that. I took a deep breath and forced myself to calm down. It was just a shadow, a trick of the light.

Someone managed to sneak up on us and grabbed my arm. Swearing, I dropped the chain and the bucket splashed back into the well. He caught my instinctive punch.

"I told you, your luck has run out." His grip on my arm and my hand tightened. It was the same guard from before. I had no idea how he'd followed or snuck up on us.

Damon jumped back and watched me.

This guard didn't make any moves towards him, at least, and I was going to use that. "Damon, run! Find Malik or Jade!"

Damon nodded and took off. The guard couldn't seem to care less, even smiling. "The fewer witnesses, the better." He dragged me towards a side road.

I dug my heels into the ground. "What's that supposed to mean?" Wasn't he just going to ship me off like all the other orphans? Why would witnesses matter?

The only answers I could come up with were not good ones.

"You have no idea how much you've cost me. My plans were set back years because of you."

"What are you talking about?" I'd never stolen anything that valuable. I wouldn't still be on the streets if I had.

He yanked me down another side street. These kinds of streets were usually pretty quiet, but there was an unnatural silence around us, like everyone had been scared off beforehand. Come to think of it, no one had been at the well, either. There were always people at the well.

Where did everybody go?

The man's grip on my arm never let up, no matter how much I twisted and pried at it. I needed to find Damon and the others and make sure they were alright. I didn't like this. Something was wrong.

"Will you stop that, you brat?" he asked, shaking me. His voice was familiar, but I couldn't place it.

I glared at him. "Let me go!"

"Ha! Not likely."

I turned my glare to his hand. He didn't wear the standard metal plated gloves normal guards wore, and I was beginning to think he wasn't actually a guard. Either way, there was a reason guards had that extra protection on their hands.

I bit him.

He howled and let go of me, and I bolted. The first drops of rain hit my face, because this day hadn't been terrible enough yet.

I aimed for the main streets. If I was going to find anybody, it was going to be there. I just needed to prove that we weren't the only two people in the city.

This man did not make it easy. He chased after me, and he was fast. I couldn't lose him, not like before.

Street rat tricks it was.

One of the roads I turned down had a fence cutting across it. I didn't even slow down. I ran and leapt at it, catching the top and hauling myself over. He got a hand around my ankle and threw off my balance. I went over head first, barely getting my hands up to protect my face.

Something cracked. Something was in pain. Something felt like fire had replaced my bones. That something was either my hand or my wrist; the lines of pain were blurry, and I didn't have time.

The guard cursed up a blue streak and scrambled up the other side of the fence.

I bit my lip and stumbled to my feet, slowly walking back into my run from before. The skies opened up, and the light drizzle turned into a downpour.

Just my luck.

I was soaked and shivering before I rounded two blocks, cradling my right wrist against my chest. It was already swelling. The pain throbbed up my whole arm, becoming the only thing I could focus on. Not even the icy rain distracted me, and it was trying really hard.

I'd only ever broken my nose before, when I'd gotten in a fight with an older kid. He'd ended it with that one punch, and my nose had been crooked ever since. The weeks it spent healing had not been fun. I wasn't looking forward to waiting for my wrist to heal.

I couldn't bring myself to run anymore, but I couldn't stop either. Turning a corner, someone bumped into me. They caught my shoulder and steadied me. "Sorry about that!"

They were gone before I could form a reply, continuing around the corner. I should have been annoyed, or ducking out of sight. Instead, I was happy to have finally found other people. A large crowd spread out on the road in front of me, covered by umbrellas and makeshift awnings. Men shouted about different items they were selling, clothes and food from far-off provinces, the most stylish jewelry in another province.

The Trader's Market. It came once every few months, and it explained where most of the missing people were. The whole town always turned up for these markets.

Once I found a cap to cover my hair, it would be the perfect place for me to disappear.

CHAPTER 4

I was the farthest I'd ever been from the palace, in a city called Gallen. It was exhilarating. Mother had no idea I'd planned to come this far, and hopefully she'd never know. Otherwise, it would be the end of these little trips.

I wore the plainest clothes I owned, dull tin goggles around my neck, and a wool cap on my head. My pocket watch stood out, but I never went anywhere without it so I tucked the chain in my waistband. It wasn't much of a disguise, but I had yet to receive more than a passing glance when dressed like this.

Lucas wore his usual breastplate and uniform under a large trench coat, but he'd traded his sword for an umbrella since it looked like rain.

The sour weather did nothing to my mood. I was raring to go at dawn and bounced in the back of the steamcar the whole way there. The second it stopped I leapt to the ground and breathed it all in.

Most of the buildings were made of brick. Shops had large windows displaying their temptations. Older shops and establishments had wooden signs hanging on black iron poles. Newer ones, or at least ones with more money, had spinning signs and eye-catching mechanics. A barbershop's sign had scissors snipping the air, steam hissing from the joints every time they clicked open. People flocked down the road, talking to each other and laughing. A group of kids rushed past me, crying "Race you!" and were followed by an exhausted looking woman with her hair falling out of its pins.

"Must be a market day," Lucas remarked, stepping closer to me.

"I hope so." I took off after the kids.

Lucas yanked me back by the collar. "Need I remind you of our rules for these outings?"

I sighed and straightened my jacket. "I know, I know. I got excited." I'd heard people talk about markets and all the things the traders brought from all corners of Wingomia Kingdom, but I'd never been to one before. I couldn't believe how lucky I was to have come on market day.

"It will still be there," he promised.

We started again, leaving the pilot and extra guards with the steamcar. We were constantly caught behind slower people, but I couldn't find it in myself to be angry. Eavesdropping on them was too interesting.

A poster pasted on a wall caught my attention. Two wrenches crossed over a gear on a bell, and printed under that read "The time for change is now! Join the Chimers and build a better future today!" A date and location followed.

Lucas scowled and tore down the poster, crumpling it and shoving it in his pocket. "Bloody revolutionists."

"Revolutionists?" I asked.

He shook his head. "No matter how good the king, there will always be unhappy folks who want change. They've gotten louder the last few years, that's all."

I frowned, trying to figure out what changes they could want, and Lucas pushed me on.

The market pushed all thoughts of revolutionists from my mind. Traders had silks from the Spodale Mountains and amber necklaces from the Ricona plains. Artisans displayed all manner of artwork, from oil paintings to gear sculptures. I didn't see it, but I could smell fish from the seas.

Hours passed by. I bought some of the silks for my mother and a horse made out of old gears for my father. I picked out an amber necklace to send to Miranda, a girl I frequently corresponded with, and then spent a solid hour looking for something for Lucas. He was a hard person to shop for, but I found a silver ring he'd be allowed to wear under his gloves.

He protested profusely when I turned around smiling, but he did finally put it on before I had to order him to.

It started raining not long after that.

"We should head back," Lucas said, holding the open umbrella over me.

"But it's barely afternoon," I argued. "It won't take that long to go back." There was still so much to see, and I hadn't tried any of the food yet. "Let's at least have lunch first, okay?"

He sighed and gave in, and I took my time picking out what I wanted to eat. His side-eye told me he knew exactly what I was doing, but his voice never stopped me.

I had my eyes on a stand of meat pies when someone snatched the cap off my head.

"Hey!" I went to grab their shoulder, but I missed them by inches. The culprit didn't look back at me, just continued on and fit my cap over their head while slipping into the crowd.

I stormed after them, earning a harsh warning from Lucas.

The thief's red hair made him easy to spot, at least, even with most of it hidden under my cap. I seized his right arm and pulled. "Hey! That's mine!"

He hissed and stumbled when turning to face me, and instantly I saw why. His right wrist was swollen pretty badly. Even though I hadn't grabbed it, I'm sure any sudden movement aggravated it.

It wasn't just his wrist that choked down my thoughts. He looked terrible. He was soaked from the rain, dirt streaking down

30

his chin. His shirt hung off his shoulder, and his collarbone stuck out. His pants had small tatters everywhere, and his boots had seen better days. A wrench hung from his belt, a habit only people in the lower class had. He didn't have a jacket or even a vest, despite the rain and the chilly temperatures.

"You can afford another one, can't you?" he asked. He had a drawl to his voice I only heard out in town, and his one foot was edging back, ready to run.

The rain pouring down on me abruptly stopped, Lucas appearing with an umbrella and his no-nonsense attitude. He held his free hand out towards the guy. "The cap, if you please."

"No, it's okay," I waved Lucas off. "If he really needs it, he can keep it."

He narrowed his eyes at me.

"Like you said: I can always get another one." I only wore them in town anyway. I wouldn't miss it.

"Jack," Lucas started.

I turned to head back towards the meat pie stall, and then I had another idea. I shrugged out of my jacket and turned back.

The kid still stood there, dumbfounded. He only stared at my coat when I held it out to him.

"I know it's already wet," I said. "But when it's dry, I think you'll need it more than I will."

He looked between me and the coat. "What's the catch?"

That caught me by surprise. "What do you mean? You need one, don't you?"

His gaze glanced down for a moment like he'd forgotten that.

I pressed it into his good hand. "I'll get another one."

His fingers wrapped around it one by one. "I don't know… thanks, I guess."

"You're welcome." His wrist still bothered me, and he could

31

do with a few good meals, but he was already disappearing into the crowd.

"That was very noble of you," Lucas said. "You're going to make a fine king one day."

A better king would have gotten that kid to a doctor. I could have at least offered him money to pay for one, or offered to buy him lunch. Just giving him my hat and a coat didn't feel like enough.

I hoped the guy would be okay.

CHAPTER 5

The rain didn't let up for hours. I made it back to Base and shivered next to the stove, trying to dry off and warm up. A spot in the corner of the ceiling leaked, steadily dripping into a puddle on the floor. The fire was warm, at least, but sitting still gave me too much time to think.

Who did that kid think he was, anyway? To just give up his cap and coat like that…and with that damn look in his eyes. I hated that look. I didn't need pity; I wasn't some sad story.

They were expensive clothes, too. That was why I'd chosen him out of everyone there, but I hadn't realized how fancy they were. I'd never felt anything this smooth and soft. The coat was probably ruined already because of the rain, but that was just as well. If a guard recognized me in it, they'd think I'd stolen it.

I would prefer it if I had.

I shifted in my corner and my wrist twinged. I should have gotten some money off that guy while I was there. He pitied me enough he would have given me everything he had if I'd asked. Normally people cursed me out and tried to arrest me. His kindness had thrown me off guard.

He must be from out of town. That was the only way he wouldn't know who I was.

Muffling a cough, I sank back against the wall and drifted off to sleep.

I woke up after the rain had stopped and Jade and Damon came back. Damon crashed in to me and wouldn't let go.

"I'm so glad you're okay," he said. "We tried to find you but Jade made me get out of the rain."

"Course I'm okay," I said.

"That's good, because you look terrible," Jade stated.

To be honest, I felt terrible, too. My wrist was killing me, I had a massive headache, and even my throat was sore.

"Let's see you almost get arrested twice in one day and how good you look afterwards," I retorted.

"Won't happen. I don't go looking for danger like you do." She sat down in front of me and offered half of a warm loaf of bread.

I took it in my good hand and bit into it. "I do not look for it. I just…don't always run away from it." So I thought stealing food from under people's noses or caps right off their heads was fun. Life would be too dull if all I did was beg for scraps at the end of the day, like Jade preferred. And the only honest jobs I could get were factory work, and no one who wanted to live long took those jobs if they could help it. Too many accidents.

"That guard was scary," Damon said. He adjusted himself so he was under my left arm, curled up against my side.

"Yeah. He really got the jump on us, didn't he?" With a few more bites, I finished up the bread.

Jade looked me over again. Her gaze landed on my wrist and widened.

I shook my head and ran my left hand through Damon's hair. If he didn't move, I could put him to sleep in half an hour. Jade could splint my wrist then.

She frowned but didn't bring it up. "So how did you get away from this guard anyway?"

I told them the story, clearing my throat so often Jade made me pause while she grabbed a bucket and went to the well. The handle had broken on the bucket, but we'd found we could jam it into the buckets kept at the well and draw it up, and then didn't have to walk four blocks every time we wanted a drink. The hard part was unjamming the bucket once it was filled with water without splashing it everywhere.

She came back and I had a long drink, and then I finished my story. Damon looked up at me with a sleepy smile on his face, and Jade shook her head in disbelief. "You have some of the weirdest luck."

"You're telling me. Check out the jacket that rich kid gave me."

She took it down from the beam I'd hung it from to dry and froze. "Holy crow, where is this kid from? You can't find fabrics like this in this town!"

I shrugged. "It was the Trader's Market. He was probably here with his dad or something."

She shook her head and hung the jacket back up. "If the rain hasn't damaged it too badly you could sell that for some decent cash."

The idea made my stomach tighten. "I lost my other jacket, though." I was already attached to the darn thing. With the money that jacket could get me, I could buy four new jackets for all of us.

"You should keep it," Damon said. His words slurred with the beginnings of sleep. "It was a present."

Maybe that was why I wanted to keep it. All my life I'd had to take what I needed. Very few people had ever given me anything.

Jade rolled her eyes, but she didn't argue. She knew what my decision was.

Malik strolled in with a surprise hunk of steak, which made him my current favorite person in the kingdom.

It woke Damon up though, and Jade wasn't willing to wait any longer before looking at my wrist. She had the most education out of

35

all of us, coming from some rich family somewhere. It wasn't much, but it did mean that on the few instances we got hurt she was the one who knew what to do about it.

Not that she was gentle while going about her work. Two seconds after she took my hand in hers, I howled and pulled it back to my chest.

"Malik, take Damon for a walk," she ordered.

"No! I want to stay," Damon said.

"Come on, Damon. We need fresh firewood anyway, and I need someone to help me carry it," Malik said.

Damon looked between us. After I jerked my chin towards the door, he went with Malik.

I turned to Jade. "We both know it's broken. Can you not make this more painful?"

"You realize I don't actually know what I'm doing right?"

"You wrap a piece of wood against it or something, don't you?"

"And what am I going to use to wrap it, genius?"

"I guess we sacrifice one of the blankets. It's starting to get warmer anyway." We'd have time before next winter to steal another one.

She glared at me and shifted through our nest to find the rattiest one. "You're also coming down with a cold, I hope you know."

"No, I'm not." The scratchy throat meant nothing.

"Ace."

"Jade." Even if I was sick, there wasn't anything we could do about it.

She picked out a blanket and ripped a piece off, then she grabbed a damp piece of firewood and bound it to my arm.

"Stay here tomorrow, okay?" she asked. "I'll bring you food, but you need to rest. You can't let a cold get worse."

"What am I supposed to do all day?"

"Promise me, Ace."

She pulled a Damon and copied his begging face.

One of these days, I would figure out how to say no to that face.

I banged my head back against the wall and gave in.

It was a good thing, too, because when I woke up in the morning, I felt even worse. I couldn't breathe through my nose or stop coughing, and everything ached. Staying at Base was the only thing I was up to doing, and even the effort of burying myself under more blankets felt like too much work.

Jade reported I now had a fever, and she brought a full water bucket within reach. Malik came back with a fresh meat pie for breakfast and made vague threats of what he'd do to me if I got him sick. Damon made me promise to get better.

And then I slept again. Not well. Weird fever dreams kept waking me up, and I couldn't get comfortable. I was barely even aware of when the others came back to check on me.

Jade put a cold hand against my forehead at some point. "He's getting worse."

"What else can we do?" Malik asked.

"He needs a doctor, or medicine at least."

"Yeah, okay, let me go fetch a doctor for a street rat," Malik snorted.

"Malik, I'm serious," Jade said. "Any fever that gets this bad this fast can't be good. And sleeping in this old place isn't helping."

There was some kind of thud.

"Kicking the wall won't help anything," Jade stated.

"If we take him to a doctor, they're going to know who he is and arrest him."

"No," I mumbled. No arresting. Getting arrested was bad.

"See? Even completely out of it and he still doesn't want to go," Malik said.

"Being completely out of it means he has no say," Jade argued.

There was a pause in their conversation. Some distant part of me wondered where Damon was, but that part didn't make it far enough for me to ask about.

"Can we wait one more day?" Malik asked. "Maybe he'll get better on his own."

Jade ran her fingers through my hair. "Okay. One day. I'll stay with him tomorrow, but if I think he's getting worse I'm dragging him to the first adult I can find."

"Best we can do, I guess," Malik said.

I drifted off after that, Jade's fingers in my hair putting me to sleep. It wasn't a deep sleep. I was coughing and sneezing and too uncomfortable for that. But I wasn't aware of anything either, not until I found myself on Malik's back.

If moving any part of my body didn't require so much effort, I would have pinched myself. This was so bizarre it had to be a dream.

"Where're we goin'?" I slurred.

Malik turned his head towards my face. "Finding you help. I'm sorry, Ace. We have to. You can be as mad at us as you want, but at least you'll be alive. If anyone can find their way back to us, it's you."

That was too many words for me to understand right now.

"Jade went ahead to try and find someone, but we didn't want to bring them to Base. That's why I'm carrying your sorry ass. And you better not get me sick."

Malik wasn't usually this chatty, but I didn't have the energy to figure out what was wrong.

"Speak of the devil, here she comes," Malik said.

I lifted my head enough to look at two people coming up the street towards us. Jade was running, and a man in a long coat followed her, one hand holding onto his hat. He placed that same hand against my forehead when he stopped next to us.

"He's definitely in poor shape," the man said. "I wish you'd gotten him help sooner, but I'll see what I can do."

"Careful with his wrist," Jade said.

The man nodded, and then he lifted me off Malik's back. "Let's get you into bed, hmm?"

Ha. I hadn't slept in a real bed since I was a kid, and those beds at the orphanage didn't count. Not that it mattered; I wasn't picky about where I slept.

I fell back asleep in the stranger's arms before we even went a block.

CHAPTER 6

It was a cold ride back to the palace without my jacket, but every shiver was worth it.

The concern from my parents when they greeted my arrival was irritating, though.

Mother fussed and demanded a coat be fetched for me at once, and no matter how much I argued we were walking inside and I was going to change before dinner anyway, she wasn't swayed.

"What happened, Jack?" my father asked.

"I ran into a kid who needed it more than I did," I said. I called him a kid but he wasn't that young; he was probably my age, actually.

They both stopped walking and stared at me. Mother slowly smiled and shook her head. Dad slapped me on the back and steered me inside.

Everyone acted like I did as much as I possibly could have done, but it still didn't sit right with me. I still felt like I should have done more.

After changing I met them for dinner and detailed the market for them, giving them the gifts I'd found. Mother was ecstatic about the silks and Dad beamed at the horse statue.

When we were done eating, Mother and I went out to the royal gardens for my magic lesson.

"Do you feel up for trying the transport spell again?" she asked. Lucas and her two guards stood watch at either entrance to the grassy courtyard.

"Actually, I was wondering if our magic could heal people?"

Her eyes widened. "Heal people?" she repeated. "Why the sudden interest?"

I shrugged and rubbed the back of my neck. "Just...saw a lot of people who needed it today, that's all." It hadn't just been that kid, either. Plenty of people walking around had nasty steam burns up and down their arms or spanning their faces.

Her surprise melted into fondness. "Oh, Jack. You have the biggest heart I've ever seen." She stepped forward to hug me, ruffling my hair. "I wish we could go around healing people. But you know our magic must stay secret. Even if you knew those spells, you couldn't have healed them today."

I squirmed out of her embrace. "That doesn't make any sense. What's the point of having this power if we don't help people?" The past generations of our family have wasted this magic, in my opinion. They'd only kept themselves safe, and the knowledge of how to wield our magic was all but forgotten. Mother had taught herself almost everything from ancient spell books.

"We do, Jack. But we have to do it more subtly than healing a town of sick people. I help fertilize the farm lands and send rains when there's a drought, and the magic in the very ground of this kingdom keeps plagues and disease at bay."

"You don't think it's time we took it a step further?"

"Jack, most of the kingdom has no idea magic exists. If we were to suddenly announce our abilities it could be very dangerous for us. There are people who would call us monsters and demand we step down, or people who would attack us and use us for their own gains."

"We live in the most fortified building of the kingdom. If they can't get to us now, why would they be able to then?" The whole

41

mindset didn't sit well with me. It sounded like cowardice.

"Determination is a powerful thing, Jack. Right now, no one in the kingdom has the willpower needed to break through our security. We don't want to give them that motivation."

"These all sound like excuses," I muttered, glaring at the ground.

"We have to keep ourselves safe first and foremost," she said. "When the royal family goes, anarchy descends upon the land. We're the first defense against that."

It still sounded like an excuse.

"All that said," she went on, "It doesn't hurt to know a few healing spells just in case. But you have to promise me that the next time you go into town, you won't heal every other person in sight."

I knew that wasn't a promise I could keep, but I made it anyway. One of her guards volunteered to be a pincushion for me to practice on, and while I got the hang of healing small cuts and bruises easily, there wasn't a way to practice anything larger without seriously injuring him. Neither I nor my mother had the stomach for that, and I think her guard appreciated us keeping the lesson theoretical.

I'd be able to practice it soon enough, anyway. One way or another I was going back to Gallen and finding that boy.

There was no immediate chance, though. The next day was Commoner's Court, and I'd been going to these since I was twelve.

It was always interesting to hear from the people directly, and to see my father rule. Most things were noted down to be discussed later with the full court. Others were dismissed as something for the provincial governor to handle.

My chance to find a way back to that town was further delayed at dinner, when Dad announced plans for a new hunt.

I rolled my eyes and pushed the broccoli around on my plate. He called it a hunt. Me and the other noble children called it forced bonding.

"Oh, don't be like that," Dad said. "This one will be different.

This time, me and the men have decided to trust you boys out there on your own."

I dropped my fork.

"Excuse me?" Mother demanded.

"Alone except for the guards that will be keeping an eye on them," Dad corrected, giving my mom a wide smile.

They wanted to let a bunch of noble kids loose in the woods? Granted, they were fairly public woods and there wasn't anything more dangerous than a rabbit in them, but this still seemed like a terrible idea.

"Absolutely not, it's far too dangerous," Mother said.

Dad reached over and placed his hand on hers. "Honey, I've already agreed to it."

"Why would you do such a thing?"

Really, why? I hated these hunts. Tramping about in the trees and shooting at small wildlife was not my idea of a good time. Especially with the children of the council.

"Because I trust our son and the highly trained guards surrounding him to keep him safe," Dad said. "This will be good for him. Those boys will soon replace their fathers on the council, and one day Jack will be leading them. They need to learn to trust each other now."

There wasn't any way to get out of this.

Mother tried. She argued every possible point she could come up with, but Dad held firm. Even if I pretended to be sick it would only postpone the event.

We were leaving in two days, rain or shine.

CHAPTER 7

The most confusing part of waking up was the smell. It was all floral, like I'd walked past a flower cart in spring. But spring wasn't for a few more weeks yet.

Unless I'd been asleep for that long? I was groggy enough to believe I'd slept for weeks.

Someone helped me sit up and tilted a cup of water down my throat. It was saltier than I expected, and I almost coughed it up.

"Easy now," a man said. "It's just medicine."

Medicine? I couldn't afford medicine. Where the hell was I?

All I saw were white paneled walls and the man sitting next to me, holding me up. I remembered him. I'd stolen his top hat. "What…"

"I'll explain later, when you'll actually remember it." He tilted the not-water down my throat again, and then gave me actual water. After, he set me back down and lifted a heavy quilt up to my chin. I buried myself in the warmth and turned my head into a pillow.

He ran a hand over my hair and said "Sleep now," and I didn't put up a fight.

I lost count of how many times I woke up like that, to him giving me medicine and sending me right back to sleep. Sometimes there was soup, nothing more than broth, but food was food and I wasn't

44

picky.

Eventually, I woke up to a dark room with the doctor nowhere in sight. It was the first time in a long time that it didn't feel like my body wanted to kill me. It was also the first time I felt like I had any amount of energy. With all that energy came the demanding urge to find a water closet.

I pushed aside the quilt and swung my legs over the side of the bed. The edge dipped under my weight and I flailed, jumping up to my feet. At least, that was the goal when I launched myself off the bed. Instead, I collapsed on the floor with my head pounding.

The doctor that had been caring for me appeared within moments, toggling the light switch next to the door. A light on the bedside table glowed warm amber.

I sat up and leaned back against the bed while he crouched down. "Are you alright? What happened?"

"Stood up too fast," I said. My gaze drifted down to my wrist, where clean bandages were wrapped around an actual splint.

"Why were you trying to stand up?" He helped me up to the edge of the bed.

"Because I need the water closet," I stated, glaring at him. Maybe he was some kind of doctor, but if he didn't recognize me as the kid who'd stolen his hat, he was an idiot.

A really rich idiot, judging by the silk pajamas and electric lights.

"You…right, of course. Let's go." He helped me to the water closet, an actual room in his house, and the next five minutes were the most awkward of my life. I had no strength in my legs, and my sense of balance had gone out the window.

"This is a good sign though," he said, helping me back into bed. I hated how I sank in it. Give me blankets on solid floor any day. "Your fever has been sweating out any extra fluid you had, so the fact you're not sweating it all out now means you're on the mend."

"On the mend from what, exactly?" I asked. I dragged my good

45

hand over my face. I was in desperate need of a bath, but I doubted this doctor was about to let me stand out in the rain. "And who are you?"

He smiled at me. "You can call me Dr. Carl. Your friends happened to run into me while looking for help for you, and I agreed to take care of you. You had a nasty case of Angrilia, but nothing I couldn't heal."

My energy was fading again, but I still had so many questions. "Why would you help us? We can't pay you. I already sold your hat." I fought off a yawn and lost.

"I don't need money," he said. "And I forgive you for stealing my hat. But we can talk about this later. You need more rest."

He pulled the quilt up and tucked me in, running his hand over my hair once before leaving and turning the light off.

If I hadn't been completely exhausted, I would have spent hours trying to figure out what he could possibly want from a bunch of street rats. Instead, I worried about it for two minutes before falling asleep.

It was the first thing on my mind when I woke up, though. Light drifted in around the edges of a curtain, still the dim gray color of early dawn. What day was it? How many had I slept through? How long had Dr. Carl been taking care of me? And why? Why would he agree to take care of someone who couldn't pay him back?

The whole thing was fishy. Stupid sickness. I shouldn't even be in this mess, but no, I just had to catch some really bad cold.

At least I finally reached a point where I could stay awake for more than ten minutes. I was able to worry about every horrible scenario that could possibly happen until the gray light turned into a calm yellow and floorboards creaked. They passed by the door to my room and kept going, fading.

The only way to get answers was to ask questions, so I pushed aside the quilt again and attempted to stand up on my own. I didn't feel as dizzy and unsteady as I had before, but I still leaned on the bedside table more than I liked. There was a chair next to the bed, and I used that to make my way to the door, shuffling it along the carpet. It was a thick carpet, soft around my bare feet and muffling my steps. Not completely, I was sure, not the way Dr. Carl's steps had creaked before.

The hallway I stepped out into was lined with plants. They hung in baskets from the ceiling and sat in planters on fancy columns. Most were leafy clumps, but some had flowers in all sorts of colors.

That explained the floral scent and creeped me out more at the same time.

Dr. Carl rose into view at the top of the stairs. "I thought I heard you. Would you like breakfast?"

As creepy as this guy was, I was not able to turn down free food. "That'd be great."

He helped me down the stairs and led me into a dining room, sitting me down in a chair with a carved wooden back. It matched the dark wood table. A gold chandelier hung from the ceiling, wax dripping down the arms. More plants were in each corner of the room, but their scent wasn't as strong down here.

This was probably the fanciest place I'd ever been in my life. It was the kind of place I felt I could ruin simply by existing near it.

Dr. Carl brought out scrambled eggs and pieces of bread. "We'll start off easy."

Hot meals were a treat in and of themselves, and I devoured the eggs almost as soon as they were in front of me. He took a seat across from me, setting his plate down and ignoring it, folding his hands in front of his face while he watched me.

"You've spent your entire life on the streets, haven't you?" he asked. There was no hint of pity in his voice. It sounded more like disgust.

"What of it?" I asked back. I tore off a hunk of bread. It was soft and practically melted in my mouth, nowhere near as stale as what I could usually steal.

47

"That means you never learned how to properly eat." He glanced down at the fork my hand was wrapped around.

"What's to know?" I asked. "It goes in your mouth, you chew, and swallow."

He lifted his gaze from the fork to my face. "If you're a barbarian, I suppose that's enough. Observe." He unfolded his hands and picked up his fork, scooped up some eggs, and brought it to his mouth.

There was a grace to his movements I could never hope to copy. I didn't even know there was a way to make eating look delicate and graceful.

It was one more thing separating me from the wealthy of the world.

"You saying if I want to eat, I have to do it like you?" I asked.

"I'm saying if you don't want to be a street rat until you die, it's time you started acting like it."

I raised a brow. "What?"

"You want off the streets eventually, don't you?"

I shifted in my seat. "Yeah, I guess." This was where he promised me incredible things, as long as I gave up everything I knew, right? And then he led me into some kind of pleasure house or something?

"Well, you can't expect anyone to treat you like more than a street rat if you don't act like more than one. That starts with manners and etiquette."

Oh hell. I needed to get out of here.

"Why do you care?"

He grinned and looked me up and down. "I believe you can help me with something. But I need to teach you some things first. Plus, you're still recovering and will be useless until you're healthy again. While you recover, you can learn."

And there were the thorns to go with this pretty flower. I knew him helping was too good to be real.

48

"What do you want my help with? And who says I'll agree to help you?"

"You will," he said. He reached for his glass of orange juice and brought it to his lips. "I hand-make the medicine I've been giving you. I can also make any number of other tonics and poisons."

And he would, if I didn't do what he wanted. He could kill me and get away with it. Jade and Malik probably had no idea where this house was. Dr. Carl could bury me in his garden and no one would ever know.

He smiled again. "I think you and I are going to get along swimmingly."

CHAPTER 8

Packs were readied and provisions procured for a week. Rifles and pistols were checked and rechecked, loaded and slung across our backs or in holsters. Mother fussed over me and kept adjusting and readjusting my jacket, even when the others started to arrive.

All in all, there were eight of us on this little hunt. Most of them were around my age, products of the nobles hoping for a daughter to eventually marry off when we were old enough.

We all shared unimpressed looks when we gathered that morning. None of us were excited. None of us had a choice, either.

I shouldered my own pack, and I refused help in mounting my horse. Ginger was a gentle brown mare, but that didn't stop my anxiety around her. She could shatter my hand in her teeth if she really wanted to. Or kick me to death.

Basically, she could cause all sorts of bodily harm, and I rightfully respected her power.

Lucas hovered. He didn't offer to help, but he stayed closer than any of the other guards did to their charges.

None of the other kids were the heir to a kingdom. One of the reasons I hated these hunts so much was because I was never allowed to forget that fact. Everything I did reflected on me and my parents. I couldn't do anything embarrassing or anything that might show weakness, like accepting help to mount Ginger.

Once I mounted, everyone else followed suit. We left on my command, trotting through the eastern gate out into the woods.

Thus began what I thought would be the worst days of my life.

The ride was uncomfortable. All of us shifted and squirmed after only an hour, and the complaints started an hour after that.

"I can't believe they're making us do this again," Jacob muttered. He was two years older than I was, dark skinned with lean muscles.

"I vote we bag something today and spend the rest of the week in the lodge," Stephen said. He was only a few months younger than me, but several inches taller, and that was before taking his curly blonde hair into account.

The lodge he mentioned was a rustic cabin in the middle of the woods, about half a day's ride from the castle. It was where we stayed during these hunts, and as old fashioned as the place was, it beat tramping through the forest all day.

"Who says we even have to catch anything?" Jacob asked. "Maybe if we don't our fathers will take the hint."

Tempting. It was very, very tempting.

If we hadn't heard the unholy screech echo through the forest, we probably would have all agreed not to hunt anything.

But we did hear it. A loud, blood curdling shriek. The horses whined and bucked. Leon, a scrappy twelve-year old, fell off his horse. Birds cawed and took off in a flurry of feathers. Startled deer raced past us. Leon scrambled back into the saddle, and our guards herded us into a tighter circle and drew their rifles.

"What was that?" Adam demanded. He was fourteen, the son of the Army General, and probably the best fighter here, besides the guards. He also knew he was the best fighter.

"We're not sticking around to find out," Lucas decided. "Back to the castle."

"Are you kidding?" Adam asked. He tightened the band holding his wavy brown hair out of his face. "This hunt is finally getting interesting."

"We should find whatever that was and kill it," Stephen said. "Imagine the looks on our parents' faces."

Oh, I could imagine, alright. Disbelief. Worry. Fear. Followed by anger. My mother would ground me for years if I hunted some weird thing in the forest. Who knew how dangerous it was?

"We should hunt it down before it attacks any people," Kurtis said. Easily the quietest of the group, Kurtis had the biggest heart of anyone here. He used to find wounded animals as a kid and nurse them back to health.

And he made a good point. If this thing was dangerous, we needed to stop it before it reached any towns.

I sighed and shared a look with Lucas.

He shook his head. "Absolutely not. If the others want to go, that's their choice. You're going the opposite direction as fast as we can."

"Is our future king a coward?" Adam asked.

I glared at him. I'd already committed to going, but now I had no choice. To leave after being called out like that would make everyone think I was scared and weak, and that would haunt me on the throne forever.

"Try to keep up," I retorted.

"Don't do this," Lucas said.

I steered Ginger in the direction all the deer had come from. Whatever they'd been running from would be this way.

"Let's go." Adam pulled his horse up next to mine with a cocky grin. Then he and his horse bolted forward, charging through the underbrush.

The rest of us dutifully followed.

We went as far as the horses were willing to carry us, but after twenty minutes, all of them pulled up short and refused to go any farther. Leon was almost thrown from his horse again, and I nearly had a panic attack when Ginger reared up on her back legs.

Horses. Give me a predictable steamcar any day.

"What's wrong with them?" Jacob asked.

"They sense something we can't," Adam said. He stroked his horse's neck.

"That's never good," I muttered. We hadn't heard anymore shrieking, or passed anymore fleeing animals.

"So, what now?" Leon asked.

Adam tried to urge his horse forward, but the steed was having none of it. "We'll have to continue on foot."

"Am I the only one who thinks this is a bad idea?" Stephen asked.

"No," Lucas muttered, low enough that no one else heard.

"We have to find out what it is, at least," I said. "And we have to make sure it's not near any towns."

"I suggest some of you stay here with the horses," Lucas said. "A small scouting team would be best. Preferably comprised of your guards and not you."

The handful of guards still with us nodded, urging their mounts ahead of us.

"You know I'm going, too," I said.

"As am I," Adam said, glaring at his own guard and daring the man to object. Most of the guards disagreed with our idea, but we wouldn't be swayed.

"Your Highness," Lucas started.

"I'm going, Lucas. That's final."

He sighed, resigned to my reckless stubbornness. Maybe after this he wouldn't complain about my shenanigans in town.

Not likely, but I could dream.

In the end, Leon, Jacob, and two others stayed behind. Only Adam, Stephen, me, and our guards went forward. We checked our rifles and pistols, I ran a finger over my watch chain, and then we started hiking through the forest. Lucas made me walk in the middle of the group, the most defensible position. It didn't feel very leader-like, but he wouldn't hear any arguments.

It was eerily quiet. Even our footsteps seemed to be muffled by the dirt and leaves. It felt like anything could jump out from behind any tree.

The trees grew thicker the farther we went, and consequently everything was also darker. The temperature dropped, too. Or maybe that was my imagination.

"Hey, take a look at this," Adam said, picking his way over to a tree. He ran his hand over a deep gash in the bark.

"I don't think a wild animal made that," Stephen said.

"Not a natural one, at any rate," I said.

Both of them turned to look at me.

"Oh, come on. Did that shriek sound like any natural wild animal to you?"

Adam shrugged. "He's got a point. But what do you think we're dealing with, then?"

"I don't think I want to know," Stephen stated.

"Perhaps this is a job better suited to the Guard," Adam's guard offered, trying once again to convince us to turn around.

"We can handle it," Adam said. "We just have to shoot first."

Was he insane? Anything with sharp enough talons to leave that big of a gash in a tree had to be ten times faster than any of us. I doubted even Adam would be able to keep up with it.

Lucas made eye contact with me. "Your Highness, we need to call this off."

He wasn't asking anymore. He demanded. As my guard, his judgment on my safety outranked my authority as the Crown Prince. Lucas was nice enough to pretend I was still in control, but his hands twitched. Any second, he'd grab me and run, reputation be damned.

"I agree," Adam's guard said, sharing a look with Stephen's guard. "It's not wise to continue on."

"We can handle it," Adam insisted. He cocked his pistol to prove he was ready.

Adam and Stephen looked to me to make the final decision.

Leaving was the smart thing to do, but it was also cowardly. And if Adam eventually inherited his father's post as the General, we would have to work together for the rest of our lives. He would never forget this moment.

My mother was going to lock me in the tower for this.

"We'll advance carefully." I mouthed an apology to Lucas.

He glared and shook his head.

I rushed forward, out of his reach.

Adam grinned, taking the lead. We found more gashes in the trees as we went, and mounds of bloody fur and broken bones. Whatever this thing was, it was a messy eater. It reeked, too. The stench of rotten meat and mildew made our eyes water.

"Did that used to be a bear?" Stephen asked. He wouldn't look away from a bloody mess at the base of a tree. Half a skull grinned at us, one round ear on top of its head.

"Yep." I swallowed bile.

"I wanted to be wrong." Stephen double-checked his pistols. He'd only come along with me and Adam because he was the best shot out of all of us. If he shot it quickly enough, it wouldn't even be a threat.

That was the plan: shoot it before it found us.

It was a solid plan. A good strategy.

It was just a shame it found us first.

CHAPTER 9

As shady as Dr. Carl had revealed himself to be, he was a good teacher. By the end of breakfast, I was 'acceptable' at proper table manners. He cleared away the plates and brought paper and pens and asked me to write the alphabet.

Jade had taught me and Malik a long time ago, if only so we could read signs and know what shop was what. That didn't mean I'd ever written anything in my life.

My letters were shaky at best, and I accidentally flipped a few. Then he made me do it again, all the letters facing the right way. Then I did it again. And again.

He only stopped because I crumpled up the paper and threw it in his face, and he agreed to move on to math.

This wasn't as annoying. I knew the basics of addition and subtraction –any street kid could figure out that much. Multiplication and division weren't as obvious to me, and it challenged me for the rest of the morning.

He sent me to the den while he prepared lunch. Large windows ran up to the ceiling, bordered with heavy dark red curtains. One wall was floor to ceiling bookshelves, with heavy tomes crammed into every space. The binding on some looked like it was falling apart, and I was scared to touch any of them to find out what they were about.

A large radio stood next to the couch, and I gravitated towards it. Some shops I'd been to had smaller versions, and when I was younger, I would spend hours listening to the music they played. My favorites were the stories they'd occasionally broadcast.

"Do you mind if I turn on the radio?" I called.

"Just don't break it."

I rolled my eyes. It was so nice to be believed in. Really.

There were a lot of dials and knobs, and I twisted a few with no effect. When I twisted one and static shot through the speakers, I almost jumped out of my skin. I scrambled to find music, and eventually the static was replaced with violins.

I collapsed onto the couch, heart still pounding. Dr. Carl stood in the doorway, toweling off his hands and shaking his head at me. He left without a word and I sagged into the cushions.

I didn't mean to fall asleep, but the next thing I knew Dr. Carl shook me awake.

He gave me a history lesson about Wingomia Kingdom and the provinces we lived in while we ate steamed green beans and pork. The only reason I didn't fall asleep again was because I was eating. I think he planned it that way.

The worst was when he *quizzed* me on everything he just said when we finished eating. Since I answered almost everything wrong, he went over everything again.

After I finally answered a few of his questions, he sent me back up to bed, and I gratefully let myself fall asleep.

He hadn't given me any hints yet as to why he wanted my help specifically, and I still didn't know what he even wanted to do. He ignored any question I asked and switched the subject.

Clearly, this was not going to be legal. Since he hadn't sent for the guards yet, I could only assume his plans were worse than getting shipped to the air force.

Days went by. He taught me how to write and do math in the

morning, discussed the kingdom during lunch, and then sent me to bed for the rest of the afternoon. He gave me books to read after dinner, and with nothing better to do I read them. Slowly. The language in the books was a struggle, sometimes, and I kept having to ask what words meant. He was always willing to explain, though. He seemed to like when I asked questions.

I was getting stronger, too, able to walk without help again. I didn't have to nap for so long in the afternoon, and my cough was all but gone. I only took medicine at night, now, and the dose was getting smaller and smaller.

That gave me my chance to spy on him. Skipping my afternoon nap, I crept down stairs and peeked into the den, where static had replaced the piano music we'd been listening to. Dr. Carl fiddled with the radio. Then the lights dimmed, or...or something passed in front of the bulb, something that threw a shadow over just the radio.

The static cut out.

Dr. Carl raised the wide end of some kind of funnel to his mouth. "General? Are you there?"

General? He knew someone in the army? Or maybe it was the air force, and he was about to ship me out.

"This is General Jenus. Lord Basil, your report is a week late."

"Apologies. An opportunity arose I couldn't pass up." Dr. Carl glanced up at the ceiling, and I had the feeling *I* was that opportunity.

Why did the general call him Lord Basil, though? What was going on?

"Does this opportunity involve feeding my people?"

"Indeed, it does. I need a few more days before I can move forward with it, keep your ships out of sight."

A few more days...until I was healthy again? Was that what he meant?

"What do you expect my men to do out here while we wait?"

"I expect you to follow orders. Or did you want your entire

58

country to collapse on itself?"

"We can't sit out here forever."

"I'll be there in a few days with more provisions. Entertain yourselves until then."

"You promised us results, Lord Basil—"

"And you'll get them," Dr. Carl interrupted. "Have a little patience, general. This plan is decades in the making."

"We'd better, or you'll find your next visit will be your last."

"Yes, yes, threaten all you want. You know I have more power than all of you combined, so do as I say and wait for my signal. Goodbye, general."

He shut the radio off, and then turned directly to the doorway.

I ducked out of sight.

The lights in the hall had the same problem as the den. A shadow formed on the wall beside me, and when I noticed it, it jumped and everything around me went dark.

I woke up in bed.

Confusion stunned me for several minutes. I had just been spying on Dr. Carl, right? It hadn't been a dream?

He knocked on my door and let himself in, carrying a tea tray. "Good, you're awake. I was getting worried you might have relapsed."

"Who's General Jenus?" I demanded.

"Beg pardon?"

"I heard you, on the radio."

He set the tea tray down on the nightstand. "I've never been on the radio in my life. Maybe you are relapsing." He placed the back of his hand against my forehead.

I knocked his hand away. "They called you Lord Basil. Why?"

Dr. Carl frowned. "Ace, it was nothing but a dream. I don't even

59

know any generals."

"I'm not making this up." Maybe I'd made up the shadows jumping at me, but all the rest had to be real.

"I believe you think it's real," Dr. Carl said. He poured the tea and handed it to me. "Perhaps I'll give you a stronger dose tonight."

"I don't need more medicine." The cup burned in my hands, but I clung to the pain, to the certainty that *this* was real.

Dr. Carl huffed. "I believe I'm the judge of that. Drink your tea. I'm going to start dinner."

He walked back out, leaving me to sit there with more questions and even fewer answers.

Maybe it really hadn't been real. I couldn't explain how I'd gotten to bed, after all. Maybe…maybe I had dreamed the whole thing up. I was worried about whatever Dr. Carl was planning. It would make sense.

It would also make sense if Dr. Carl realized I'd been listening and was pretending it never happened. I'd have to watch him closely and see what else I could find.

Of course, from that point on, Dr. Carl added even more lessons into the day, and I barely had time to think. The etiquette lessons were the worst. Now I had to learn how to properly bow and address people, and anytime I said something he deemed 'street language' he slapped the backs of my hands. I figured out pretty fast what he didn't want me to say, and made myself sound more like him. Any time I corrected myself he'd nod and smile.

He gave no indications that the radio conversation ever happened, and I never caught him doing it again. The incident slipped to the back of my mind, not forgotten, but put aside until I had more information.

My time here was…nice. Living in a house with regular meals, not having to worry about the weather. Not being covered in dirt all the time. There was still the worry about whatever he wanted me for, and I knew I had to leave soon, but it was hard to be worried about that when he taught me math or history, or when he pulled out a map to show our city, Gallen, not even a half a day away from the palace in Chiari.

Five days after I first came down for breakfast, a stray thought passed through my mind.

This was what having a father would have been like.

I dropped the book I was reading.

A father?

"Ace?" he asked, looking up from his own book.

We were both reading in the den together. He had reading glasses perched on the edge of his nose.

I swallowed. "Nothing. Just sleepy, I guess."

He pulled out a black pocket watch and checked the time. "It's still a little early, but perhaps you'd best go up to bed."

I nodded. "Yeah, I think I will. Um, goodnight." I brought the book with me and took careful steps up the stairs, down the hall, into my room.

A father. Did I really think of him that way? I couldn't. He was only doing all of this for his own selfish reasons. Whatever he wanted a street rat for, it probably meant bad things for me. No one would care what happened to me, after all. Only other street rats.

I had to get out of here. I was becoming attached.

The thought made my heart sink. The food…and the bed…It was almost worth it to stay just for those.

Almost.

He didn't go to bed for a few more hours. I dozed while I could, but when his steps passed by my door, I was wide awake. I waited another two hours after that, just to make sure he'd fallen asleep and was going to stay that way. Then I carefully snuck out of my room.

The stairs creaked, so I slid down the banister. The front door was only feet away, but I glanced towards the kitchen. Was I terrible person if I stole food from him? He'd been feeding me for over a week now, plus medicine was never cheap. And he wasn't asking for money in return.

Then I remembered why I was running away in the middle of the night in the first place and I didn't feel so bad. I grabbed a sack and stuffed it with bread and salted meats.

Slinging the sack over my shoulder, I bolted for the front door. The locks clicked noisily and the hinges squeaked. I winced and slipped through the smallest gap.

As I shut the door, I saw Dr. Carl sitting in the stairwell, elbows on his knees, fingers laced together in front of his face.

I hesitated, but when he made no move to come after me, I shut the door and ran for it.

The street was unfamiliar. That was pretty impressive since I usually prided myself on knowing every nook and cranny of Gallen.

I kept running for as long as I could, which wasn't nearly as long as I was used to. I wasn't at full strength yet, and the sack of food on my back wasn't the lightest thing in the world. Dr. Carl didn't seem to be coming after me, so I slowed to a walk.

By dawn, I was ready to pass out. My arms ached from carrying the food. My feet dragged on the sidewalk. I listed from side to side. Worst of all, I still didn't know where I was. I hadn't realized this city was so big, or that there was so much of it I hadn't explored.

I sank down on someone's front steps, hunched over my knees. It physically hurt to keep my eyes open. Maybe I could get a little bit of sleep here.

It was a terrible idea, bound to go wrong, but before my mind could convince the rest of my body, I was asleep.

A guard shook me awake. I didn't recognize her, but she recognized me.

"Hey, kid, come on. There are better places to sleep than this," the guard said. She was smaller than me, with a high-pitched voice. I didn't think I'd run into her before. If I had, I would have escaped her easily. She was far too small to hope to hold onto me.

But right now, I was exhausted. Running away before Dr. Carl released me had been a bad idea. I doubted I could even make it down the street before passing out again.

She placed a hand against my forehead and frowned. "You've got a fever. That explains it. Come on."

She helped me stand and took the bag of food out of my hand.

"Don't." I tried to hang onto it, but I'd reached my limit. The world tilted under me.

"Where in the world did you steal this much food from?" she asked.

Her voice sounded distorted, and her features blurred.

She swore and caught me before I hit the ground. That was the last thing I remembered.

CHAPTER 10

I would have died immediately if I didn't have such a good personal guard.

The screech came from the canopy only a few meters ahead of us, and some creature leaped from the tree branches straight at our little hunting party.

Straight at me and Adam.

"Shoot the damn thing!" Lucas hauled me aside and shoved me down behind a tree. Adam and Stephen's guards performed similar maneuvers.

I hit the ground hard, knocking my head on a tree root. Lucas threw his body over mine as the creature landed. Tree bark tore, and one pistol shot rang out.

Lucas swore and dragged me up, pushing me back further while he fired his own shot. Either Lucas missed, or the bullet had no effect, because the creature didn't react.

"Hey!" Adam yelled, wielding a pistol in one hand and a rifle in the other.

"Stay back, sir!" his guard yelled.

He'd earned the thing's attention, luring it away from me and Lucas and giving Lucas the chance to stash me behind another tree with strict orders not to move.

I peered around the other side to watch, drawing my own pistol with shaking hands.

Everyone was spread out, mostly behind trees. Stephen took deep breaths across from me, his hands trembling too much to ever get a good shot. Adam stood in front of the creature, taunting it.

Call it brave or foolhardy, but whatever he was doing seemed to be a novelty to the thing. I guessed it didn't have many animals try and taunt it. I certainly didn't want to. The thing was taller than I was. Its shape resembled a bird, mostly, but where wings would have folded against its sides long, gangly arms hung instead. Its beak curved, and the edges were serrated like a knife. Black and dark gray feathers covered the thing from head to toe.

Three pairs of bright red eyes gazed at us. They all moved independently from each other, so the creature could literally keep an eye on all of us at once.

My mouth went dry. What the hell was this thing?

"You smell worse than a gutter," Adam said. "And I bet all those feathers hide the fact you're scrawnier than a branch, aren't you?"

From the corner of my eye, I saw a glint of black steel. Lucas aimed his pistol and fired.

The bullet bounced off the creature's head.

It screeched again and slashed at Lucas. Its claws caught on a tree though, slowing its swing down long enough for Lucas to duck behind an oak and for one of the others to distract it. Adam had been yanked back to some kind of shelter, but his taunting hadn't ceased.

We were in trouble. If bullets weren't going to be enough against this creature, we were going to die. Guns were all we had.

Well. *I* had magic. Magic I was forbidden to use in front of anyone. Such a dumb, stupid rule. What ancestor of mine thought that had been a good idea? Why had all my other ancestors allowed it?

Lucas cursed and crawled beside me. "I want you to run. I'll distract it. You run back to the others and get back to the castle."

65

"No!" I wouldn't leave them to die. He couldn't ask that of me.

He would have argued more, but we didn't have time. The creature leaped around the tree, beak opened wide to chomp us both to little pieces.

I panicked. Instead of firing my pistol like any sane, normal person, I threw the thing at it. It was a decent throw, sailing straight down the creature's throat. The beast was so surprised it drew up short, hacking like a cat with a furball.

Lucas spared me an incredulous look.

I shrugged. There was no time for thinking. Act now, question everything later.

The creature shook its head.

One of the others fired at it, nailing it in the eye. Those were apparently fair game, as the red orb exploded in a shower of bright yellow blood. It whirled on the others with a pained howl, but the sound was tinny, like a bad radio connection.

My gun. It was still stuck in its throat. Shame I couldn't try and reach in and shoot straight down the beast's throat. The inside probably wasn't as bulletproof as the outside.

Actually, that wasn't a bad idea. Who said I had to physically reach down the creature's throat? This kind of telekinesis was child's play.

I grabbed my watch, thumb resting over the familiar grooves of the sun and moon display on the cover, and reached for the magic stored within. A sixth sense rushed over me, connecting me to the world. Channeling it, I focused on the gun in the creature's throat. It wasn't angled well for what I wanted to do, so I shifted it slightly. This did nothing to please the creature. It stumbled from side to side, still shaking its head wildly. Yellow blood splattered the ground.

Then I cocked the pistol and pulled the trigger. It didn't feel any different from shooting a gun in my hand, except for the lack of recoil.

The shot was still distinct in the air. The guttural choking sounds

66

stopped. It went still. Blood trickled out of its mouth, mixed with some kind of black oily substance.

I expected it to fall over or collapse. I did not expect it to melt into a goopy mess.

If Adam had thought it smelled bad before, that was nothing to the smell we were treated to now.

"What happened?" Stephen asked. He and Adam walked up behind me, eyes trained on the mess.

"Someone must have gotten a lucky shot," I said. My voice shook. So did my hands when I pocketed my watch. Energy buzzed through me. I wanted to run and never stop. Maybe I'd be able to outrun the nightmares that were sure to come from this.

"Wasn't us," Adam said. "We didn't have a clear shot with the tree."

I shrugged.

"In any case, it's dead now," Lucas said.

"But what *was* it?" Adam asked. He grabbed a twig and approached the goop, hesitantly poking the black mess. The goop sucked the twig out of Adam's hands. "Really glad I didn't use my finger."

"We should meet up with the others," Stephen's guard said. "And then I think we need to call this hunting trip over."

"Why?" Adam demanded. "We killed the thing already."

"We don't know if there's more," the guard said. "What if it's part of a pack? We could have just angered a dozen of them for all we know."

Lucas spoke up, "This needs to be reported to the King. He needs to know creatures like this are walking around."

I winced. Hopefully he meant *just* the King needed to know. If we could not tell my mother about this, I might be able to see the outside of my room again.

But he did have a point. Duty first. There was a potential threat to Wingomia, it needed to be investigated.

I pushed myself up, acting more put together than I felt. "Lucas is right. It's not like any of us really wanted to go hunting anyway."

"I would if it was always like this," Adam said. "This was actually interesting!"

"I think you mean terrifying," Stephen said. "I thought we were really going to die there for a minute."

"That was more excitement than I think our parents were planning on," I agreed. "Come on, let's meet up with everyone else."

None of the others were disappointed with the decision to head back home, and they were all enthralled with the story of the creature, especially the way Adam told it. He painted me like some kind of coward hiding behind a tree, and I attempted to set the story straight. It was hard to do when, as far as anyone else was concerned, the only thing I did was throw my gun at it and make it choke.

Not exactly what heroic songs were made out of.

Adam continued with his version of events. Lucas clapped me on the shoulder. He probably assumed I'd done something with magic, but we couldn't discuss it with the others listening.

This left me with far too much time to think. That creature, whatever it was, wasn't natural. No normal animal would just *melt* when killed like that. And yellow blood? What was that about? Even bears and rabbits all bleed red. Not to mention the unholy shrieking. The sound alone sent every animal within range running for the hills.

Where had it come from? I wouldn't claim to have explored every inch of these woods, but I feel like I would have run across something that deadly long before now.

What if it wasn't the only one? What if there was a whole pack somewhere? If they were bulletproof, and the guards went after them, they'd be in serious trouble.

I started chewing on my thumbnail. It was an old habit all my tutors had tried desperately to break, but when I was lost in thought the habit reemerged.

68

If the creature wasn't part of a pack, that was almost worse. At least with a pack there was a logical explanation for where it had come from. But if it was by itself? It couldn't have just sprung up out of the ground, like some kind of monster or demon.

This was going to be the start of some very long conversations with my parents.

CHAPTER 11

I wished I could say I didn't know where I was when I woke up, but the smell was unmistakable. Dirty diapers, mold, and too many unwashed bodies created an odor that was hard to forget.

That, and the sound of a dozen kids screaming and running through the halls, made this place unmistakable.

The Orphanage.

My worst nightmare.

I shut my eyes again and hoped if I went to sleep, I'd wake up somewhere else. It happened enough lately that it seemed like a valid option.

It didn't work. I was still here. My heart pounded just knowing that, and I hadn't even seen the caretakers yet.

Someone had placed me on the bottom bunk in a room and put a wet washcloth on my forehead. Since I couldn't picture any of the people in charge doing that, I assumed one of the other kids had.

My bunk was one of four in the room. A single bare bulb screwed into the center of the ceiling. Worn chests sat at either end of the bunk beds, full of whatever belongings these kids had. I hoped I hadn't stolen some kid's bunk.

Loud voices erupted outside the door, followed by fast shushing. Hinges creaked when someone poked their head in.

I sat up.

They yelped and disappeared from view.

Taking a deep breath, ignoring how my whole body shook, I stood up and approached the door. Before I could pull it open more, a girl burst through, coming up short when she saw I was so close. Her hand tightened on the doorknob.

She looked around eleven, with long dark brown hair in two braids. A beauty mark dotted her cheek under one of her wide dark brown eyes.

"You're not supposed to get up," she stated.

"I'm not staying." I knew where the orphanage was. I could find my way back to Base from here.

"You're sick," she said.

"I'll be fine." I'd rather be sick anywhere else than be even remotely healthy inside this building. I'd even willingly walk myself to the air force rather than stay here.

"Mama and Papa weren't happy to see you," she said, still standing in the doorway, still blocking my way.

Mama and Papa. The caretakers of this place. They insisted all the kids call them that. "I don't want to see them." That was the last thing I wanted, ever. Being stabbed a hundred times was more preferable.

"But the guards that dropped you off also had a bag of food, so they said you could stay."

King's beard. That food was supposed to be for my friends. Mama and Papa would keep half of it for themselves.

"Where'd you get the food?" the girl asked.

"Stole it from a rich guy," I said. "If you let me leave, I can bring more." I would do no such thing. I would never come anywhere near here if I could help it.

"How'd you steal it?" she asked.

"Went in the kitchen while he was asleep and took it." I pushed her out of the way, but a whole group of kids stood outside the door, blocking the hallway.

71

The girl spun me around, standing on her toes to get in my face. "Can you steal it again?"

"From Mama and Papa?"

She nodded.

"Do you want to die? That is how you die."

"You slept in my bunk. You owe me." She jutted her chin out, like she was trying to be taller.

"I didn't choose where I slept, so no." I pushed past her and all the other kids. It was time to leave, before Mama and Papa knew I was awake.

"It smelled so good, though," one of the kids said. He was a little blonde boy, missing a front tooth.

"And you're not getting a bite of it if you try to steal it," a deep voice said. Heavy steps came up the stairs.

My entire body froze. I wanted to run and hide, jump out a window, crawl into the walls, anything but actually face him. But I couldn't go anywhere. The kids scrambled behind me, mouths snapping shut as we faced the top of the stairs on the other end of the hallway.

A giant of a man stepped into view. His presence took up the whole second floor. Papa. His arms and legs were thick with muscles, straining against his shirt and pants. An old scar cut his eyebrow, a remnant from his days in an illegal fight club, the stories went. He ran his fingers over a whip coiled at his waist.

"Not to mention your actual punishment if you try it," he said.

The sound of the cracking whip echoed in my mind. He'd never been afraid to use it. If the room was too small, he'd get a poker from the fireplace.

His gaze met mine, and his face twisted. "The brat's awake, huh?"

This is the part where I should *do something*, say something, at least. Maybe something witty like 'Anyone with eyes can see I'm awake.' The best I could do was not whimper.

"You've caused a lot of trouble, runt." Papa moved closer.

I didn't know if it was fear or stupidity that kept me rooted to the spot.

"The guards said you've been a thorn in their side for years now, making them look like fools. And, of course, they blame *us*, because we didn't keep you here like we're supposed to."

He stood right in front of me. I had to crane my neck to look up at him.

"So, here's what's going to happen. You're going to be on your best behavior. If you put even a shadow out of line, I'll whip you until I find bone. Then, once your fever breaks, you can join all the others doing the King's work in the air force."

Anyone unfortunate enough to stay in the Orphanage until they came of age had this fate waiting for them now. They used to go to some mill outside town, but once the air force had been established a few years back, that became their fate. Sent to the coast to build flying ships, never to be heard from again.

A lot of us wondered if there even was an air force out there.

"Or," I coughed to clear my throat. It felt like I hadn't had anything to drink in years. "Or, you let me walk out the front door right now. You don't want me here, and I don't want to be here. Let me go, and we both win."

He grinned. "Nice try, runt. But the guards will be back for you in a few days. I can stand you that long."

"Sure they aren't coming for you?" I regretted the words as soon as they left my mouth. It was a defense mechanism, so no one would know how terrified I really was at the threat. It just didn't defend against much when in front of Papa.

He grabbed my shirt collar and leaned in my face. "Watch it, runt. I've whipped people for less before."

"Yeah, I know." Anger burned in me. There was a mass grave in the backyard full of 'tragic accidents' to prove it. I'd had good friends end up in that grave before I ran away.

If I stayed, I'd be in that grave long before my fever ever broke.

73

He narrowed his eyes at me. "Maybe you need a demonstration."

"I've seen plenty." I grabbed his wrist and dug my nails in.

He let go of my shirt just to punch me, but at least stumbling away gave me some distance from him.

The kids gasped and scattered back.

"Don't ever do that again," Papa said. "Or you really will get the whip." He patted the thing at his side.

All of us flinched.

Satisfied, he walked away, pausing at the top of the stairs. "By the way, none of you get dinner tonight since you were planning to steal it. Can't let thoughts like that go unpunished, now, can we?"

He disappeared down the stairs again.

I sagged against the wall and slid down to the floor. I felt drained, like I'd run all through the city. Except worse, because I was emotionally spent. I needed another nap.

One of the kids sniffed. "I missed breakfast, too."

"We always have to share, why don't the grownups?" a little four-year-old girl asked.

"Guess we'll just have to steal it after all," the older girl with the beauty mark said, looking to me. "He'll help."

"Excuse me?" I'd barely survived that encounter. I had no desire to go poking a hornet's nest.

She crossed her arms and looked down at me. "You'll go hungry, too. And you know what you're doing, so you have to help."

The kids all looked to me, eyes pleading.

One of these days, I was going to have to figure out how to say no to that look.

CHAPTER 12

I expected my parents to overreact when we all returned much sooner than planned. I expected my mother to put me under extreme security, for her to fuss, for everything to be unbearable for days.

I expected all this, and yet, somehow, I was still surprised.

We arrived at the palace after sunset. Mother came running out to meet us, hair unbound and flying behind her and her shoes unlaced.

"Are you hurt? What happened?"

I dismounted and found her hands on my face, running through my hair.

The guys snickered.

"Mom, I'm fine. We're all fine. No one is hurt."

She let out a deep breath and pulled me into a tight hug. "You nearly gave me a heart attack. I thought something must have happened. What are you doing back so soon?"

My father hurried into the courtyard to meet us, looking much more put together than mother, but showing almost as much concern.

"Something did happen," I started. As much as I didn't want to tell her, there was no way she wouldn't find out. Especially if magic was needed to fight off any more creatures. We were the only two magicians in the entire kingdom, and I certainly didn't know what to do.

"But everyone is okay?" Dad squinted through the darkness to look for hidden injuries.

"We're fine," Adam groaned. "We found some...monster, thing, out there."

My parents stared at us for a moment. Glanced at each other. "What?"

I explained as best I could. Servants came out to lead all of our horses to the stables. Some were already on their way to the Villa outside the palace to let the other boys' parents know we were back already. Two came out with lanterns.

My mother shook her head. "I knew letting you go was a mistake. You never should have hunted that beast. You should have returned as soon as you heard it." She looked at all the boys. "I'm very disappointed in all of you. This was a poor decision that you made."

Adam stomped forward. "I don't think we did anything wrong. We found a problem, and we handled it. That's the purpose of these little hunts, isn't it? To build teamwork between all of us?" He remembered who he was speaking to a moment later and stood up straighter, tacking on a curt "Your Majesties."

My father stroked his beard, and Mother shot him a glare. He'd be getting an earful from her later, that was for sure.

"Your Majesties," Lucas said, putting a hand on my shoulder. "With all due respect, the boys handled themselves well out there. Maybe it was foolhardy, but Lord Adam is right. They assessed the problem and calmly planned a course of action. Grown men could hardly have done better."

That was high praise coming from my bodyguard who'd been begging me to turn around the whole time.

Not that my mother cared.

"Selena," my father interjected, using his stern King voice. "You can berate them all you want; it doesn't change what already happened. We have to decide what to do next."

"We need to find out if there are more," I said. "Make sure they're not going after any towns."

My father nodded. "I agree. Adam, perhaps you'd like to inform your father of what's happened?"

Adam stood straighter and puffed his chest out. "Of course."

I rolled my eyes.

"Tell him to start a thorough search of the woods immediately."

"Right away!" He and his guard hurried away, which was the signal for the others to start heading home.

Soon it was only me, my parents, and our guards. Mother wrapped me in a hug again and started leading me inside. "I'm so glad you're safe. I never liked this hunting trip anyway."

"Your Majesties," Lucas began, pitching his voice low. "I have a few more observations I want to share with you."

Mother tensed. "I think we could all do with a nice cup of tea, hmm?"

"That sounds wonderful," Dad said.

We relocated to one of the first floor sitting rooms, and servants set out a tea tray for us. My parents sat on a small couch together. I sat across from them on a twin couch, a dark mahogany coffee table between us. The blue wallpaper in here always reminded me of the river.

Lucas perched on the edge of a wing backed chair, a cup of tea in front of him going cold.

"It wasn't just any creature that attacked us," he said after the servants left us alone. "It was a demon."

I froze, teacup halfway to my mouth. I'd had the passing thought out in the forest, but it couldn't actually be a demon.

Mom spilled her tea over her skirts, but she didn't even notice. Dad jumped to take the cup out of her hand and started sopping up the mess with a handkerchief.

I didn't know much about demons, only that they were bad omens, usually preceding major wars and bloodshed.

77

"You're certain?" Mom asked.

Lucas nodded. "Yellow blood, turned to black goop when we killed it." He must be paying more attention to my magic lessons than I did to remember that. His chin jerked towards me. "I don't know what he did, but I doubt any of those boys would be alive today if it weren't for him."

My ears burned. I hid behind my teacup as much as I could. "After it swallowed my gun, I just used magic to shoot it from inside."

"That was smart thinking," Dad praised.

Mother rigidly controlled her breathing. "You fought a demon."

"We didn't know it was a demon," I countered. "And you can't tell me it would have been better if we'd left it alone to wreak havoc out there."

She stood up and started pacing.

"Selena." Dad grabbed her hand. "We would have done the same thing if we'd been there. We can't fault him for that."

"But why was it there at all?" she asked.

"I don't know. Perhaps you could explain more of what you know about demons? I don't remember much about them."

I nodded. Dad knew less about this than I did. He and Mother had studied all they could years ago, but Mother had kept up with it to train me while Dad had turned his attention to the rest of the Kingdom and more traditional lines of defense.

Mother took a deep breath and agreed. "Yes. That's a good place to start." She resumed her seat and refilled her teacup, adding in a sugar cube and stirring. "Demons are from the Underworld. They are beings of pure chaos."

The Underworld? I'd never heard it described as an actual, physical place before, not the way mother described now.

"It's normally impossible for them to cross into our world. But occasionally, cracks appear, and demons crawl through."

"So, that one we saw today might have been the only one?" I

asked.

"For now, possibly."

Well, that wasn't a strong vote of confidence.

"You must understand that cracks between the worlds aren't because of time or some kind of erosion. They're formed when very strong chaotic energy converges in a single location."

"Where does that energy come from?" Dad asked.

Mother traced a finger around the edge of her cup. "People, usually. Their thoughts."

"So, it builds over time until it creates a crack?" Lucas asked.

Mother shook her head. "No, all the sources I've read say they're the result of a single person. They alone possess thoughts strong enough and chaotic enough to cause these cracks."

"So, if we don't want more demons, we have to find this one person?" I asked. Talk about a needle in a haystack. There were millions of people in this kingdom.

"Ideally, yes," Mother said. "But obviously that's difficult."

"There have to be countermeasures we can take in the meantime," Dad said. "Some way to notice when more demons appear."

I glanced at Mom. She continued to trace the rim of her cup.

Tracking spells weren't easy. The larger the scale, the less likely they'd work. It was why she hadn't been able to track my twin brother when he was kidnapped. I'd only asked about them once. She'd shut down when she answered, becoming a shell of herself and losing all emotion for a few hours. I think she considered it her biggest failure. All this magic, and she still hadn't been able to find her son.

Maybe it would be different with something like a demon. It wasn't human, after all. And we wouldn't be tracking, per se. We'd be setting an alarm, something that would ring a bell when it crossed into our world and at least let us know.

That would never work. The world was too big for any one of us to cast a spell that large. These demons could appear anywhere. Our magic only reached so far.

"I'll have to think about it," Mother answered.

It was one of her diplomatic answers. One of those, 'We'll consider it, but we can't make any promises.'

Dad frowned. He'd noticed, too. "Selena, what aren't you telling me?"

I looked between them. My parents never fought or kept secrets from each other. Or at least, that was what I'd always assumed. It seemed naïve to believe that now. They ran a kingdom together. They couldn't possibly agree with each other a hundred percent of the time.

Mother took a deep breath. "Any spell that large would have consequences. People would notice something, not to mention the toll it would take on the caster."

Dad ran his hand up and down her arm. "Okay. You take some time to think about how you want to handle it. But tell me what I can do to keep people safe in the meantime."

"Can't we warn people?" I asked. "Just tell them to be careful and not to go into the woods alone?"

"They'd wonder why and investigate anyway." Dad shook his head. "We can warn them that there's a dangerous animal, maybe. But then they'll try and go after it, and we don't want to cause *more* people to go into the woods."

"Tell them the guardsmen are doing a training exercise," Mom said. She laid a hand over Dad's on her arm. "They're training in the woods, and in order to avoid accidental injuries civilians are advised to keep out."

"Wait, we're going to blatantly lie?" I asked.

They both smiled at me, their eyes softening. I felt six years old again. I wanted to pout like one, too.

"It's the hardest thing about being in charge of a kingdom, Jack," Dad said. "You try to be as honest and just as you can, but sometimes lying is the best way to protect everyone."

80

I understood that. It made sense not to tell the kingdom about demons crawling around. But telling them something else instead… it felt like an insult, almost. Like we couldn't trust them with the truth.

Which, maybe we couldn't.

The idea still didn't sit right with me. It shouldn't bother me so much, not when it was the most logical course of action, but it did. "I understand."

"That's enough for one night, I think." Mom set down her teacup, still mostly full. "You've had an exciting day, Jack. You should get some rest."

I nodded. There was no way I'd be able to sleep after all this, but being away from everyone was its own relief.

Dad stroked his beard. "We'll have to figure out what you'll be doing for the next few days. Your tutors took up some extra work in the Villa this week.."

Oh, that was right. I was supposed to be gone for the whole week, which meant now I had a free schedule for the first time in ages.

Maybe I could go back and look for that kid after all. Not that mom would let me out of the castle right now. I didn't see how I could sneak out, either. Not without someone covering for me.

I eyed my dad. "Can I shadow you?" He had to have at least one day where his schedule didn't mix with my mom's.

His eyes brightened, and I immediately felt like the worst child in the world. Here I was complaining we were going to lie to the whole kingdom, only to turn around and plan to deceive my parents.

"That's an excellent idea," he said.

The guilt sank in a little deeper.

CHAPTER 13

I made the kids wait until after everyone went to bed. Before anything else, I needed another nap. Plus, Mama and Papa needed to see them hungry at dinner. A small, hopeful part of me wanted to believe they'd have a change of heart and let the kids eat something, at least the little ones, but no such luck. They were still rotten people.

Mama glared at me all through dinner. There was an infant strapped to her back, crying off and on. In her defense, I'd be a cranky person too if I always had a kid screaming in my ears. But against that defense, taking care of the kid would help stop them from screaming. My sympathy for her was limited. At least she never hit the kids. She left that to her husband.

Her brand of torture was crueler. She wanted to be called mama, but she never acted like a mother. She scoffed at scraped knees, laughed at us when other kids teased us, insulted us night and day, blamed us for all her problems.

The fact she didn't hit us was her only saving grace.

It was an uncomfortable dinner, mostly silent. And then the kids went to bed, so Mama and Papa could have time to themselves.

I told most of the kids to sleep if they could. Only me and the older girl, Sara, would steal the food. Any more would be too noisy, and we'd be caught for sure.

Sara and I sat on her bunk, waiting until the house quieted down. Even then, I made her wait another hour. Papa had to be expecting us to do something. We had to wait until even he fell asleep.

Finally, when the moon shone through the window and we hadn't heard any creaks in the house for a long time, we snuck down to the kitchen.

It was dark and hard to see anything, but we didn't dare turn on a light. We kept our hands out instead, carefully feeling in front of us and sliding our feet over the floor. But as quiet as we were, it didn't stop the kitchen door from creaking open.

Or the crash from the stack of pans the door knocked over.

He'd set a trap for us.

"King's Beard." I grabbed Sara's arm and bolted for the stairs.

A light clicked on above us. Papa stood at the top of the stairs, still dressed, whip uncoiled in his hand. "I knew you brats would try something."

Sara grabbed a fistful of my shirt and cowered behind me, muttering a prayer under her breath.

Papa came down the steps one at a time.

"Come on!" I turned on my heel and raced back to the kitchen. The front door would be locked with padlocks, keys on a necklace under Papa's shirt. But the backdoor was only bolted from the inside. When I was a kid, I'd escaped by climbing the fence and dropping down in a neighbor's yard.

I hoped Sara could climb.

We tripped over the pots and pans in the kitchen.

"Where do you think you're going, brats? I'm going to teach you what it means to be part of civil society!"

I crashed into the backdoor. My fingers fumbled with the lock.

Papa kicked a pan out of the way, and it clattered over the

floor.

We swung the door open and launched ourselves into the night air. I took a running leap at the fence and hauled myself up, straddling the top and reaching back for Sara.

She grabbed my hand and tried to climb up, but we weren't fast enough.

The whip cracked down on her back. She screamed and let go of my hand, crumpling on the ground.

"Sara!"

The whip cracked again. And again.

Her shirt tore. Strips of fabric flittered in the air, stained crimson.

"Stop it!" I screamed. "You'll kill her!"

Papa looked up at me, anger glinting in his eyes. He raised his arm to crack the whip again.

I flinched back so hard I fell off the fence into the neighbor's yard. Air rushed out in a painful whoosh. For a second, all I could do was curl on my side and remember how to breathe.

It wasn't a second I had to spare.

Sara screamed again. The whip cracked down relentlessly.

"You better get back over here, boy, or I *will* kill her!"

I croaked out a desperate "Stop," and clawed at the fence. "I'm coming!"

My feet scrambled for purchase, and I shook so badly with fear that I couldn't climb up again as easily as I had the first time.

Sara went quiet.

How many times had she been lashed? How much could her small body take? I hoped she'd fallen unconscious and escaped the pain, at least for a while. I hoped it wasn't worse.

My feet slipped, and then a fist pounded against the fence and I lost my grip.

"Well, boy? She's not moving, are you going to leave her

84

here to die? Are you going to let a girl die for you?"

"I'm coming, damn it, just give me a second."

A light flicked on in the house next to me, and someone came out on the back porch. "What is going on out here?"

I froze, hanging off their fence, Papa cracking the whip on the other side.

The man looked from me to the fence.

Something in my brain started working, thankfully. "Call the guards! Get help!"

Those were words I thought would never leave my mouth.

"What was that?" Papa demanded.

"Oh, not again," the man whimpered, retreating inside.

Please don't let this man be a coward. Please let him be calling for help.

Papa hauled himself up on his side of the fence, and he leered down at me. He reached one hand over the fence for me.

I dropped to the ground and scrambled back.

He swore at me. "Don't make me take it out on little Sara anymore!"

"Leave her alone!" I yelled.

He dropped out of sight. The whip cracked.

"No!" I jumped for the fence again.

The man came back out of his house, wrapping a bathrobe around himself. "Don't do it, boy! He'll kill you, too!"

But if he killed Sara, it was my fault. I brought the extra food; I started this mess. I promised to help, and I only made things worse. I couldn't get her out. *It was my fault.*

I swung a leg over the fence, but the old man grabbed my other one and yanked me back to his side, just as the whip cracked the air I'd been in.

"Help is on the way," the man promised. "I sent my maid for

the guard."

"Whittaker, is that you? You better stay out of this, you hear me?" Papa yelled. The fence rattled.

"He can't do anything to me," Whittaker promised.

"Sara, I have to help her!" I fought his grasp. Energy still surged through me, but I could feel the end of it coming. I wouldn't be able to last much longer. I was already pushing myself far past what I should be doing considering I still had a fever, especially when I didn't have the medicine anymore.

Whittaker lifted me off my feet and hauled me away from the fence. "The guards are coming; they'll take care of her."

"They won't be able to do anything if she's already dead!" I yelled. I squirmed in his grip. Kicked his knee caps. But either I was even weaker right now than I thought, or he was a lot stronger than he looked, because I couldn't wriggle free no matter how hard I tried.

"Oh, she will be," Papa promised, "if you don't get your ass on this side of the fence in five seconds!"

"I'm trying!" I sobbed.

"George, you leave that little girl alone!" Whittaker yelled.

"Stay out of this, old man! This doesn't concern you!"

"It does now!"

"Let me go," I begged. "I have to help her!" She was hurt and bleeding, and it was my fault. I'd sat there on the fence, watching it happen, grateful it wasn't me. I could have jumped down in front of her. I could have stopped her from trying to steal the food in the first place.

Whatever scars she bore, they'd be my fault.

If she died, *it was my fault.*

CHAPTER 14

The first day, I did shadow my father around. I felt too guilty to try to come up with a decent excuse right away. And this was stuff I was going to need to know, so it wasn't like shadowing him was a waste of my time.

But it was *a lot* of time. My father's schedule was packed tight, every second accounted for. Without his head advisor and the pocket watch all but glued to his hand, he'd never have made it to all his meetings.

"I thought Mom ran half the kingdom," I said during our brief lunch. We had twenty-six minutes exactly before we met with the head of the Infrastructure Committee.

"She does," Dad said. "She handles more of the social issues, like the guilds and the justice department, and the nobles. I handle the infrastructure, like bridges and trade routes and taxes."

I still didn't understand how he was busy enough to meet with people back-to-back like this all the time, even though I attended all his meetings that day. His meetings mostly seemed to be about letting people talk and promising them an answer at a later date. If an answer was needed at all. Half of them seemed to be just updating him on what was going on.

Wouldn't it make more sense to have them send in a report for him to read on his own? When I became king, that was how I'd do it.

But that wasn't going to be for a very, very long time, because nothing was going to happen to my father. Never. He was immortal.

"Jack?" my father asked.

My head snapped up. "What?"

He smiled at me and rubbed the top of my head. "It's been a long day. Why don't you go see if you can get some fencing in before dinner?"

I wrinkled my nose. Fencing was not a favorite activity of mine. I didn't have the balance or grace for it.

"After what happened on the hunt you cannot get out of it now," he stated.

That was an excellent point. "Yeah, okay. I'll see you at dinner?"

"Of course." He gave me a quick one-armed hug and continued with his advisor while I went up to my rooms, Lucas a silent shadow behind me.

After changing into my fencing gear, I trudged down to the courtyard. Lucas and I both picked up some practice foils, and he drilled me until dinner.

While sitting at the table, rolling peas around on my plate, I realized I never came up with an excuse to not follow my father the next day. The only thing that could remotely work was pretending to be sick…except even then a doctor would be checking in on me all day. And what excuse could I have to go into town?

I was a terrible liar anyway, so I asked them straight out if I could.

Mom blinked and lowered her fork. "You were just there last week," she said.

"I know, but…"

Dad chuckled. "You want to find that boy, don't you?" He sipped his wine.

My cheeks reddened. Was I that obvious? "He really looked like he needed help."

"You can't help everyone, Jack," Mom said softly. "And the

88

chances of finding him again…"

I lowered both hands under the table so they wouldn't see my clenched fists. "Maybe I can't help everyone, but I should help everyone I can, shouldn't I?"

Mom geared up to say something else, but Dad beat her to it.

"You can go, but you can't give the shirt off your back again, deal?"

"Just my shirt? Does that mean I can give him my pants?"

"Don't you dare come home without pants, young man, or that will be the end of these trips," Mom stated.

That was fair, I decided. "I won't give him anything I'm wearing," I promised. That didn't mean I wouldn't still *bring* him stuff, but this pleased my parents.

Later that night, I went through my clothes, looking for the slightly worn ones or ones I didn't like anymore. My wardrobe was usually kept up to date, so it wasn't a large pile. Still, it filled a cloth bag Lucas found for me, so I hoped it would be enough.

I could barely sleep. I was too busy making plans in my head of the places I would check, spells I would use to try to find him, and other ways of tracking him down. Then I was too busy imagining how our next meeting would go, trying to figure out how I would hand over the clothes without looking like I was pitying him. He didn't seem like the type to accept charitable donations.

Come morning, I was out the door as soon as I could be. I only had the day to find him, I had to make it count. The flight lasted forever, and the steamcar barely stopped before I jumped out.

"Your-wait!" Lucas jumped down after me.

I smiled back at him. "We've only got so much daylight, come on!" I raced into the crowd, bag clutched in my hand.

Lucas grabbed my shoulder and hauled me back. "Please don't run off like that."

"I'm not running off," I said. "You're right here!"

He pinched the bridge of his nose. "Just…stay near me, please.

We don't need another hunt incident."

The mention of the hunt sobered me, but it wasn't like a demon would be in town. We'd know if there was by the mobs of screaming people. We didn't even know if there were more like it, or if that had been the only one. So, what was the use in worrying about it?

"We'll be fine," I assured Lucas. "Now, where should we start looking?"

He sighed, but suggested we ask a guard if they knew of any poor kids with red hair. It was an unusual enough color it would narrow our search down by a lot.

As it turned out, plenty of guards knew of a poor kid with red hair about my height. And they did not think of him favorably.

"Little devil, that one," one guard said, thumbing his nose. "Don't know what you'd want with him, sirs"

"That's our business," Lucas said. "Do you know where we can find him?"

"Naw. He comes, he steals whatever he can get his hands on, and then he disappears. Would love to get that rat off the streets."

Another guard swore he had to be part phantom. "I've chased him around half the city, and then he vanishes!"

"Climbs over the roofs like a monkey," his partner added. "Just the other week, we had him cornered at the river. He jumped in and used the water wheel to get out!"

All the stories we heard were like that. The guards were more than willing to rant about the red-haired devil, but none of them knew where he lived. They'd checked orphanages, and they searched the alleys all the time, but they'd never found him.

I was starting to think he *was* some kind of phantom. Maybe my meeting with him hadn't been real.

Lucas thanked the last guard and then sighed, scanning the road. When he spotted the Chimer shouting at the corner, he took my arm and crossed the street. "Honestly, Jack, I'm liking the sounds of this kid less and less."

"You saw him that day," I said quietly. "He was hurt, and sick."

"He sounds resourceful enough to be fine," Lucas insisted. "He *plays* with the guards. He doesn't need your help."

Maybe he didn't. But I couldn't let this go so easily. Something was drawing me towards him. I still wanted to find him, if only to learn his name.

"Let's keep looking," I said, turning on my heel.

Lucas sighed but dutifully followed.

We walked half the city, even down some of the narrow side streets that made Lucas nervous. We stopped into a few churches, risking off-the-cuff sermons about preserving life and the dangers of destruction.

Their message fell flat when half a dozen people missing arms or legs or sporting horrific steam burns dotted the same street, holding cups out for some shred of generosity.

I emptied my wallet and Lucas's before we left. When my hand drifted to my watch and I gave the people long, considering looks, Lucas clapped a hand on my shoulder and steered me away.

"Oh, no you don't. None of that special talent of yours. Your Mother would have my head."

I sighed but didn't fight him. She'd have both our heads if I used magic so publicly.

"You've done all you can today," Lucas said.

"It's not enough," I said. "A handful of coins doesn't solve their problems."

"No," he agreed. "But you did make them happy. Don't underestimate that."

A token prize, but the best I could hope for about all of this.

The Gallen clocktower rang four times. I turned towards it automatically, thumb running over my watch chain. The clock didn't sound anything like the Palace clock, but there was still something familiar and calming about the sound.

"Jack?" Lucas shook my shoulder.

"Huh?"

"You drifted for a second there," Lucas said. He looked me up and down, frowning.

"Sorry. Disappointed we didn't find the kid, that's all."

"It was a longshot," he said, gently coaxing me on.

We had to take a detour around a Chimer rally in front of a warehouse on the river, and Lucas refused to let me close enough to hear what they shouted. After that, he couldn't get me in the steamcar fast enough.

I eased back in my seat, goggles over my eyes and wind whipping through my hair. The flight back gave me too much time to think of today's failure. Longshot or not, I'd still wanted to find that boy.

At dinner, Dad asked how it went. The way I stabbed my chicken was answer enough.

"I'm going back tomorrow," I stated. I would go back every day until I found him.

My parents glanced at each other.

"I don't think it's such a good idea," my father said.

"Please, let me do this," I said. "I can't explain it, but I have to do this."

Dad sighed. "You have the rest of this week. After that, promise me you'll drop it."

Find one kid in a big city who could apparently disappear like smoke? In a week? And just…give up, if I couldn't?

But on the other hand, if I couldn't find him in a week, maybe I never would. He could already be dead for all I knew. A deadline might not be a bad idea.

"Okay. I promise."

CHAPTER 15

Porch lights lit up the street, even though it was three in the morning. People hovered in doorways or peered out of windows. A fleet of steamcars had parked anywhere they could all over the street. Papa and Mama had both been arrested, both dragged out of the orphanage in handcuffs.

Sara was carried out in a red and white sheet.

I'd collapsed on Whittaker's front steps and hadn't moved since. He stayed by my side, patting my shoulder or rubbing my back.

Sara was dead. Because of me. Because of all the choices I'd made.

A few guards came to talk to Whittaker, and they tried to talk to me. Words…didn't really reach me, right then. None that made sense anyway.

She'd just wanted food. She was hungry. She was trying to survive. I'd stolen almost everything I'd ever eaten, so why was she dead?

An older guard leaned down on the steps below me. He had a scruffy white beard and round cheeks, and wrinkles around his eyes. "Rough night, huh?"

I glared weakly at him. That didn't even begin to describe how this night had gone.

"What's your name?"

"Ace." The sound barely made it out of my mouth.

"That's a good, strong, name. I'm Officer Jacoby. I've heard from a few of the other kids what they think happened, and it sounds like you were right in the middle of it all."

"What will happen to them?"

"The other kids? They'll stay here. We're working out a rotation of guards to keep an eye on them for a day or two until new caretakers can be appointed. And once this story hits the papers, I'm sure many of them will be adopted."

That was good. They deserved real homes, not this house of nightmares and death.

"Can you tell me what happened?" Jacoby asked.

"We just wanted food," I whispered. In bits and pieces, I told him what happened. My arrival, my bag of food, my plan, my fault. Sara's death.

He stayed quiet and let me talk at my own pace, until I said every last gory detail. He patted my knee. "I'm sorry you had to go through this. I hope you know it wasn't your fault. George made his own choices. And the Guard should have been checking in more to make sure he and his wife weren't abusing their power. But we'll make it better now, I promise."

Liar. Sara was dead. They couldn't change that.

Officer Jacoby stood up and talked with a few other officers.

Whittaker, still next to me, let out a deep breath. "Well, I don't know about you, but I'm exhausted. I've got a spare couch you can sleep on if you want. I doubt you want to go back next door any time soon."

Never would be too soon. But I didn't want to stay with Whittaker, either.

I wanted my friends. I wanted Jade and Malik and Damon.

"Ace? Where are you going?"

My body moved on its own. Down the steps, up the street, shrugging off a few half-hearted attempts to grab me. My pace quickened when I rounded the corner.

By the next block, I was running.

By the one after that, I was blinking away tears.

It took me an hour, but I finally stumbled back to Base.

Malik and Jade both jumped up when I shouldered the door open, my feet shuffling over the floor, and Malik pulled a knife on me. It clattered to the ground when he got a good look at me.

"Ace!"

"You're back!" Jade said.

They tackled me, and once Damon woke up and realized what was happening, he jumped on the pile, too.

I clutched all of them as tight as I could until exhaustion finally made me pass out. When I woke up hours later, sunlight poked through the crack over the door. My head was in Jade's lap, with Malik beside me and Damon curled up on top of me.

"Not the return I was expecting," Malik said.

"Especially when you still have a fever," Jade added, pressing her hand against my forehead. "Did the doctor kick you out?"

"No, he was just weird." After drinking some water, I explained everything to them. They prodded me until I told them about the orphanage, too. At least, I told them the bare details. I didn't want to freak Damon out.

"I can't believe you ended up back there." Malik squeezed his fingers around a wrench.

"Or that you were there for less than a day and managed to flip the place on its head," Jade said.

Even Damon had his own two cents to share. "I can't believe you came back without shoes. You always tell me never to walk around barefoot."

Blinking, I glanced down at my feet. I'd been in such a daze with everything going on, I'd never noticed I didn't grab my boots.

Well, that was just great. I was lucky I hadn't stepped on any broken glass.

"I'll try and find some for you today," Malik offered. "You should get some more rest."

It felt like all I did anymore was sleep, but I couldn't deny how drained I was, despite the nap I just had. And not going out and facing the world sounded like the best idea I'd heard in weeks. "Thanks."

Jade asked Malik to bring back food, too, and with a quick salute he was off.

Damon started telling me everything I'd missed. The most exciting thing seemed to be his successful pickpocketing adventures and Jade slugging a handsy drunk across the face. But Damon went day by day, making sure I knew everything, and it wasn't long before I nodded off.

The nightmares didn't take long either. Only a couple hours later, I woke up gasping in a cold sweat. Jade's lap had been replaced by a folded blanket, and another had been laid out over me. She and Damon were by the stove, fingers covered in ash, practicing Damon's letters on the wall.

A pair of boots and a stale loaf of bread wrapped in paper sat next to my head. One of the boots didn't have laces, and the other had a weird green stain on the side.

"Are you alright?" Jade asked.

I took a deep breath. "Yeah. Just a dream." A horror featuring Dr. Carl and Sara and too much blood, but only a dream.

"Ace, look, I can write the alphabet!" Damon beamed. He rubbed more ash on his fingers and started writing in a blank space of wall.

"That's great, Damon. You're doing really well." I sat up and tried on the boots. They were a little snug, and I'd have to find some way to lace up the one, but they'd work. Then I tore into the bread, and my stomach angrily reminded me I hadn't eaten since dinner two days ago at Dr. Carl's house.

My thoughts spiraled after that, thinking back on the bread I'd stolen, which had been brought to the orphanage, that Sara had wanted to steal, and everything that happened after.

The bread turned to dust in my mouth. Sara…

Damon finished the alphabet and beamed at me.

I tried to smile back, but my face wasn't working. "Great job, buddy."

Jade tilted her head at me, eyes narrowing. She knew something was wrong.

I couldn't do this again. "I'm going for a walk."

"Ace-"

"Alone," I added, and all but ran out of Base. My hands shook, and I couldn't take a full breath. The whip cracking down over and over echoed in my head.

I walked on instinct for a while, turning corners and sticking to the shadows. I slowed when I reached the bridge, bracing myself on the railing and trying to teach myself how to breathe again.

Normally I pay attention to my surroundings, and it's pretty hard to sneak up on me. But the tap on my shoulder almost sent me over the side.

"Whoa, easy, it's just me!" a kid said, raising both hands and taking a step back.

"Are you trying to give me a heart attack?" I demanded. Who was he? He acted like we knew each other, but I'd never seen him befo…wait. "You're the one who gave me his jacket."

He smiled and held a hand out to shake. Behind him, the same servant from before kept a lookout. "Yep. My name is Jack."

I glared at his hand. "You want it back or something?" I'd barely taken it off since he gave it to me. It was warm, and wearing

97

something that wasn't worn through was a nice change.

"What? No! Not at all, the exact opposite, actually." Still smiling, he held out a bag for me. "This is for you, too."

I eyed the bag and then him. What game was he playing?

"This stuff is all old, and I don't need it, but I figured you would, or you would know someone who would, and it would be more useful to you than to me," he said.

I slowly took it from him and looked inside. It was all clothes, but it was all as well made as the jacket I wore. I eyed Jack again. Had he sought me out just to give me more clothes? Didn't he have anything better to do? And why *me?* There were plenty of other kids who needed this even more than I did. He must have passed some of them to find me.

"I know it's not much." Jack scratched his cheek. "I just... wanted to do more than I did last time. I'm glad your wrist is better."

My wrist? There wasn't anything...wrong...with...

There had been. I had broken it. I remembered Jade setting it.

I did not remember anyone taking the splint off. Even if I did, it wouldn't have healed this fast. I glanced down at my wrist, turning it back and forth. Nothing hurt.

"Is it better? I thought it looked better. If it's not I can give you money for a doctor?"

Seriously, what was up with this kid? Why was he so determined to help me?

"It's fine," I said.

"Oh, good. I'm glad." And he smiled a genuine smile.

Was there something wrong with his head? Normal people didn't act like this.

Movement behind Jack caught my eye, and I saw Dr. Carl striding up the bridge, hands clasped behind his back. The grin splitting his face made me back up a few steps. I'd seen that smile on Papa's face more times than I could count. That smile said he'd

98

already won, and someone was about to hurt.

The servant behind Jack shifted, fully facing Dr. Carl and keeping Jack behind him.

This wasn't just a servant; he was a bodyguard. Who exactly was this kid?

"I'm glad I found you again, Ace," Dr. Carl said. "You had me worried."

"I bet."

"And I see you've already met Jackson. You've done your part very well."

"My part?" I repeated. Had I somehow done exactly what he'd wanted me to do, even without knowing what he wanted? And how did Jack figure into his plans?

"Who is this?" Jack asked.

"Doesn't matter, we're leaving," the bodyguard said. He steered Jack around me, but Jack twisted back and broke out of his grip.

Dr. Carl waved his hand.

The bodyguard went flying off the bridge, splashing into the river.

"Lucas!" Jack yelled. He peered over the edge of the bridge.

I stepped back, eyes locked on Dr. Carl. "How did you do that?"

"I'm one of four magicians on this continent," Dr. Carl said.

"*What?*" Jack demanded, whirling on him.

"Oh, yes, Jack. Your mummy didn't tell you about me?"

So now Dr. Carl knew Jack and his family? And magicians? Magic? Magic wasn't real, no one could wave their hand and cast real spells.

But Lucas had been blasted off the bridge with only a hand wave. No one touched him.

My head had never hurt so much in my life.

Dr. Carl took slow steps towards us. Jack and I backed up together.

Jack looked as confused as I felt, at least. "She knows about you? But wait, who's the fourth magician?"

Dr. Carl smiled at me.

Okay, this guy was insane. It was a miracle he hadn't killed me when I was sick.

Jack looked at me, too, and then glanced at my hair. His mouth fell open. "No…"

"Indeed," Dr. Carl said. "It surprised me, too. And with both of you, I'll be able to bring this kingdom back to its former glory."

I was missing something important, some key to understanding this conversation. I also had the feeling that we needed to get out of here, now, which Jack seemed to agree with because we both turned and started running, turning downstream to follow his bodyguard.

"What's going on?" I asked.

"It's complicated," Jack panted. "There!" He spotted his bodyguard hauling himself up out of the river, soaking wet but otherwise alright. "Lucas!"

"Your Highness!" Lucas exclaimed. "Are you unharmed?"

I tripped. Did he say what I thought he said?

"I'm fine," Jack said. "What about you?" He helped Lucas to his feet.

"Fine, but we need to get out of here."

"You're not going anywhere." Dr. Carl reappeared in front of us in a swirl of shadows.

I swore and stumbled back until I fell. He really was using magic.

Lucas pushed Jack behind him again and pulled a dagger. "Jack, get out of here. Use that transportation spell."

"All the way back to the palace?" he asked.

Palace? Oh, no.

Lucas swiped at Dr. Carl, but Dr. Carl vanished and reappeared behind him. He flicked his wrist, and Lucas's shadow went taught. Lucas froze with it.

"Shadow magic," Jack breathed, backing up next to me.

"Jack, go," Lucas grunted.

"Not without you," Jack insisted.

Dr. Carl turned to us.

"He wants you. Go."

"I'm willing to bargain," Dr. Carl said. "You two come with me, and I let him live."

"So, if we don't, you'll kill him?" Jack asked.

"*Jack*," Lucas growled.

"What will it be?" Dr. Carl asked.

It was the same bargain Papa had tried to make me. Go with him, and he wouldn't hurt Sara.

"Live, Jack, for Wingomia!" Lucas said.

Jack inhaled sharply.

Oh hell, he *was* the Crown Prince, wasn't he? I was in so far over my head.

"I won't ask again." Dr. Carl twisted his hand, and Lucas twisted with it, grimacing.

The whip echoed in my head. I launched myself at Dr. Carl. We almost went into the river, but he'd lost his grip on the spell holding Lucas and Lucas grabbed my arm.

Dr. Carl went into the water with a splash.

Lucas hauled me back to safety, practically throwing me to the ground.

"Ace, are you okay?" Jack asked.

"He won't be for long if we don't move." Lucas strode to Jack's

101

side. "Jack, the spell! Anywhere is fine."

"He has to come with us," Jack said, pulling out a pocket watch.

How in the world was a *pocket watch* useful right now?

"Whoa, wait, what?" I backed up a step.

"That guy wants him, too. We can't leave him," Jack said.

Lucas frowned and nodded, then reached out to grab my arm again.

A dripping Dr. Carl reappeared in front of us.

Lucas pushed both of us behind him and flashed his dagger again. "Jack, do it now."

"You're coming, too," Jack insisted. He grabbed my hand tightly and held out his other for Lucas.

"What is happening?" I asked.

"Alright." Lucas reached his hand back, wrapping it around Jack's fingers and the watch.

My vision blurred on the edges, and I felt lightheaded.

Lucas pulled out of Jack's reach.

Jack screamed "No!"

And then we were falling.

CHAPTER 16

I screwed up the spell.

That was my only coherent thought after crashing into a tree and knocking every branch down in my fall.

Ace groaned in a heap a few feet away, mumbling a lot of swear words under his breath.

Lucas wasn't here.

He'd slipped out of the spell as I casted it, when it was too late for me to stop.

He was probably dead now.

What a *stupid* way to die. I might not have been able to get all three of us to the castle, but I could have gotten us out of there, at least.

"What the king's beard just happened?" Ace demanded. He shifted and glared at me.

I carefully sat up, frantically checking my watch for damage. It was intact, but the hand pointed to eight. That transportation spell cost me a third of my magic, and it didn't even work right. It would take hours of meditation to bleed that energy back into the watch.

"Where are we?" Ace asked.

I slipped my watch back into my pocket.

"That's an excellent question." The only thing around us were trees. It could have been the forest outside the castle, but it didn't have the same impression. These trees felt older, wilder.

Ace took a deep breath and rubbed his hands over his face.

I stared at his hair again. It was a lighter shade of red than my mom's, and it desperately needed an introduction to a hairbrush. But he was around my age, and something about him was familiar.

"Did that actually just happen?" Ace asked, dropping his hands. "Magic? That's real?"

I sucked in a breath. Technically, no one outside the royal family and our personal guards were supposed to know that magic was real.

Yet that man had used it, and he wasn't part of our family. And if what he said was true, if Ace was the fourth magician he'd been talking about…it wasn't impossible to think he was my missing brother. Which meant he was part of the royal family anyway, so I didn't need to hide it from him. Even if he wasn't, it was hard to deny it at this point, especially when we were lost together.

"Yes, magic is real. Rare, but real."

"O-kay. Sure. Why not?"

"Can I ask you a personal question?"

He stiffened, face going blank. "Depends on the question."

"You live on the streets, right?"

"Yeah…"

"Do you know your birth family?"

"No."

The reply was quick, clipped, an immediate end to the conversation. But not an end to the thoughts running in my head, because unless I found some proof that he wasn't my missing brother, I was going to assume he was.

I debated telling him, but I didn't want to get his hopes up in case he wasn't Alex. It wouldn't be fair for me to tell him he might

104

be a prince and then rip that dream away from him later. His life was cruel enough as it was.

Mom would know what to do. She probably had a spell we could use to find out for sure.

Ace pushed himself up to his feet, swearing and wincing the whole time. It did not encourage me to do the same, but he held out a hand to me anyway.

"My turn to ask a question," he said.

I took his hand and painfully stood up. "Shoot."

"Are you…I mean…your bodyguard called you…" He took a deep breath. "Are you…*Prince* Jack?"

When had Lucas given me away? I'd never even noticed. Granted, I'd had a lot on my mind at the time, but still. "I am, yes."

Ace paled and abruptly dropped my hand. "Aw, hell. I have to get you back to town. Can you do the magic thing again?"

"Um, I don't know if I can. It helps if I know where I am first.". It wasn't a step I usually had to worry about, but it was hard to go anywhere when you didn't know where you were starting from. Besides that, attempting another spell would likely cost another third of my magic, and after the last one, I wasn't confident I could get us where we wanted to go

"Can't you use magic to figure it out?" Ace asked.

In theory, yes. "I don't know the spell for that. I'm still in training."

He gave me the most unimpressed look anyone has ever given me. Apparently, being Prince didn't mean much in his world if I couldn't back it up.

It wasn't an unreasonable expectation, I guess. But I was only fifteen.

"Okay. So, we're in some woods, we don't know where, and we don't know how to get back," Ace summed up. "Unless you know how to get out of these woods, we're dead."

When he put it that way, it did sound like we were in major trouble.

He sighed and rubbed his hand over his face again and mumbled "I *just* got back to the others."

"We'll be fine," I said. "We have to find a town eventually, right?"

The unimpressed look was back.

"Do you have a better idea?"

He tilted his head back and took a deep breath. "No."

"Alright then. Let's…start walking, I guess."

It didn't matter which way we went, so we set off, in silence at first. We both needed time to accept our current situation. Nothing about it was ideal. What would we do if night fell and we were still out here? What would we eat? What if we weren't anywhere near civilization? Could we survive out here for days on our own?

Could that magician find us out here?

"Hey, Ace?"

He grunted.

"You knew that magician, didn't you?"

"Yeah. He's a doctor. He was taking care of me while I was sick. In return, he wanted me to do something for him, but he never explained what, and I left before he really had a chance. Overheard a conversation with a general though, something about the general staying put until he was ready." He shrugged. "Still not sure it wasn't a fever dream. That general called him something weird. But…after what just happened…I think there's a reason my friends found him so easily when I needed help."

There were so many concerning things about everything he just said, but my mind fixated on the start. "You were sick?" I knew he hadn't looked well the first time we met. "Are you still sick?" It sounded like he left before he should have.

"Not really."

"Not—what does that mean?" I demanded. Was he sick on top of everything else?

"I'm fine. If you're worried, get us out of here faster." He pushed past me and kept walking.

He was definitely sick. I didn't know how badly, but I would be watching him a lot closer from now on.

We marched on through the underbrush. While keeping a hand in my pocket to siphon my magic into my watch for storage, I asked more questions about Dr. Carl, and Ace answered as well as he could.

Whatever conversation Ace overheard, it didn't bode well. Dr. Carl wielded shadow magic, and he potentially had connections with our military. That screamed coup in the making.

We had to get back and warn my parents, as soon as possible.

Easier said than done.

Daylight faded, and my stomach growled. Breakfast had been a long time ago, and it didn't help to think that we might be without food for a while. All the walking only made us hungrier, plus, now my feet were sore.

"Can we take a break?" I asked.

"We need to find water," he said.

If I couldn't have food, I would settle for water. If we could find it. We ended up following a deer trail for over an hour before it led us to a stream.

A dozen warnings about unclean water ran through my mind, and I ignored all of them and cupped handful after handful and brought it to my mouth.

Ace laughed. "Wouldn't think a prince would stoop to this kind of thing."

"Have to drink, right?"

"Yeah, but you're a prince. Don't you have to do everything gracefully or something?"

107

"You show me a way to do this gracefully and I'll do it."

He did try a few different ways, and then I did, and then we were splashing each other, which felt amazing until a stiff wind reminded us it was only early spring.

Ace sneezed, and my humor vanished. I was an idiot. He was sick, and here I was splashing him with water. I apologized, and he splashed me again.

I wiped the water from my face. I wouldn't apologize for worrying, but I would remember not to be obvious about it. Ace was one of those types that didn't like people fussing over him.

Besides, what was I going to do about it out here? The best thing was to get him back to civilization. Maybe I could convince him to let the castle doctor look him over, and that way Mom could meet him and figure out if he really was my missing brother.

"We should figure out where to sleep tonight," Ace commented, looking up at the sky through the trees. What was left of the day was fading fast.

"I wouldn't stay here," someone said.

We jumped to our feet, Ace swearing up a storm.

There was no one there.

"Who…What?" I asked. My heart pounded in my chest, trying to calm down after that scare.

"Up here," they said, drawing our gazes up to the trees again.

I still didn't see anyone, but there was a curved flash of white floating on a branch. Two ears faded into view as I watched, melding into a green face. A bushy tail swung back and forth under the branch.

Three red eyes opened in the dark. Ace swore again.

My hands shook. Was this another demon? The eyes looked the same, but this one wasn't immediately trying to kill us like the other one had.

It jumped from its perch and drifted down to the ground. It sort of looked like a fox, if foxes were black and green, had three red eyes, and had long ears that bent halfway up, and smiled from ear to ear.

"Sel?" Ace asked.

"You know this thing?" I demanded.

He shrugged. "I've seen it around town a few times, but I have no idea how it got out here. The red eyes are new, too."

"I am wherever I need to be," the fox responded.

Ace's jaw hit the ground. "Since when can you talk?"

"I speak when there is something to say," Sel said.

Ace muttered some choice swears under his breath.

"So...you're not going to attack us?" I asked, struggling to wrap my head around a talking demon that didn't want to kill us right away.

Sel drifted back up into the air, paws crossed beneath him. A gold collar gleamed on his neck, half hidden under his fur. "Not today."

That was so comforting.

"Are you here to help us?" Ace asked.

"What? No, we're not listening to some weird demon fox," I declared. "He'll probably lead us into a trap or something." Not attacking us was one thing, but that didn't mean we had to trust it. I didn't care if Ace did apparently know this thing, it was still a demon.

"I can be helpful," Sel said.

I could put up with a lot of things, but demon foxes were not one of them. "I think we'll be going now." Grabbing Ace's arm, I started off down the stream.

"Not the way I would go," Sel said.

"Good thing you're not coming with us," I stated.

"Are you okay?" Ace asked.

"I'm trying to save your life. You really think a demon fox wants to help us?"

"You don't know he's a demon," Ace said.

"I am," Sel interjected.

I raised an eyebrow.

Ace took a deep breath. "Yeah, okay."

Sel floated past us, rolling gently through the air. "My intentions towards you are pure."

All I could do was stare at Sel for a few moments, mouth opening and closing. Where should I even begin with that kind of statement?

"Can you prove it?" Ace asked.

Sel turned to look at us upside down. "There's a bigger, meaner demon downstream, where you are currently heading. He'll eat you."

"That seems like a good reason to not go this way," Ace said.

"Unless he's lying so he can lure us wherever he wants to eat us," I countered.

"I don't want to eat you," Sel said. "You're all bones. Not appetizing at all."

We went a little green at that.

"Then why do you want to us to go with you?" Ace asked.

"I'm not taking you anywhere. I'm just warning you that certain death lies ahead. Very unpleasant."

I tilted my head. He didn't want to lead us anywhere? Was he really just warning us about another demon? But what was in it for him? Why would he bother?

"Try not to die," Sel said. His body dissolved into shadows and blew away with the wind.

Ace and I stared at the spot he'd vanished for a long moment.

"That was…bizarre," Ace said.

I nodded. "Weirdest thing ever."

"Should we go now?" he asked.

"Yeah, quickly." We turned to head upstream instead, and we doubled our pace. Whether there was a demon the other way or not, it wasn't worth the risk. I didn't like our chances against one. Neither of us had a weapon, and I didn't know how to fight with magic. It would not end well. Avoiding it was our only hope.

CHAPTER 17

We didn't make it far before we couldn't see anything in the dark. Taking shelter under a tree, I offered to stay up while he slept for a while. Jack made me promise to wake him in the middle of the night to switch, and then he was asleep in minutes.

For being a spoiled prince, he was doing pretty well out here. I had expected him to start complaining almost as soon as we started, but he hadn't whined once. He wasn't what I expected from royalty.

Of course, I hadn't expected magic or demon foxes, either, so that didn't mean much.

The night grew chilly. I paced around the tree a few times to keep warm and stay awake. Most of my body ached in some way, and I wished I could lay down and sleep the way Jack did. Even if I did, it wouldn't take long for nightmares to ruin it.

Sara was killed yesterday. It had only been a day, but it felt like a lifetime. In a way, I was glad my view had been blocked by the fence for most of it. But the sound would echo in my head forever.

I'd planned to let Jack sleep all night, but I started coughing and accidentally woke him up.

His hand found my forehead and he frowned. "I'm sorry. I wish I could do more for you."

"It's not like I've never had a cold before." I curled up on the ground with my back to him. The problem was, this wasn't a cold, not if this was still the same thing that had sent me to Dr. Carl in the first place. Hopefully a little sleep would be enough to let me get by. If I kept getting worse, I'd be in real trouble. There wouldn't be any convenient doctors around this time, not even an old woman who would feel bad for me.

Luck was on my side for once. I was so worn out I didn't have any dreams. Sunlight woke me up hours later.

Jack was gone.

I bolted upright. "Jack?"

My imagination ran wild with all the terrible things that could have happened. The demon Sel mentioned might have eaten him. He could have abandoned me. Some other creature might have snatched him. Maybe he was never real to begin with.

"Jack!" I yelled, and then immediately coughed. Using the tree, I pulled myself upright. My head felt like it weighed a hundred pounds and was stuffed with bread. Sleep had not helped as much as I'd hoped.

"Coming!" he answered, voice distant.

It calmed me down though, and I slid back against the tree until I was on the ground again. While I waited, I tried to force my nose to work right.

I heard Jack before I saw him, his footsteps heavy in the underbrush. He came from behind me, plopping himself on the ground without a care in the world, his arms full of a ridged fruit.

"Do you know what these are?" he asked, holding one out to me. It was long, like a lemon, only a deep maroon color, and ridged along the sides. From the bottom, it looked like a star.

"Star fruit, I think." They were pretty rare. I'd only had one a handful of times.

"So, they're safe to eat?" he asked.

"They are now," I decided, taking the one he offered me. I bit into it like an apple, even though I was pretty sure the peel wasn't

113

for eating. I was too hungry to care.

"You can't just decide if it's safe or not," Jack muttered, eyes narrowed.

Since I didn't fall over dead, he took a bite of his own. They were sweet and juicy, but the insides were white. Clear juice ran down my chin, and I wiped it on my sleeve.

Jack pulled out a handkerchief, but after the night we'd had it didn't look much cleaner than my sleeve.

"So, I was thinking," Jack started, dabbing at his mouth with his handkerchief. "If we climbed one of these trees, we might be able to see the direction of a town or something, so we can at least know which way to go."

That was logical, and normally I wouldn't have a problem with it. But I doubted my ability to climb anything right now without breaking my neck.

He saw the look on my face. "Did I say we? I meant me. *I* will climb a tree."

"Do you even know how to climb?"

"Of course I know how to climb. Just because I'm a prince doesn't mean I didn't have a normal childhood."

He said it as if I'd had a normal childhood, and I didn't believe him either way. When you grew up with all the power and money you could ever want, never struggling for anything, you didn't have a normal childhood.

We ate the rest of the star fruit he'd found, and then he picked a tree to climb.

The first few branches went fine. He pulled himself up with his arms and pushed with his feet, carefully not looking down. I was ready to be impressed, but then a branch cracked under him.

We both froze.

The branch gave way and he plummeted ten feet back to the ground.

"King's beard, are you okay?" I hurried over to him.

114

He groaned. "That wasn't fun."

"I didn't think it was," I said. Had he hit his head? Was I going to have to deal with a loopy prince on top of everything else?

I offered a hand to help him up, and then he brushed himself off. "Alright, new plan. I'll use magic to levitate up there." His watch was back in his hand.

I stared at him. If that had been an option this whole time, why hadn't he done it in the first place?

Before I could ask just what, exactly, was wrong with him, he lifted off the ground. I took a few startled steps back, and he rose above my head and kept going, pushing branches out of his way. Somehow, when the demon fox had ignored gravity last night, it hadn't bothered me. It had been sort of a *why not at this point* kind of thing. But watching Jack float up like a steamcar without any machine helping him? That was unnatural.

He drifted back, landing without a sound, and pointed behind me. "I saw smoke coming from that way. Could be someone who lives out here. They'll be able to tell us how to get to town."

"You didn't see a town?" I asked. I knew I wasn't the greatest with geography, and I had almost no idea of what existed in the kingdom outside Gallen, but I was pretty sure a giant forest wasn't anywhere near my city or his palace.

He shook his head. "No. Actually…I saw mountain peaks. I don't know how, but I think, somehow, we ended up in the Spodale mountains."

"Right. So, I know exactly where those are, but can you explain it to me anyway? How far away from home are we?" Jade, Malik, and Damon had to be worried out of their minds right now. They already had been, and for me to run off and not come back was about the worst thing I could do to them.

He crossed his arms and looked at the ground. "Pretty far. They're a week's journey away from the palace."

My mouth dropped. Yesterday, he'd made it sound like we'd be lucky if he could even make it to the palace. How had he blasted us

115

a week away in the wrong direction?

He rubbed his forehead. "I'm sorry. I don't know how this happened. I shouldn't even be *capable* of doing this, I don't have this kind of training. I don't know if it's because I was panicking, or if something else interfered, or what."

"If you figure out how it happened, can we get back the same way?" I wasn't looking forward to a week of traveling with him, especially when I knew I was getting sick again.

"Maybe...I'd be willing to try if you are," he said. "But it doesn't make sense, such a big spell should have used up more of my magic." He looked down at his watch, as if the thing had any answers.

If I let him, he'd stay there all day thinking like that. But since I didn't want to spend more time out here than we had to, I started walking in the direction he'd pointed, dragging him along.

"Unless you really are Alex, and you somehow amplified the spell with your own magic, and we just got blown way off course..."

I nearly stopped walking. "I'm sorry, what? Who's Alex?" Why would he think that was me?

Jack made a funny sound in the back of his throat. "I wasn't going to say anything until I was sure. Dr. Carl said you were the fourth magician in the kingdom, which is only possible if you're part of the royal family. Though I'm not sure how *he* uses magic..."

"Jack."

"Right. Anyway, if you're a magician too, and you're part of the royal family, then you'd be Prince Alex, my twin. He was kidnapped when we were infants, and we never found him."

I couldn't help it. I laughed. Me? A prince? What a joke.

Jack tore his arm out of my grip. "Oh, sure, most traumatic thing to ever happen to my family, go ahead and laugh about it."

I forced myself to calm down. "Sorry. You have to admit, though, the idea of me as a prince is pretty funny." Even after a night in the woods, Jack looked far more regal than I ever would.

"I don't find it funny," Jack stated. "If you're my brother, that's going to be huge. It...you don't know what it would mean to my parents. To me."

To them? What about to me? To find out that after all this time, after all the terrible things that happened to me, I actually had a family who wanted me? A family that I would never fit in with, because I could never be like Jack. I would never be prince material. A family I half feared because of what they did to people like me?

Besides, we didn't know if I really was or not. "Dr. Carl is insane, remember? He was probably lying. Or he was wrong." I was a street rat. I always had been, and I always would be. Pretending otherwise would only be painful for everyone involved.

"That's why I didn't want to say anything," Jack muttered.

"Well, we can forget about that, at least." I stalked ahead. Me, a prince. What a dumb idea.

We were quiet for several minutes, and Jack stayed behind me. I didn't look back at him. There was some kind of tension between us, and I didn't understand why.

"Would it really be so awful if you were a prince?" Jack asked quietly. "Most people would kill for the chance."

"I don't want to pretend to be something I'm not," I stated. "I'd never fit in at a castle as anything other than a kitchen boy." Even then, it wasn't like I would know what I was doing.

"But you'd have food whenever you want it, a place to sleep at night, people to care about you--"

"I have people who care about me," I cut in. Those people were probably terrified for me. They probably thought I jumped in the river and drowned or something.

Jack raised his hands. "I'm not saying you don't."

"This is a stupid conversation." I walked a little faster. I wasn't a prince, so there was no point trying to convince me I was.

Thankfully, Jack dropped it. We walked in silence until we found a cabin. It wasn't a moment too soon; I wasn't sure how much longer my strength would hold out. I'd barely been awake for an

117

hour, but I was ready for a nap.

A dog flew out from behind a tree, barking at us. I yelped and stumbled back into Jack, knocking us both to the ground. The dog, a big, brown monster with large teeth, pounced on us. Claws shredded my arm, ruining the sleeve of my jacket and drawing blood. I kicked out, and the dog latched onto my boot. He tore it off and shook his head, tossing my boot into the bushes.

"What'd ya find there, boy?" an old gravelly voice asked.

The dog backed down, but its hackles were raised and teeth bared. A low growl rumbled in its chest.

A man walked into view, leaning on a tall walking stick. He wore old denim jeans factory workers usually wore, and thick flannel shirts. His gray beard looked like it could sand the edges of scrap metal, and his gun could definitely shoot a hole through some.

He looked as surprised to see us as we were to see him. "Kids?"

Jack peeked over my shoulder. "Um. Sorry to bother you, sir, but we were hoping you could help us?"

The man blinked. "What are a couple of kids doing here?"

"We got lost," Jack said with a little laugh.

"Now there's lost, and then there's being dumb enough to get lost all the way out here. I'm a day's ride away from anything."

Of course he was.

"Yeah…we went the wrong way for a while?" Jack asked more than said.

This kid could not lie to save his life. Which was a shame, because our lives might actually depend on it right now.

"We lost control of our steamcar and crashed out here," I said. "We got turned around and just started walking, but we didn't know which way to go. We still don't."

He looked at me, took in my bleeding arm, my missing shoe, the general dirt and grime that never really went away. Then he looked at Jack, whose shirt was neatly tucked in, shoes properly tied, and he must have washed up at the stream while I slept because even his face didn't look that dirty.

He put a hand on the dog's head, and the growling stopped. "I don't buy it for a second, but I ain't about to let you bleed out. Come on."

Jack fished in the bushes for my boot, which had a few new holes, and then he helped me up. We followed the stranger into his cabin, which screamed bad idea to me, but we were out of options. I was sick enough without letting my arm get infected.

The cabin had one room. An iron stovetop fireplace sat in one corner on a brick step. Pelts littered the floor like carpets, and antlers on the walls held up coats and other guns.

He told us to sit at the table, which only had one chair, while he fished out bandages from a chest at the foot of his bed. Jack pushed me into the chair.

The dog started sniffing around us. Jack knelt on the ground to pet him, and the beast dropped to the ground and rolled onto his back, paws flopping through the air.

The man snorted. "A little love and he eats out of the palm of your hand. Real intimidating, Killer."

The dog's ears perked up.

"Aw, you were just protecting your friend, weren't you?" Jack said, rubbing his hands all over Killer's belly. "You didn't mean to hurt Ace, you were being a good boy, yes you were."

I raised an eyebrow at Jack. He was too wrapped up with the dog to notice.

The man dropped bandages and a bottle on the table. "Jacket off." He popped open the bottle, releasing the unmistakable scent of alcohol.

I shimmied out of my jacket, and he yanked my arm to start cleaning. There was nothing gentle about it, no warning before he wiped an alcohol-soaked rag over the bleeding wounds.

"So, Ace, want to tell me what you and your friend are really doing out here?" the man asked.

119

"No." I hissed when he dabbed a few extra times over my arm.

"We really are lost," Jack said. Killer's head was now in his lap. "I can't explain how we ended up all the way out here, but if you could point us in the direction of town, we'll be out of your hair in no time."

"It's a day's ride south of here," the man stated. "But you'll never make it before the monsters get ya."

"Monsters?" we repeated.

He wrapped a clean white bandage around my arm. "Don't know how else to describe them. I been lucky so far, they've left me and Killer alone. But they're scaring off all the game."

"Do you know how many there are?" Jack asked. He'd gone still on the floor, his face blank.

"I've seen at least two, but I haven't been looking for 'em."

"No, don't. They're dangerous. Guns don't work, unless you can shoot inside their mouth," Jack said.

I glanced at him. So did the man wrapping my arm.

"You should head into town," Jack went on. "It'll be safer there."

"If you know so much about 'em, why don't you get rid of 'em?"

"I didn't know there were any out here, and I've only fought one before. I only beat it because I got lucky." Jack looked up at us. "Why are you out here in the middle of nowhere anyway?"

"Don't like people," the man retorted.

That was fair. A little extreme, I thought, but I could understand it.

"Well, if a demon comes after you, it'll kill you. It's only a matter of time," Jack said.

"You just want a ride to town," the man spat.

Jack's intense glare lessened.

The man pulled the ends of the bandage tight and tied it off. "You're not subtle, boy."

"Will you take us?" Jack asked.

120

"Don't want to," the man said. He gathered the extra bandages and alcohol and carried them back to the chest.

"But you shouldn't be out here anyway!" Jack jumped to his feet. Killer jumped up as well.

I rubbed my arm, content to let the two of them battle it out. A ride to town would be nice, that meant I could sleep, but I didn't see how Jack could win an argument against this man.

"Neither should you." The man slammed the chest closed.

"We're *trying* to leave," Jack argued. "We'll walk if we have to. Would you be able to live with yourself if you just let us go? Just let whatever demons are out there come get us?"

"Boy." The man stepped towards him, wagging his finger. He lowered his finger, mouth twisting in a frown. "Damn you."

Jack grinned and pulled his shoulders back.

Did...did he just win? Against this angry old man?

"I need some stuff from town anyway," he muttered. He pulled down an extra flannel shirt and tossed it at me, to replace my ruined jacket. "I'll take you to town, but that's it. I'm not doing any other favors for you."

"That's fine," Jack agreed. "This is all we'll ask of you."

The man harumphed and started gathering things together.

Jack turned a beaming smile towards me.

I rolled my eyes, but I had to admit he'd done a pretty decent job. We knew how to get to town *and* we had a ride, however unwilling. Not bad at all.

CHAPTER 18

The old man, Don, put us to work. He had an ancient steamcar, one that needed us to manually pour water into it and then crank the generator to get it started. Most modern ones had a suction that you could place in a bucket and it would fill itself up. Some you still had to crank, but the latest models only needed a few spins to get them started.

We got it running, but the loud humming didn't inspire confidence. It didn't sound like this thing should still be working. It was large enough for all of us, at least, and any distance it could take us was better than walking, so I didn't complain.

Ace and I sat in the back row, squished together. This close, his fever was obvious, and that made me nervous, too. Killer sat up front with Don, tail wagging as we took off. Don didn't have extra goggles for us, and I wasn't sure when I'd lost mine, so Ace and I would just have to make do. Ace fell asleep right away, which wasn't surprising. He needed the rest.

He needed medicine, too, and a doctor, which I would hopefully be able to find for him when we were back in civilization. Assuming anyone believed I was the prince, way out here. I didn't exactly look the part at the moment, and I couldn't prove it. We'd be in trouble if they didn't believe me, since I wasn't carrying money. I couldn't pay for anything. And it would still be a long trip to the palace from this town.

It was a long trip there in the first place. The steamcar was so loud, we couldn't talk. I didn't think anyone was too upset by that. I recharged my watch for a few hours, bringing the hand back to ten o'clock, before I drifted off, too. Sleeping on the ground outside hadn't been restful.

Not that I would call dozing in the steamcar rejuvenating, either, but at least I was able to get a lot of it, however poor. Enough so that when we arrived, well after midnight, I was ready to run off wherever we had to.

No one else was as eager as I was, and I didn't have any place I could go this late at night anyway. We stayed by the steamcar until the sun was up and it was an acceptable time to start wandering the streets.

Don made saying goodbye pretty easy, all but chasing us off.

Here, in town, Ace was in his element. We passed a few shops just opening, and he suggested ducking inside one real quick, and before I knew it we were racing out of there because his arms were full of bread.

"When did you even grab them?" I demanded. I'd barely registered it was a bakery before we had to run.

He laughed.

Bread alone didn't make the best breakfast I'd ever had, but any food was welcome at this point.

I took the lead again after we popped the last pieces in our mouths. If I could get my hands on a map and figure out where we were, I could try transporting us again. We might not make it all the way to the castle, but even a few miles were better than nothing.

The problem was, I didn't know where to find a map of the whole kingdom, so I led us in circles all morning.

"What are you doing?" Ace finally asked.

I explained my abysmal plan. "Do you know where we could

find a map?"

He shrugged. "A school, maybe. Or a library, if this town has one."

A library. Ace was a genius.

It wasn't weird at all to go up to a stranger and ask how to get to the library, and Ace managed to steal some meat pies along the way, but I had no idea where he'd stolen them from, since I definitely hadn't seen them. Ace hadn't been seen, either, as no one chased after us and we didn't even have to hide our meal.

"You're terrifying, you know that?" I asked.

He shrugged. "It helps that no one here recognizes me. They aren't on guard the second they glimpse my hair."

I glanced at his red hair. I'd only considered how similar it was to my mother's. The idea that it would make him unmistakable in a crowd had never occurred to me. "Is that why you stole my hat?"

Grinning, he nodded. "Already lost it, though, so I hope you didn't want it back."

I rolled my eyes. "You lost my jacket, too."

"A dog shredded the jacket, there's a difference."

"I'm still getting the impression I shouldn't give you anything important to hold onto," I stated. We walked up the steps to the library, and I held open the door for him.

"If it's valuable I make no promises."

"I feel like I shouldn't even have anything valuable near you," I muttered. His hands were fast. If he wanted something, he had a good chance of getting it and getting away before anyone even noticed it was missing.

Hopefully he wouldn't think anything in here was worth taking. Books should be pretty useless to him.

We found the atlas section, and I picked out the most recent one and unrolled the map over a table.

Wingomia spread out before us. We were an island kingdom made up of five provinces. Towards the center, a little illustrated castle marked my home in Chiari. The Spodale Mountains covered the north, and I tapped on the dot marking the town we were in.

The distance between this town and the castle looked so small on paper, but in reality, it would take almost a week to travel between them. My parents would have the kingdom in an uproar long before then, if they weren't already demanding answers for my whereabouts.

I traced a straight line between us and the palace. It would be a long jump with magic, but it was shorter than the one I'd done to get to the Spodale Mountains in the first place. Gallen was marked on the map, too, bordering the river a little way north of Chiari.

"Okay, I think I'm ready."

"You're really going to try and just magic us there all the way from here?" Ace asked.

"It beats walking." I rolled the map back up. "Besides, I have to tell my parents about Dr. Carl. We're the only ones who know he's after the crown."

He hummed. "I suppose I'm stuck with you until he's dealt with."

"That's probably for the best." For several reasons.

"Alright, let's go see your palace."

I narrowed my eyes at him. "You're being strangely eager all of a sudden."

"I'm still hungry and you said they have food whenever you want."

That would do it.

I put the map back. "Alright, let's go."

We went back outside and found a quiet side street. I wasn't sure what this would look like to anyone watching, but the fewer witnesses the better.

My hands were sweaty, and I rubbed them on my pants before grabbing Ace in one hand and my watch in the other. Then I focused on the castle. The courtyard, the throne room, the garden, my room, *anywhere*, it didn't matter, as long as we ended up there. I just wanted to be home.

Magic flowed out of my watch, like opening a tap on a reservoir. It seeped around me, encasing me and then traveling down and jumping up around Ace. Once it wrapped around both of us, the world faded away. Colors blurred into nothing until reforming elsewhere, and everything was solid once again.

Solid, and about a hundred feet beneath us.

Ace swore and clung to me as we dropped out of the sky.

"Why can't I ever transport on the ground?" I demanded the air.

All that came out of Ace's mouth was a string of curse words.

Of course, landing on the ground was only relevant when I transported us over ground in the first place. It would have been bad enough to end up a hundred feet over the courtyard or something, but I'd messed up the spell again. There was no courtyard or palace room beneath us.

No, the only thing beneath us was a giant lake, the only one in Wingomia, and a hundred miles south of the castle I'd been aiming for.

At least landing in the water would hurt less than solid ground, I hoped.

CHAPTER 19

Jack was going to be the death of me if I survived this.

I would definitely be the death of him. The second we were out of this damn lake, I was going to kill him.

First of all, the lake was not as soft a landing as water should have been. I've fallen off a roof and been in less pain than after smacking into this lake.

Second of all, there seemed to be

no bottom. We kept sinking, tossing and turning so much I lost track of the way to the surface.

Third of all, *I didn't know how to swim.*

My chest already ached from lack of air, and we were still going down. Maybe. I wasn't sure where we were going anymore.

Also, I didn't know where Jack was. I lost my grip on him when we hit the water.

Something, hopefully Jack, grabbed the back of my shirt and yanked. I risked opening an eye. The water burned, and I regretted it. But I did glimpse Jack towing me up towards the sunlight with him.

It was impossibly far away. My lungs burned, demanding air. There was no way I could last that long without breathing. How could Jack last this long? How was anyone able to hold their breath like this?

The thing about needing to breathe when underwater was that even though I knew opening my mouth wouldn't help, that there was nothing to breathe but water, I still wanted to, desperately. My body demanded air, and it wouldn't listen to my head telling it *not yet*.

Pressure burst in my chest, and I let out the breath I was holding.

Water rushed into my mouth and up my nose. I grabbed at my throat.

Jack kicked out wildly next to me, moving us faster.

I coughed, trying to spit up the water, but it didn't do much good. Any attempt at a small breath made things worse.

Of all the stupid things I'd done in my life, this was how I was going to die. Unbelievable. I should have died trying to save Sara, not lost devils only knew where in the kingdom.

Jack tugged on my arm, and then, instead of being pulled up, we were falling again, crashing onto a roof and tumbling over the edge to land in overgrown bushes.

"King's beard, come on, Ace!"

I was still trying to figure out which way was up when Jack dragged me out of the bush and onto solid ground. Air had never tasted so good, even if the smell of sap overwhelmed everything else.

"You're okay," Jack panted beside me. His head dropped on my shoulder. "You're okay."

I coughed again. "Did you swear?"

He grimaced. "You're a terrible influence."

"What happened?" I asked. My throat felt like I'd garbled broken glass, and my voice didn't sound much better.

Jack sat up and pushed his hair back. His left hand clutched his pocket watch. "I transported us. Used the last of my magic, though, so we're stuck here for a while until I recharge."

128

'Here' was beside an old forgotten church. The windows were broken. Ivy and moss climbed the sides of the stone building. Trees and bushes had grown around it, hiding it from view. Through gaps in the trees, I saw other vague building structures. This whole area probably used to be some sort of village before it was abandoned for whatever reason.

"Recharge?" I asked.

He showed me his watch. A sun and moon overlapped each other in the design on the cover, and when he flipped it open there was only one hand on the clock face, pointing right next to the twelve. "Magicians are always leaking magic, but watches like this can catch it and store it. Then the gears inside convert the raw magic into something more malleable that I can cast spells with. All the transporting around the kingdom drained what I had stored, and it'll take me a few hours to build it back up."

I blinked at the watch. Looked at Jack. Looked back at the watch. "That makes no sense."

"Magic rarely does."

That was not an explanation, but okay. I pinched the bridge of my nose, trying to figure out if my headache was because of his magic or everything else. "What now?"

"We either wait here while I recharge, or we start walking and hope we find help," Jack said.

Neither option was appealing. We didn't know what direction to walk in or what was around us, but waiting to transport again wasn't guaranteed to be safer.

Jack pushed his hair back again. "I think we should rest here for a while. You're still recovering, and now you've nearly drowned. We can spare a few hours to rest up."

"Are you sure that's a good idea?"

His mouth twisted. "No. But you need to take it easy, so we'll make do. Come on, let's see what the inside of this place looks like."

He stood up and brushed off his pants, holding a hand out to me.

129

Sighing, I accepted the help up. My vision spun, for once unrelated to his magic. A little nap might not be a bad idea after all.

"Easy." Jack steadied me and kept close as we searched for a way in.

Old wooden doors had rotted away, and moss covered most of the inside. We startled a few rabbits when we tripped over the steps at the threshold. The inside of the church was several feet lower than the ground outside. The broken windows and holes in the ceiling left plenty of light to see, and the center of the floor was taken up by a large pond. Dull windchimes dangled from what remained of the ceiling, but ivy strangled any sound they might have made.

"This place must have been beautiful before," Jack said.

"They put a building around a pond," I stated.

"Yeah, that's a little odd."

One of the corners furthest from the door was still intact and mostly free from debris, so I curled up with my back to the wall. Sitting was a huge relief, and closing my eyes helped my headache.

"I'll keep watch," Jack offered, still studying the church.

That shouldn't have comforted me as much as it did, but I admitted knowing someone else would be awake in case anything happened was a huge relief. With any luck, there'd be a way back home when I woke up.

CHAPTER 20

This church fascinated me. The outside bore resemblance to the modern churches I'd seen, with similar steeples on the roof and large windows. But the inside was completely different. The pond, for one thing. A sundial had crumbled into the pond, too, and now lay in pieces under the water. Modern churches had benches or something to sit on, and big gathering rooms with worktables for people to create and invent things. This one had the single room with the pond, like the water had been the focus centuries ago.

Maybe it had been. One of the holes in the ceiling right over the pond was perfectly circular and intentional, so rainwater could keep the pond from drying out. But why did people worship the water? How could the church have evolved so drastically to switch their idol from water to creation?

I couldn't find any old books or writings when I explored, and the few etchings and paintings I found on the walls were ruined with age and exposure to the elements.

The quiet started getting to me after a while. There was no city hum, no banging pipes along the floor. Even the rustle of trees sounded distant and muffled. It had started as a calm quiet, and I'd been at peace while I explored. But the longer we were here, the less comforting it felt. There wasn't anything I could do about it, though, not until I built up my magic again.

I channeled a steady stream of magic into my watch all day. It caught my excess magic naturally, and at the palace I never had to worry about it, but I could speed up the process when needed. It took two days to fully charge the watch, but by sunset I was halfway there.

Ace slept the whole day. When I wandered close to his corner, I could hear his raspy breathing, and the flush on his cheeks was obvious.

Mother had taught me to heal cuts and broken bones, but the same logic applied to fevers, right? Theoretically, I should be able to heal sickness, too.

I sat next to him, hesitating. I had enough magic to either try and heal him, or transport us again. Neither option was guaranteed success. I'd never healed an illness before, and was just as likely to mess it up as actually help him. Transporting hadn't been any better, considering where we were now.

But if I transported us to the middle of nowhere again, and Ace was still sick, we'd be in the same position and I wouldn't be able to do anything about it. At least if I tried to heal him and failed, we wouldn't be any worse off than we already were. Hopefully.

"Don't hate me for this," I muttered, placing a hand over his burning forehead. Taking a deep breath, squeezing my watch, I sent the magic to him. Instead of focusing on stitching a cut together, I told it to lower his temperature, to sooth his throat, to lighten his bruises.

Ace blinked awake halfway through. "Jack? What the hell—"

"Shh. Concentrating."

He closed his mouth and let me work for a few more minutes, until I finally pulled my hand away again. The hand in my watch was back between eleven and twelve, but Ace looked more lucid and the flush on his cheeks had faded.

"What did you do?" he asked.

"Tried to help. How do you feel?"

"A lot better," he said. He rolled his head around. "Not all the way, but...thanks."

I'd take it. "You're welcome."

He stretched his arms above his head. "So can we get out of here yet?" He jerked his chin towards my watch.

"Oh, uh, I just used what I built up on you..."

Blinking, he opened and closed his mouth a few times. "Oh."

The tips of my ears burned, and I looked away at the pond. "If you're up for it, we can try walking somewhere in the morning. It's kind of late, now."

He nodded. "Yeah, okay. Um. I'm going to...look for something to eat, then."

"There's nothing in here, but I didn't look outside." Dear gods I hoped he could find something. My stomach was about to eat itself.

We went together to search the surrounding woods with what little light we had left. All we found were a few questionable berries and tree bark my friend Miranda had once told me was edible. Assuming I recognized the right tree...they all looked the same to me. The berries were tart, and the bark was dry and chewy.

Starving might have been better.

Ace ripped into the bark like a tough loaf of bread, and I watched in horror as he popped a few berries right after. "What? Food is food."

"We're not even sure this is food."

He shrugged. "If it dulls the hunger pangs, I'll eat it."

Fair, but I physically could not put another piece of this bark in my mouth.

Note to self: learn how to cast agriculture spells. If I ever got stranded in the middle of nowhere again, I did not want to resort to eating tree bark.

133

Not that I even had any magic to cast those spells with right now, anyway, but I was still going to learn them the second we made it to the palace.

After 'dinner,' Ace volunteered to stay up while I caught some sleep. I managed a few hours, but it was hard to get comfortable on mossy rocks, and the smell of dirt and mucky pond water kept tickling my nose. I knew Ace had been sick, but how had he slept half the day in a place like this?

I switched with him again in the middle of the night, and jealously watched him fall asleep again in minutes. Was this what he used his magic for? The ability to sleep anywhere, at any time? Not fair.

Come morning, we were as rested as we were going to be. I had three hours in my watch, not enough to attempt transporting the two of us again, especially if we needed another quick getaway like last time with the lake. So, we set out on foot, hoping something lay ahead of us.

'Something' turned out to be a grounded airship in the late afternoon. By then we were cranky and sore from walking all day with no food or water, and we stumbled blindly into a makeshift camp before we knew what we'd found. We'd just heard voices and ran for it.

It was hard to tell who was more surprised, us, or the thirty men who froze at our entrance.

Crates were spread around the clearing, and a large fire pit had a spit roasting a wild pig over it. It looked like they'd been camped here for some time, small paths worn into the grass where they'd trekked the most.

"Uh, hi?" I waved. "Do you have anything to drink?"

The closest one to us pulled a knife out. "State your name and business."

My gaze zeroed in on the knife. "Uh…"

"I'm Ace, this is Jack. We've been lost for a few days. Do you

134

have any water or food you can spare?"

"King's beard, Horace, they're just kids," someone else said, stepping up behind Horace and pushing his arm down. "Look at 'em, they've had it rougher than we have."

"Kids make the perfect spies," Horace said, lowering the knife but not his glare.

The second man snorted. "Right. They've starved themselves just to gain our trust. Oi, Thomas, bring some flasks! And the Captain!"

We were allowed to sit on some crates, Thomas passing us some flasks of water. It was warm, but it was still the best thing I'd had in days. They promised us some of the pig they were roasting when it was ready.

Before that, their captain approached us and had us follow him into the airship and his personal quarters. A tall man, his very presence commanded respect from the crew.

His quarters were neat and orderly, but lived in. Piles of handmade quilts covered the bunk, and pictures of the captain and a beautiful woman covered the room. A lot of the pictures showed a little girl in them.

The captain turned extra chests on their side to use as chairs around the table, which was covered in charts and other sailing instruments I wasn't familiar with. Ace reached out to poke one, and a piece went swinging back and forth on it. I made a note to keep an eye on the instruments; the last thing we needed were Ace's quick hands snatching something to try and sell later.

The captain stared at us. His fingers tapped on the table. "Jack and Ace, was it? I'm Captain Kendall Ryan. You two are a long way from anything."

"We've been lost for a few days. Crashed our steamcar and got all turned around," Ace said.

I was glad he took over. My first thought was to tell the captain the truth, which I couldn't do because of all the magic, and I'd been about to panic. But Ace used the same story we'd told Don without missing a beat, like lying was as easy as breathing for him.

Captain Ryan nodded. "Whereabouts did you crash?"

Again, panic flooded me. We had no idea where we even were in the kingdom, what would sound believable right now?

"If we knew that, we wouldn't be lost," Ace quipped.

Ryan hummed. "I'm going to be honest with you two. In return, I'd like the same honesty. I don't trust either of you. It's suspicious that you showed up here, coming from the direction you did."

I swallowed. What could we possibly tell him that wouldn't make him more suspicious?

Ace leaned forward, letting his exhaustion weigh on his shoulders and using his roughed-up state to his advantage. Not that it was an act; fever colored his cheeks again, and I wanted to shove him into a proper bed as soon as possible. "Okay. The truth is, we were kidnapped."

Ryan sucked in a breath.

"Our kidnappers wanted to use us to ransom our father."

I nodded along.

"We didn't say anything because we're not sure we can trust you," Ace went on. "You and your crew might hold us against our father, too." He elbowed me. "*He's* just a terrible liar."

Ryan looked back and forth between us, disbelief written all over his face.

"Our father really is wealthy," I said. That wasn't even a lie, if Ace turned out to be Alex. "If you help us get back home, he'll pay you whatever you want." Also not a lie. My parents would gladly pay Ryan for whatever trouble he went through because of me.

"Whatever I want, huh?" Ryan crossed his arms and leaned back in his chair.

I may have made that promise a little prematurely.

"So, I'm supposed to take you wherever you want to go, and you'll have your unnamed wealthy father pay me when we get there."

Ah. I could see how this sounded from his point of view. He wanted a guarantee we'd actually pay him when we got there. I wasn't sure how to promise that, though. I didn't have anything to offer as collateral. We could work for it, but neither of us knew anything about sailing. Plus, with Ace getting sick again, he wouldn't be much help.

I had no idea how to convince this man to help us.

Beside me, Ace whispered "Please." I thought he was talking to me at first, or that he hadn't meant to be heard at all, but he lifted his head to look at Ryan. He leaned forward on his knees, lower lip trembling like he was about to cry. "We just want to see our family again. We want to go home."

Actual tears slipped out of his eyes, and I was no longer sure if he was acting. I didn't know where he considered home to be, but it clearly meant a lot to him.

"*I have people who care about me.*"

He'd said that. Maybe whoever these people were, they were like family to him. If he loved his family half as much as I loved mine, then no wonder he'd been so offended at my Alex theory. I'd be unhappy if someone tried to rip me from my family, too.

I laid an arm around his shoulders and squeezed. "I'll get you home, I promise." Wherever home meant to him. Dr. Carl or not, I would make sure he could go back.

Ryan stood from his chair and turned to face out the port window, his hands clasped behind his back. He took several deep breaths. "Who's your father?"

I froze again. It was a fair question, but I didn't know if I should lie or not.

Ryan turned back to us. "I'm going to need to know if I'm going to take you to him."

My inner thoughts were nothing but wordless screaming. Of course he needed to know where to take us, but it still wasn't a good idea to just announce that I was the prince. I could lie and list one of the other nobles, but if we showed up there and they didn't play along, Ryan would catch on and he might kidnap us for real. Besides, if he was going to be paid by the King and Queen, he was going to find out sooner or later.

Ace watched me, waiting to see what I wanted to do on this one.

Oh, to hell with it. "My father is the King. I'm Prince Jack. Ace isn't actually my brother, but he is a good friend and he is coming to the palace with me." It was the best I could do to protect him at this point if things were going to get ugly.

Ryan whistled and stroked his beard. "The prince, huh? You would fetch a pretty ransom."

Was that a general comment or was he considering it? "My father will pay you for my safe return."

"And you need a ride anyway," Ryan went on. He stroked his beard for another minute, turning it over in his mind. "Alright. You boys have a deal. I'll take you back to the palace."

The relief his words caused was incredible. I sagged against Ace and gave him a weary grin.

Ace did not return the grin, eyeing Ryan warily.

I elbowed him before he said something to change Ryan's mind. If the Captain refused to give us passage, we had no back-up plan. We'd end up wandering this unending forest until we died.

Thankfully, Ace got the hint and kept his mouth shut.

Ryan showed us to the first mate's quarters, where we'd be staying for the trip. The timing couldn't be better, because Ace's fever spiked again. He curled up on the bunk and tried to rest, but a little girl with brown hair in braided pigtails burst in before he could fall asleep.

"Samantha!" a woman scolded, chasing after her.

The girl stopped at the foot of the bed, looking up at us with big brown eyes. She was maybe five or six, and missing one of her front teeth.

The woman had cut her hair at chin length, and she wore a worn leather apron, her sleeves rolled up. "I told you not to barge in here." The woman took Samantha's hand and smiled at us. "Sorry to intrude."

"It's no problem," I said.

"Daddy says you're gonna stay with us!" Samantha giggled.

The woman shushed her.

"Daddy?" I asked, looking up at the woman.

She sighed and put a hand on her hip. "Kendall is my husband. This is our daughter, Samantha. I'm Petra."

"I'm Jack, and this is Ace," I said, shaking Petra's hand.

"Pleasure," Ace croaked.

"Oh dear, you need some tea for that throat. I'll be right back," Petra said. "Come on, Sam."

"I want to stay!" Sam pouted.

"She's alright," Ace said, smiling softly at Sam.

Sam beamed back at him.

I stared in confusion as Petra slipped out, wondering how the sick grump I'd been traveling with was replaced with…this. He let Sam climb into the bed with him and played some kind of clapping hand game with her, all the while wearing the softest expression on his face.

It baffled me, and I stared at him and Sam until Petra came back in with a steaming cup of tea and medicine. "You look like you've got a fever, so I figured better safe than sorry. Once one person gets sick on a ship, it's not long before everyone else does."

Ace accepted both without complaint, thanking her in a whisper.

"How long will it take to reach the palace?" I asked.

"We're about three days from Chiari," Petra said. "It'll take us a few hours before we can launch, and we might have to stop partway for supplies. Then we'll dock in Chiari and walk the rest of the way."

The capital city was more than close enough. I could handle walking through town. Taking three days to get there, though…I was tempted to try magic again, but one look at Ace convinced me not to. He needed rest, and if we ended up lost in the woods again, I wouldn't be able to care for him. This wasn't ideal, but it was the smartest option at the moment.

"Is there a radio or something I could use to call ahead?" I asked. I hated to think of my parents worrying about me for so long, but I didn't have the mechanical knowledge needed to conjure a working radio.

Expecting one on this old ship was asking a lot, anyway. They'd only hit the markets around five years ago.

"Afraid not," Petra said.

I sighed. "So much for that."

"Kendall's already planning our course. We'll be launching to the skies by nightfall."

"That long?" They obviously hadn't been expecting to leave so soon, considering all the crates outside, but I still wished we could move faster. My parents had to be worried sick.

"As long as everything stays on schedule. Speaking of, there's some pre-launch tasks I need to take care of. Excuse me. Come on, Sammy."

Sammy pouted but took her mother's hand and walked out with her.

I fussed over Ace for a few minutes, taking the empty teacup and pulling the blankets up, until he snapped at me to leave him alone in his usual grumpy way. How could the five-year-old he just met get him to be so gentle, and yet he does nothing but snap and roll his eyes at me?

I left the cabin fuming about it, but the anger faded as I explored

140

the ship. Iron pipes against the ceiling occasionally spit out puffs of steam, and sailors hurried about the ship. Someone swore and yelled about not having food for this kind of trip, and someone else yelled back that they'd better make do.

I went the opposite direction of that argument and headed back to the deck. Sailors climbed through the rigging and unfurled the sails and balloons for flight, and Petra went around with a clipboard. Sammy followed with her own little clipboard, and she nodded and made checks at the most random times. They'd both grabbed a pair of goggles and had them sitting ready on their heads.

I moved into the corner of the cabin and the deck, hopefully out of the way of everything, and watched as Captain Ryan shouted orders from the top deck and men scrambled to follow them. The anticipation built in me as they readied for launch.

It would still be a while, so I went back below deck to get out of the way.

Ahead of me, one crew member crashed into another, and they dropped the crate they carried. A rifle fell out onto the floor.

"Watch it!" one of them chastised, scrambling to pick up the rifle and stow it away. "These kids don't know what kind of ship they're on, we don't want 'em ratting us out!"

I ducked into an open room, one of the men's quarters, my heart pounding. A crate full of rifles? What kind of ship were we on? I'd just assumed they were part of the air force, but what if they weren't?

I waited a few minutes before chancing the hall again, and then I rushed back to our room.

CHAPTER 21

I napped until the ship was ready to launch. Sleep plus the water and medicine did wonders for my headache, and the promise of watching the launch had me excited. I climbed up on deck with Jack, and we found spots against the rail out of the way.

All the crates outside had been brought onboard, and the balloons and sails were all unfurled and ready. The engines made the floorboards shake, and the steam from the masts came out dark and thick. Wings unfolded from the sides with creaks and groans.

"Wings ready, Cap'n!" someone shouted.

"Boiler at a hundred twenty degrees and climbing, Captain!" the helmsman called.

Ryan appeared at the rail of the top deck and yelled, "Archer, ready to launch on my signal!"

"Ready, Captain!" a voice echoed up a hollow pipe.

"Launch!" Ryan yelled.

The ship jolted. I grabbed the rail for balance. Steam billowed up into the balloons, and wood creaked and groaned. The trees around the clearing shrank, inch by inch, until we cleared them altogether. Another quick order, and the ship jerked forward, sailing over the trees and gaining altitude.

142

Heights had never bothered me before, but something about being this high with nothing but an old ship between me and death made me nervous. I couldn't seem to find my balance, either, and my stomach cramped uncomfortably.

Crewmen went running around, double checking this gauge or another. Everything seemed to be normal, and things calmed down pretty quickly after that. Jack and I wandered up to the top deck and found Captain Ryan with Sammy on his hip, making faces and rubbing noses at her. Petra noticed us and waved us over.

"What did you think?" she asked.

"That was amazing!" Jack said. "I've never seen a ship launch before, let alone been on one!"

She laughed. "It's something to behold. Gives us a thrill every time."

He nodded and continued talking shop with her about how the ship worked. I didn't pay much attention, hearing something about steam and thermodynamics. Jack didn't look like he understood either, but he politely kept talking with her about it.

"Do you two want a tour of the ship? I need to check in with some people before dinner."

Jack went with her while I stayed behind to play with Sammy, who seemed thrilled to have a new playmate.

For dinner, Captain Ryan invited me and Jack to the Captain's table. Jack eyed me for a bit, ignoring my pointed glares back, until we were served and I picked up my silverware. When he finally looked away after that, I tried not to be too upset. I had only learned to use them properly a week ago, after all.

Petra asked questions about our families, and Jack carried most of the conversation, describing his life as a prince and what the King and Queen were like. He was oblivious to the way the rest of the table reacted, their smiles growing forced and insincere.

So, they weren't fans of the royal family, either. I'd have to warn Jack to keep his mouth shut around the rest of the crew later.

"I feel like I'm doing all the talking," Jack joked. "Tell me about yourselves. It's unusual for a wife and child to be on the ship, isn't it?"

Petra hummed. "Not so much nowadays. It just didn't make sense anymore to own a ship and a house, when we could just live on the ship. I learned different duties on board to be useful, and we sold our house for extra coin."

"It's tough out here for us merchant folk," Captain Ryan said. He twisted a goblet in his hand, examining a dented rim. "Too many people, not enough jobs. Not enough jobs that pay what they should, either. And too many jobs are just plain dangerous with those boilers. Makes people desperate. I couldn't leave my family where I couldn't protect them."

It was a common story on the streets, but Jack frowned.

"I like living on a ship!" Samantha proclaimed, slamming both little hands on the table next to her plate. "I get to see all kinds of things!"

The tension eased at once, Samantha's outburst startling laughs out of us.

"We do get to see some amazing places," Ryan admitted. "Just last month, we took a big shipment up to Spodale. You ever see the mountains covered in snow?"

There was a way to make those mountains *worse?*

Ryan went on to describe it, and various other amazing wonders of the kingdom. He had Jack's undivided attention, longing shining in his eyes, even when Ryan switched from snow-capped mountains and gorgeous seas to homeless kids and working people who still couldn't afford to live comfortably.

I bowed out of the conversation once my plate was clean, choosing instead to go back to bed. Petra stopped me to give me another dose of medicine, and then I curled up in the bunk again.

The good thing about being stuck on this ship was that I had all the time to rest that I wanted.

144

The bad thing was that too much sleep meant nightmares.

I woke with a strangled scream in the middle of the night, a cracking whip and Sara's cries echoing in my mind. My heart pounded in my chest. It took several minutes for my breathing to even out, but I was still keyed up. The walls of the cabin felt like they were closing in on me.

Without a second thought, I threw off the blankets and made my way on deck. I paused there, unsure of where to go. If I were home, I'd walk around the neighborhood to work off this energy. But the ship was only so big, and I didn't want to be stared at for pacing the deck. I couldn't bear the thought of being below deck anymore, so I went to the railing and wrapped my hands around it.

Jack appeared out of nowhere next to me. "Are you okay?"

I swore and managed to stop myself from punching him. "Stop doing that."

He frowned and put a hand against my forehead. "You're still warm, you shouldn't be out of bed, yet."

"I don't want to sleep anymore," I insisted. My throat was marginally better, at least. Petra had been giving me lots of tea, and it seemed like it was working.

His frown persisted. "Until we get the right medicine, it's all we can do to try and keep your fever down."

"I'm fine." I'd had colds in much worse conditions than this. "A few minutes on deck isn't going to kill me." Jack playing mother hen, however, might.

He shrugged out of his jacket. "At least take my jacket, it's pretty cold up here." He held it out to me.

I looked from the jacket to him. If he considered this cold, he would never survive a winter on the streets.

He pushed the jacket at me when I didn't reach out to take it. Was giving me his jackets going to be a thing? Why did he feel he had to give me the clothes off his back?

145

"You're going to be a lot colder than I am," I said.

"Nice to know you care, but you're still putting this on. I'll force you if I have to."

This was more trouble than it was worth. I snatched the jacket and slipped it on. It wasn't as nice as the one he'd given me before; this one had seen some rough days.

Jack shivered.

All I could do was laugh and put my face in my hands. "You're such an idiot."

"It's not that bad." He crossed his arms over his chest.

A nicer person would have given him his jacket back. I, however, was ready to see how long it took before he asked for it back or found a different one. How tough was the little prince?

I waited in silence, leaning on the rail and looking out over the towns beneath us. These towns weren't as crowded as Gallen, the roads wider and the houses more spread out.

"It's beautiful, isn't it?" Jack asked softly.

I barely heard him over the wind, and I glanced over at him.

He looked out over the horizon, like it was the most beautiful thing he'd ever seen.

I didn't know what he saw that was so impressive. One room in his fancy palace had to be nicer than a bunch of trees and old buildings.

"Just think of all the people who live down there, all their hopes and dreams."

I rolled my eyes. "How many do you think are dreaming of their next meal?" How many hoped to survive the winter?

He frowned at me. "What's your dream?"

"Huh?"

He gestured out over the land. "What do you want to do with your life? When this whole thing with Dr. Carl is over."

146

I tightened my fingers around the rail. It was hard to let myself have dreams. Most things seemed impossible, and I could die any day. I didn't want to make plans and then have them ripped away from me.

That didn't mean I hadn't dreamed in the darkest hours of the night, and the words tumbled from my mouth. "I want to make a shelter for homeless kids. Some place they can come and go as they please, get a good meal when they need it, have a place to sleep when the weather is bad. But there'd be no pressure to stay if they didn't want to, no false promises about being adopted by a loving family, and safety from the guards." I'd give them the life I wished I'd had.

"What if we could keep kids from being homeless in the first place?" Jack asked.

I snorted. "Yeah, okay." Talk about dreaming. No matter what he did, there would always be abandoned kids, or kids who ran away from home.

"I'm serious," Jack said. "You know so much more about the lower class, more than any of my father's advisors. Whether you're Alex or not, you could make a difference."

He said that now, when we were miles away from our lives and nothing seemed real. It sounded believable, until I thought of actually standing in front of the nobility. It didn't matter what I could offer them, they'd laugh me right back onto the streets. Jack didn't understand that.

Jack sighed and crossed his arms over the rail. "You'll see when we get home."

I shook my head and turned my back to the rail, gazing out over the ship. This late at night, things were calm on deck. Only the watchmen and helmsman were about.

"Have you ever played cards before?" Jack asked. "I played with some men after dinner. They're pretty nice."

"A few times," I said. Some of the men from back home would

147

invite us sometimes. Malik and I had gone, and I had thought of learning some of the tricks to gamble better. No one was about to let me or Malik into a gambling hall, though, so there hadn't been any rush with that plan.

"I'm really bad at it," Jack said with a small laugh. "My face gives me away all the time."

"That's because you are the world's worst liar," I stated.

"You say that like it's a bad thing," Jack said.

I shrugged. Lying was a survival skill for me. Jack didn't need that in his world of servants and silver spoons, and it was one more thing separating us.

I was starting to regret leaving the peace and quiet of the cabin, but I felt better on deck in the open air.

"You should get back to bed. I'll come get you for breakfast, okay?"

I took him up on his offer and retreated below deck, still wearing his jacket, despite Jack's growing shivers. It was freely given; it was mine now. Hopefully, this one wouldn't meet the same tragic fate as the last one.

It took me until I burrowed under the blankets to remember why I'd left the cabin in the first place, and my mood fell. Jack had distracted me from thinking about the nightmare, but there was nothing to distract me now.

I sat up again. There would be no sleep anytime soon.

"You're a long way from home," someone said.

I jumped, eyes landing on Sel perched on the back of a chair. "How did you…" Following us in the mountains was one thing; seeing him here in the cabin, thousands of feet in the air, was straight up unbelievable.

Sel stretched his forelegs in front of him, arching his back. "I come and go as I please."

That wasn't really an answer, but hearing him talk also shouldn't be possible in the first place.

I was not made for this kind of stuff. Shaking my head, I scooted back against the wall. "Why are you here?"

"Your mind is a mess. It's attractive." He licked his paw.

I blinked. "I don't know what that means."

"You know an awful lot of things." Sel stretched his back legs before leaping into the air. "But you don't believe half the things you know."

I must be losing my mind, because this conversation made no sense. "What the hell does that mean?"

"It means you're stubborn."

I glared at him. He made it difficult by turning see-through.

"It also means you don't want to know half the things you know."

A headache beat against my forehead, and I took a deep breath and rubbed my hands over my face. I should have stayed on deck with Jack. "I hate riddles."

Sel rolled onto his back in the air. "Just because you don't want something to be true doesn't mean it isn't."

"Do you have a point with all of this?"

Sel rolled back onto his front and crossed his paws under his chin, his face-splitting grin glowing. "Princey is right."

I furrowed my brow. "About what?"

He cackled and dove into the floor, vanishing into the wood.

"Uh, Sel?" I waited for him to reappear, but he didn't. "Alright then."

I paced around the cabin to keep myself awake. Jack would not have been pleased with me, but I couldn't handle another nightmare so soon. Pacing turned to poking through the first mate's things, and I found a few books in one of the trunks. I picked one out to read and settled on the bed again, which is where Jack found me for

149

breakfast.

"You're supposed to be sleeping," he stated.

"Didn't feel like it."

He pinched the bridge of his nose. "Do you even know how to read?"

I slammed the book shut. "I may not have the fancy education you do, but I know basics."

"Sorry, that was insensitive. I just assumed…I mean, if you were on the streets, how could you, where would you have…"

"My friend Jade taught me," I cut off his rambling. "And Dr. Carl went over a lot of stuff with me."

"Right. Sorry, again."

I ignored him and opened the book again.

He sighed and came forward. "I'm sorry. I spoke without thinking. I didn't mean to offend you."

I didn't look up from the book. "It doesn't matter. Once Dr. Carl is dealt with, we'll never see each other again." It wasn't like a prince could be friends with a street rat.

"Maybe, maybe not. I guess it depends on if you're really Alex."

"Don't start with that again." I glared at him over the book.

He held his hands up in surrender. "You can't prove you're not him."

I tugged on my hair. "We look nothing alike, number one."

"No, we're definitely fraternal twins."

"We're not any kind of twins."

He leveled me with a hard look. "You look like my mom."

That drew me up short. I didn't have a comeback for that kind of comment. "What?"

"I didn't notice until after you'd cleaned up a little, but you do. She has the same hair, and you have her eyes."

150

The Queen had red hair? I hadn't known that.

It didn't mean anything though. It was a coincidence.

Sel's voice cackled around us.

Jack jumped.

I only sighed and marked my place in the book.

The fox appeared on the ceiling mid-stride.

"What the--did he follow us from Spodale?" Jack asked.

I shrugged. "What do you want now, Sel?"

He jumped down from the ceiling and landed in my lap. I froze, hands up in the air above him.

"Don't be stubborn," he said. He turned in a circle, and as he laid down, he vanished, the weight disappearing.

"That is the creepiest fox I have ever seen," Jack stated. "How are you not more concerned? Where did he go? Where did he come from? What is he?"

"I don't think we're going to figure that out," I replied.

Groaning, Jack rubbed his hands over his face. "He doesn't act like other demons. He's not vicious and bloodthirsty. And why was he telling you not to be stubborn?"

"Hell if I know," I said. A thought wiggled in the back of my mind, replaying the prior conversation in my head. The conversation hadn't made sense before, and it didn't make sense now. He was just a demon fox being weird and creepy.

"Are you not bothered by this?" Jack asked.

"If he wanted to hurt us, he would have."

"He followed us halfway across the kingdom. That doesn't freak you out?"

"So what if it does? What am I going to do about it?"

He opened and closed his mouth. "Fair point, I guess."

I shook my head and laid down, hands behind my head. Of all

the things to worry about, why was he focusing on this?

"In any case, we're invited to Captain Ryan's table again."

Not one to turn down food, I followed him to the captain's quarters, where an eager Sammy waited to tell us all about her dreams. She took up most of the conversation, which didn't seem to bother anyone. I doubted any of us knew what to talk about with one another.

I had a headache by the time we finished eating, and sleep started to sound like a good idea again, nightmares or not. But Jack came with me back to the cabin and was soon pacing like I was earlier.

I tried to read to distract myself from him, but it wasn't easy. "Will you sit down already?"

"Sorry." He sat in the one chair in the room, fingers drumming on the desk next to it. "I'm…curious about this ship."

"Don't ask me how it flies. I don't understand that stuff."

"No, I mean…the cargo. I saw rifles in their crates. A lot of rifles, and ammunition. And I overheard someone say to watch what they said around us, we don't know 'what kind of ship' this is. We aren't flying any flag, and none of them are wearing the air force uniform."

This sounded like something we should leave alone. If I stumbled into a large gang intentionally keeping secrets in Gallen, I'd turn around and forget I ever saw anything. That was how a street rat survived. "It's not really our business, is it? They're getting us home, don't ask questions."

He frowned. "If they're not a legal ship, it is kind of my business."

"What are you going to do?" I demanded. "They find you sniffing around, they'll throw you overboard."

"I know." He grimaced. "But I can't just ignore it."

"Yes, you can," I said. "Just play cards with them and keep your mouth shut until we land."

He ran a hand through his hair. Anymore, it was as messy as mine.

"Forget what you saw and what you heard," I told him. "It's not worth it."

"Yeah, I know. It's not that easy, though."

"Then think of something else. Tell me about the palace. What do you do all day?"

"Lessons, mostly," Jack shrugged. "My tutors teach me everything they can about the different provinces, Wingomia's history, all the ins and outs of politics and what makes a good leader." A soft smile grew on his face. "And Mom teaches me magic."

Is that really all he did all day? He just learned things? When did he ever do anything? "You aren't in charge of anything?"

He shook his head. "Not until I'm eighteen. Then Dad will transfer some responsibilities to me."

I wasn't sure what made me ask, some kind of twisted curiosity. "Do you only become king when he dies?"

Jack's face darkened. "He can choose to step down if he wants. He doesn't have to die."

"What if he goes missing?"

Jack glared at me. "If the King goes missing and there's no queen, then the eldest child can choose to rule in absentia or choose a regent. After a year, they can be crowned. Not that it matters, because nothing is going to happen to Dad."

Clearly, I'd hit a nerve. I wasn't eager to dig deeper, so I let the silence stretch on and went back to my book.

CHAPTER 22

The cabin only had the one bunk. When Captain Ryan first offered it to us, we'd said we'd be fine sharing it. That was before we knew how narrow the bunk was. Since Ace was still sick, I took half the blankets and made a nest on the floor, mourning my real bed back home at the palace.

It wasn't comfortable. I stole a few hours of uneasy sleep, and my body protested. Everything ached, and I wanted nothing more than to soak in a hot bath.

Ships were, surprisingly, not stocked with bathtubs. They weren't stocked with any kind of tub, and when I asked a sailor about it, he'd laughed and offered to dunk me in a water barrel if I wanted.

We had to drink out of those barrels so I respectfully declined.

But as I lay in the blankets, feeling the grit and grime and the aches and pains of the last few days, I was tempted. Drinking water or not, I felt *disgusting*. It made it hard to sleep.

Ace didn't seem to have that problem. He was practically comatose, curled up under the blankets without a care in the world.

I almost regretted letting him have the bed. *He'd* have no problem sleeping on the floor. I felt terrible for thinking it. He was *sick*, and this whole mess was my fault to begin with. The least I could do was let him have the bed.

Rolling over to face the wall, I watched the swaying shadows caused by the dim oil lamp until drifting off.

A hard thud woke me up some time later, followed by a sharp "*Shit*" and heavy breathing.

I sat up and turned to Ace, who now sat on the floor, face in his hands, tangled in the blankets. "Ace?"

He started, dropping his hands and whipping his head up to face me. "Jack."

"Are you okay?"

"I'm fine." His voice had that tight, clipped tone to it he got sometimes when he didn't want to talk about something.

"Did you have a nightmare?"

"I'm going to get some air." He jumped to his feet and ran out the door.

I blinked from my spot on the floor, lowering myself back down. He clearly didn't want to talk about it, and he wanted to be alone. It wasn't like we were that close; I wouldn't want to explain my dreams to him either.

But we were all each other had out here. I probably would have told him anyway. Ace wasn't like that, though. Should I push him? Maybe he thought I didn't want to listen. Maybe he'd at least appreciate not being alone.

He had looked pretty shaken.

I breathed deeply, debating a few moments longer before following him. He was easy to find on deck, curled around the railing. He still had on my jacket from earlier, had apparently never taken it off. I didn't know what to think about that, so I filed it away for later and joined him.

"You didn't have to come out here," Ace said. He didn't look at me.

"I know," I said. "Just thought you might want company."

"Not really."

"I won't say anything." I wanted to, though. I wanted to ask

155

what his nightmare had been about, or offer comfort if I could. But words didn't seem to work much with Ace, so I stayed quiet.

After a few minutes, he relaxed next to me. I waited a few more minutes for him to make the next move.

"Can you…distract me?" he asked in a quiet voice.

"Sure." My mind raced for a topic, something that wouldn't upset him. "Did I ever tell you I paint?"

"No, you didn't. What do you paint?"

"Landscapes, mostly, and flowers. We have a ton around the castle."

"Are you any good?"

I laughed. "Depends on your idea of good. You can always tell what I painted, at least." My best paintings were of flowers my best friend Miranda sent me from her garden. I seemed to put the most effort into those. But I didn't practice as much as I should, so my skills could only improve so much.

"Do you ever paint people?" he asked.

"No, people are hard," I said, pulling a face and making him laugh.

"Okay, I have another question. What are things you're bad at?"

"Why?"

He lifted a shoulder. "I expect you to be good at everything, so it's kind of nice hearing the things you're bad at."

My face twisted again. I didn't follow his logic. But, to be fair, I was decent at anything I tried, or I had the best tutors possible to help me learn to be decent. "Well, I'm not that great at horseback riding."

"But that's so easy," Ace said.

"And where have you had the chance to learn how to ride a horse?" I demanded.

"There's an inventor outside town. He keeps a horse in case he can't fix his steamcar and lets me ride when I stop by."

Was he for real? "You know how to ride a horse?"

He nodded. "Usually bareback."

I couldn't even ride bareback, though that had more to do with my respect of the large creatures and their deadly hooves. "That's impressive. Can you do jumps and stuff?"

A smile warmed his face, something I hadn't expected to see. "Yeah. Old Harry would set up tracks and jumps for me sometimes."

I shook my head in disbelief. "You are full of surprises." He'd get along with Dad, at any rate. Dad was crazy about horses and went riding every morning before breakfast. He'd tried to pass on that same love to me, to no avail.

Ace shrugged. "It's not like it's a useful skill to have."

"Doesn't mean you can't enjoy it," I said. "You're allowed to do things because you like them, you know. Not everything has to have a purpose."

He hummed, which wasn't an agreement, but it wasn't an argument either, so I'd take it.

"So, what else are you bad at?" he asked.

I sighed. Of course this would be the one thing he wants after having a nightmare. At least it seemed to be working; he was more relaxed now. "Fencing, I suppose. I can hold my own in a duel, but I think everyone expects me to win all the time."

"You mean you're not one of those dashing princes off to save the princess?" he asked.

"What princesses?" There'd been only one royal family for the last eight hundred years, ever since the end of the Civil War that united all the provinces under one banner: my family's. The upside to no other royal family was that we weren't married off for political alliances, and everyone in my family had been able to choose who to marry.

"Ah, I see, lack of motivation," Ace said.

I rolled my eyes. "Can you fence? You seem to know how to do plenty I wouldn't expect."

157

"Of course I can't fence. I'm good at running away, though."

I laughed. "I guess you'd beat me in a race, then."

"Easily," he agreed.

We fell into silence. I shivered in the night air.

"You can go back inside, you know," Ace said. "I'm fine. You… helped a lot." His face scrunched as he said it, like he didn't want to admit it.

I bumped my shoulder against his. "You're welcome. Are you ready to go back to bed?" The medicine Petra gave him had worked, and his fever had broken earlier that day, but he was still pale and exhausted.

He snorted and shook his head. "Not a chance. But that doesn't mean you shouldn't go get some more sleep if you can."

"I'm not that tired right now." Even if I was, it was hard to sleep in that cabin. So, I stayed on deck with him, telling him more about what my life in the palace was like. I dropped small things about my parents, too, like how Dad loved horses and Mom loved to read.

He didn't act interested in these tidbits, but he didn't get upset when I talked about them either.

We stayed on deck until sunrise, and then we went back to sleep for a few hours. When I was up, I played cards with the sailors again. I was still abysmal at it, which they found endlessly entertaining. If they were some kind of smuggler ship or pirates, then they were really good at hiding it. They seemed so friendly; I couldn't imagine them attacking another ship.

After I grew tired of losing so much, I abandoned the card game to explore the ship a little more. Previous attempts ended with crewmen shooing me out of the way; the corridors were narrow, and with all the pipes and boilers, there wasn't room for an extra body. That didn't sate my curiosity, and I kept wandering down for another look whenever I could.

This time, no one stopped me as I went below deck. Excited, I kept going, examining every gauge and tank to figure out what their purpose was.

"…needs to be visible," someone said. They had to talk loudly to be heard over the boilers, and I couldn't make out what direction it came from.

"We could probably get him up in the crow's nest," someone else replied. "Be easy to lure him up there and tie him to the mast."

"Good. We can lock the other boy in his room," the first voice said, and I realized it was Captain Ryan. "He's not important."

A stone sank in my stomach. Why did I feel like the boys in question were me and Ace?

More importantly, why were they tying anyone to the mast? What did they need to be visible for?

"Are you sure we can pull this off?" the second voice asked. Was that the first mate? "Attacking the palace directly is a huge risk. We should call in reinforcements at least."

My blood turned to ice. They wanted to attack the palace?

Oh, King's beard, these guys were chimers, weren't they?

No wonder they wanted me nice and visible on the mast. They knew my parents would never allow anyone to attack this ship once they knew I was on board. They'd decimate the palace, kill hundreds of servants and dozens of nobles, maybe even my parents themselves.

"No time," Ryan replied. "We have the ammunition; we need to strike while we can."

I backed up one foot at a time. They hadn't noticed me because of the boilers, but I didn't want to risk hanging around.

Once my foot hit the stairs, I fled back to the cabin.

CHAPTER 23

I was dozing when Jack burst into our room, slamming the door behind him and leaning against it like someone was after him.

"What's wrong?" I demanded.

Jack panted, looking at me with panic written all over his face.

I didn't want to know what could rattle him this badly. Getting thrown into the middle of nowhere with no supplies didn't shake him, and learning some crazy doctor was after us didn't even warrant this much open fear. What was worse than no food and someone trying to kill you?

"We're on a chimers' ship," he hissed.

I blinked. The news did not exactly surprise me, not with what he said before about the crates of rifles, and Captain Ryan had agreed to ferry us home too easily. Still, they were taking us home. Whatever secret reason they had couldn't be that bad, and we could handle it when we got there.

"Okay?"

He dug his hands into his hair and paced the small floor of the cabin. "We're on a chimers' ship," he repeated. "And they want to attack the palace."

That got my attention. Now his panic made more sense. "What the hell?"

He laughed, a little hysterically. "They're planning to tie me to the mast so the palace knows I'm on board, so they won't fight back. They'll decimate the palace and everyone inside it, and then probably kill me so they can take over unopposed."

Well, that sounded terrible. "King's beard." Was that really their plan? What about Petra and Sammy? Was Captain Ryan really willing to risk starting a battle with his family on board?

He nodded. "What do we do? We can't let them open fire on the palace, there are too many innocent people there, our parents are there."

Now wasn't the time to correct him about the 'our parents' thing, but I did flinch at the mention. He didn't notice.

"What can we do?" I asked. "We can't take down a whole ship full of people."

He tugged at his hair. "I don't know. I don't know. The two of us can't launch a mutiny, and neither of us know how to fly an airship anyway."

"Do we need to know how? Crashing seems just as effective at stopping them."

"We're still on board," he hissed.

I shrugged. "We can use your teleport thing right before we crash. Ship goes down, never makes it to the capitol, and we end up somewhere else in the kingdom, no worse off than we are now."

He checked his pocket watch. "We could just teleport right now, without doing anything to the ship."

"That works, too." It made no difference to me if we decided to leave before wrecking anything or after.

He nodded. The panic on his face had been replaced with consideration, and he continued pacing. "We could make a clean getaway right now. But." He bit his lip and turned to me, finally standing still. "I don't want this ship anywhere near the capital. They have so many rifles on board, I'm worried they'll attack anyway even if we're not here."

"Okay, then we bring the ship down." I hoped we found a way

161

to do it with minimal casualties. I would hate if Sammy or Petra got hurt because of this.

He took a deep breath. "Yeah. We'll bring the ship down. How exactly do we do that?"

I laughed and unclipped my wrench from my pants. "Are you kidding? Crashing a ship is the easy part. Just break stuff."

He eyed my wrench. "Without getting caught?"

I grinned. "Who do you think you're talking to?"

He didn't look convinced. "I want to get up to the helm and steer the ship off course, maybe try and get us away from any towns."

"That's a good idea," I said. Bad enough we might accidentally kill some of the crewmen, I really didn't want to kill any innocent townspeople below us.

"Okay." He shook his hands out. "Give me ten minutes to get the ship off course, and then…break stuff, I guess."

I twirled the wrench. It was a shame Malik wasn't here, he lived for this kind of stuff.

Jack hesitated at the door. "I can do this. I can do this."

"You'll be fine," I told him. "But we're running out of time, so you better get going."

He took one more deep breath and then slipped out the door.

I waited about ten minutes, and then I did the same. I couldn't tell if the ship had turned at all; the constant rocking all felt the same to me, so I hoped I'd given Jack enough time.

Sneaking down to the boiler room was easy. A few guys were working down there, but I crept around them and started twisting every gear I could find.

Steam hissed out, and the pipes rattled.

The men came running, and I made myself scarce. While they fixed my first mess, I got to work wrecking everything else. I unbolted a pipe altogether, scalding my hands when I didn't pull them back in time and the steam billowed out.

The ship groaned and shuddered. The floor tilted under me, and an alarm started ringing. I ducked out of sight as more people came running down to the boiler room, and then I crept out into the hall again. Most mechanics were probably helping in the boiler room, which left me free to start destroying the pipes in the halls.

Steam quickly filled the air, and the ship pitched violently. I scrambled to climb back up to the stairs and get myself on deck.

Men ran back and forth up there, which seemed normal to me, until I realized they weren't running to the rigging or anything, they were chasing Jack.

"Oh, king's beard," I muttered, watching him duck under one guy's arms and dance around someone else. He did better than I would have thought, but he couldn't keep this up forever. There were too many crewmen after him.

There was a crash behind me, and the ship lurched to the side. Everyone lost their balance and went sprawling on their hands and knees.

We were losing altitude, fast.

What have Jack and I done? This was a terrible plan; we should have just left when we had the chance.

"Jack!" I yelled, struggling to reach him.

He whipped his head around to find me and scrambled to meet me halfway. At this point, all the crewmen gave up on catching him and were more concerned with saving themselves. Someone was at the helm, desperately trying to right the ship.

Jack's hand found mine, and then the nauseating sensation that accompanied this horrible spell overtook me.

When it ended, we were still falling. We were at the kind of height where you have time to realize you're falling, but not enough time to do anything about it. We landed hard in the middle of a cobblestone street.

Steamcars hummed over us, and pilots swore at us to get out of the road.

Either they hadn't seen us appear out of nowhere, or they

163

decided that wasn't their problem and didn't care.

Jack groaned and cradled his head.

I grabbed his arm and forced him to his feet, dragging him to the sidewalk so we wouldn't get flown over. He leaned against a shop window and pulled his hand away from his head, wincing at the bright crimson on his palm.

"Great," he muttered. "Where are we?"

"Don't know," I said.

"The airship?"

"No idea."

Sammy's face flashed in my mind. She better survive that crash, or I'll throw myself in the nearest river and drown.

He prodded his head, pulling faces at the bump. "Guess we need to figure out where we are and how to get to Chiari from here."

"Yeah," I said, glancing up at the sky. The shadows were getting pretty long, which meant night would fall soon. "Food first, unless you want to skip dinner tonight."

He sighed. "Not particularly. You're going to steal it, aren't you?"

"Do you have money on you?"

"No," he pouted.

"Then yes, I'll be stealing." We had to find a place to shelter for the night, too. I didn't want to sleep, but Jack looked like he needed some time to rest, and I didn't like the idea of wandering an unfamiliar city in the dark.

I looked up and down the street, weighing our options. This whole time, I'd been off balance in the woods and on an airship, but this time, we were in a city.

This was my kind of place.

CHAPTER 24

My head throbbed. I landed hard on the street after the teleportation spell, and the disorientation remained for a while. Long enough for Ace to drag me around whatever city we were in and shove some fruit in my hands.

I narrowed my eyes at the apples in confusion, and then I looked around the street we were on. "Where did you find apples?"

"There's a market on the street over," he said, wiping apple juice from his chin. He was halfway done his already. "You should eat something."

Apples didn't sound like dinner, but it was better than tree bark and questionable berries.

"We need a plan to get home," I said, finally biting into an apple.

Ace hummed, his attention on the rooftops. "I'm going to scout the city from above. Stay here, okay?"

He didn't wait for an answer before using a shop window to jump up to a sign, hauling himself up from there and scampering onto the roof.

I stared at the spot he'd disappeared, trying to track the invisible handholds he'd used to get up there. "What?"

He returned about five minutes later, jumping down in front of me out of nowhere. "This way." Gesturing for me to follow, he took off down the street.

There was an energy to him in this city he'd been lacking for the last few days, and not just because he'd been sick. The city brought him to life in a way the woods hadn't. He moved differently, slipping effortlessly between people, hands slipping into the occasional pocket.

I frowned at the thievery. "Ace."

He glanced back. "What?"

Catching up to him, I pointed at the change purse now in his own pocket. "Give it back."

"We need it more than they do," he said.

"That doesn't make stealing okay," I hissed.

Shrugging, he continued walking. "Survival isn't about what's right or wrong. It's about what works."

That was a depressing comment that got me to shut up for several minutes.

He continued to lead us through the city, away from the crowds and to the more rundown part of town. The streetlights weren't lit over here, and I saw no evidence of a lamplighter anywhere. People huddled in doorways, and the shop windows were boarded up or broken.

"Where are we going?" I asked. I failed to see how anything around here would get us home. It seemed more likely we'd be murdered than anything else.

"Finding some place quiet to sleep. Unless you want to pass out in the cold?"

I didn't, but I'd also prefer not to pass out at all. "We should keep moving."

"Neither of us know this city. It's not a good idea to wander around at night."

Fair point, but it still didn't sit right with me. That was too much time sitting around doing nothing when we could be pleading with

166

guards for a ride or something. At the very least, we should figure out where in Wingomia we were.

"We'll figure something out in the morning," he said.

If we lived that long. I eyed the dilapidated buildings. "But why here?"

"Because you're not going to find an unclaimed spot in the middle of town," he said.

He stopped in front of one of the houses, tilting his head as he considered it.

The house in question looked one good windstorm away from being a pile of rubble. We saw straight through to the back, each window nothing more than a hole in the siding.

"This could work," he said.

I gaped at him. "Are you serious? I thought we were looking for someplace warm!"

"Relax, I'll rig up a stove and board up the windows, it'll be fine. Let's check it out." He bounded up the steps and knocked on the front door.

"Check it out?" I repeated. "Are you insane? This place is going to collapse any minute!"

Snorting, he gave the door frame a few good kicks.

I winced, expecting the place to topple over and crush him.

The house remained standing.

"It's not going anywhere," he said. "Doesn't sound like anyone is inside, either. Good news for us."

"Yippee."

Unperturbed by my lack of enthusiasm, he climbed in through one of the broken windows and unlocked the door from the inside for me. Because whoever owned this house was clearly concerned about thieves these days.

I missed the palace and having nice, sturdy walls. When we get back, I will never take solid walls for granted again.

"You coming or not?" Ace called from inside the house.

Gripping my watch in case I needed a quick save, I stepped into the house.

Ace rummaged through the rooms, tossing things into nonsensical piles. It all looked like trash to me, but he clearly saw something different in the sofa upholstery and stuffing.

"What exactly are you doing?" I asked.

He nodded at the upholstery. "If we tack that over the windows, it will help keep the wind out and the heat in. Some solid boards would be good, too, but I don't have any nails."

I lifted up the sofa stuffing. "And this?"

"Fuel for fire," he replied, moving into the hallway. His hand trailed along the paneling on the wall, thoughtful, and then he continued into the dining room. "Excellent, the chairs are still here."

"Why are chairs—"

My question was interrupted by the sound of something smashing and wood splintering.

I ran into the dining room. Ace had slammed a chair against the floor, breaking the legs off. He kicked loose pieces free and piled them all by the door to the kitchen. "Why?" was all I could ask.

"Firewood," he said.

"Aren't there easier ways to get firewood?" I asked, watching in horror as he methodically broke every single dining room chair. He'd probably have broken the table, too, if it wasn't so thick.

"Unless you've got an ax and some trees, not really," he said.

He continued like this throughout the house, breaking anything he thought would burn and stealing whatever he found useful.

In the end, he dragged one of the dirty mattresses from upstairs down to the kitchen and started shoving chair legs and couch stuffing into the ancient iron stove. The dining room table was propped up like a door to the kitchen, rather than boarding up all the windows, because that was less suspicious and we only needed to heat the one room anyway.

I sat on the mattress in awe, watching him coax a fire to life in the stove with the aged flintstones.

He had no hesitation about any of this. For him, it was routine, just another day.

If I'd been out here on my own, I'd have ended up on someone's doorstep, freezing through the night, possibly killed by some crazy person.

He made surviving like this, with nothing but the clothes on our backs, look easy. And it's heartbreaking to know he had to learn all this the hard way while I was tucked safely into my own bed at home.

The fire sparked to life, and he slapped the little door shut. Heat started to fill the room.

"That should do it," he said proudly, joining me on the mattress. He finally noticed the look I'd been giving him all night. "What?"

"I don't know whether I should be impressed or heartbroken right now."

His face twisted. "Why would you be heartbroken?"

"Because you know how to do all this stuff, and you shouldn't have to. Someone should have been taking care of you."

His face went blank. "Yeah, well. Life didn't pan out that way."

He started to get up to go do something, maybe just sit on the other side of the room, but I grabbed his arm and dragged him back down. "It will from now on."

Ace blinked.

"I promise, someone will be there to take care of you now," I said.

He pried his arm free. "I don't need anyone to take care of me."

169

"It's not about need."

He gave me a long look.

I made sure to keep my face determined. There would be someone from now on, whether he stayed in the palace with me or not. I wouldn't let him go back to sleeping in abandoned houses with broken furniture for firewood.

"Do what you want," he finally said.

His words made it sound like he didn't really care, but there was a look in his eye, half curious, half doubtful, that made me think he meant it more as a challenge.

Challenge accepted.

CHAPTER 25

It wasn't the worst place I'd ever spent the night. Anything with a roof over my head and walls to block the wind was okay in my book.

Judging by the bags under the prince's eyes, he disagreed.

His stomach growled loudly in the morning, and he sat with his head between his knees for half an hour before he was willing to start the day.

"Do you want me to just bring breakfast back here?" I offered. I was hungry, too, but I was used to it.

"No," he groaned. "The faster we get going, the sooner we get home." With a great show of effort, he pushed himself to his feet.

"Well, good news," I said, shoving the dining table out of the way so we could get out. "We can buy breakfast."

"You stole that money," he grumbled.

"Do you not want a hot breakfast?" I asked.

He put a hand over his stomach and glared at me. "…Fine."

Stomachs always win in the end.

I led us back to the main part of town, where we were more likely to find something good.

"Did you actually remember the way back here, or was this a lucky guess?" Jack asked, squinting at a shop.

"…Did you *not* remember how to get back here?" I asked him. It wasn't that many turns. I thought everyone could retrace their steps like that. Maybe he just wasn't paying attention.

He shook his head. "Never mind. Breakfast?"

Amazing how little he cared about the source of our funds now that he wanted food.

I found the market, and we bought more fruit, some meat pies, and some cooked sausages. I also took the opportunity to pick more pockets and replenish our funds.

Jack did a double-take at the new change purse. "Where did you—no, I don't want to know."

Grinning, I swiped a loaf of fresh bread from someone's shopping bag and broke off a piece, holding it out to him.

He eyed it for a moment, sighed, and then took it. "I want to head to the guard house. Maybe word has gotten around that I'm missing, and they'll be able to escort us to Chiari."

A guard house? My whole body recoiled at the idea. "What if they don't believe you?"

"Then they laugh and chase us out on the street, I guess," Jack said, shrugging. "And we're no worse off than we are."

"Orrr they realize we're street rats and try and arrest us?" I said. That seemed like the far likelier option.

"We're not street rats," Jack said.

"I am," I reminded him. "And you can't prove you're not."

"That's still no reason for them to arrest us," Jack said. "We'll tell them the same thing we told Captain Ryan, and hopefully this time they don't turn out to be Chimers."

Could he have said that any louder? I glanced around nervously to check if anyone heard, but no one was watching us.

That was the beauty in being someone the rest of the city wanted to ignore. Sensitive conversations stayed private.

"Let's just try the guard house and see what happens," Jack said. "It can't be any worse than what we've already gone through."

"Easy for you to say," I muttered. I still doubted this plan, but I went up to the rooftops to find the guard house anyway.

The city sprawled out before me. Up here, it was easy to think I was back in Gallen, just a few rooftops away from Base.

I wished I could be that close to my friends, instead of however many miles were between us now.

But maybe Jack's plan would work.

Jumping across a few rooftops, I found the guard house only a few streets away. I went back for Jack, dropping down beside him and making him jump.

He put a hand over his chest. "Are you trying to give me a heart attack?"

"You should be paying attention. That's a good way to get robbed, just standing around like that."

He snorted and stuffed his hands in his pockets. The chain for his pocket watch still hung off his belt, so at least that hadn't been taken. Tracking that thing down if it were stolen would be a pain in the neck. "Like I have anything worth stealing. Our stench alone is probably keeping people away."

"See? Being smelly has its uses," I said. "Guard house is this way." I started walking, and he scrambled to keep up.

"Thanks for finding it," he said.

I shrugged. "It wasn't that hard. And if it gets us home faster, then whatever."

"Yeah. This should work, I know it."

I wasn't so convinced. Like he pointed out, we looked and smelled like street rats. Any guard who believed some random kid was the prince should resign.

I led him across a few streets, nabbing a few change purses along the way. It was amazing how much easier this was in a city where no one recognized me. Back home, just about everyone knew to avoid the street rat with red hair. I could never reliably pick-pocket, because everyone was on guard around me. Here? No one knew who I was. They held their hands over their noses when I came near, but that left them open to my quick hands.

"Will you stop that?" Jack hissed when I pocketed a lady's sapphire ring. If I could find a pawn shop, it would sell for a ton of money.

"This could buy us a real bed for the night," I told him.

"I don't care. Stop stealing from people."

Rolling my eyes, I shoved my hands in my own pockets for the duration of the walk. I had a decent enough stash for now, anyway.

Outside the guard house, we paused at the bottom of the steps. It was one of the older buildings on the block, large columns on either side of the doors. Steamcycles were parked along the road out front, all marked with the guard sigil on the front panels. The same sigil was etched in the glass on the doors.

"Good luck," I said, patting Jack's shoulder and then turning to find a spot to wait somewhere else.

He grabbed my hand. "Please come in with me."

He was joking, right? "Me and guards don't mix."

"They don't know you here," he reminded me. "And I'm worried if we get separated, we'll never find each other again."

Ridiculous. He knew I needed him to get back to my friends. I wouldn't run off at this point. But that might not stop him from being dragged off unwillingly.

Sighing, I nodded and followed him up the steps inside.

The place was, unsurprisingly, crawling with guards. Desks were pushed up against each other. Civilians sat beside them, or waited in hard wooden chairs on the side of the room.

Jack went up to the first guard he found, a man in his early thirties with a mustache wrapping up into his hair and a bare chin. "Hi, excuse me."

The man barely looked up from the paperwork he was filling out. "Can I help you?"

"I hope so," Jack said brightly, pulling out his big, innocent

174

smile. "My friend and I are lost; we were hoping you could arrange a ride home for us?"

The guard sighed and put his pen down, getting a better look at the two of us. I could tell the moment he registered the tattered clothes and offensive stench, and I saw the conclusions he drew for himself.

"What are you trying to pull?" the guard asked.

"Nothing, we really do need a ride home. To the capital city, Chiari," Jack said.

The man laughed. "Uh huh, sure. You want me to just fly you halfway across the kingdom. Do you think I'm an idiot? Get out of here."

This went about as well as I expected. I turned to go, but Jack set his shoulders.

"I'm telling the truth," Jack insisted. "There's too much to explain now, but I'm Prince Jackson, and I need help to return home."

The guard held in a snort. "You? You're the prince?"

Jack stood as tall as he could. "Yes."

That was all the guard could take. He doubled over his desk in laughter.

Other guards started looking at us.

"What's the matter, Moyer?"

"This kid," the guard we'd been talking to, Moyer apparently, pointed at us. "This kid thinks he's the prince!"

Some of the other guards started chuckling.

One of them, an older gentleman with gray hair and a neatly trimmed beard, came over to us. "Alright, boys. You've had your fun. The prince is safe and sound in the palace, so why don't you just run along back home? Do you need a place to stay?"

"I know I'm a mess right now," Jack said. "It's been a rough few days. But I assure you, I am Prince Jackson, and I need to get back to the palace."

175

The guards shared looks of amusement with each other. "That's enough, son," the new guard said. "What's your real name?"

"Crown Prince Jackson William Meciare."

The humor started to die out in their eyes. Moyer stood up. "We're done messing around. If you need a place to stay, we'll take you to the local orphanage."

I jolted like someone pulled on my puppet strings, grabbing Jack's arm and yanking him back towards the door. The second they started throwing the word orphanage around, it was time to go. "We'll be fine, thanks."

"Ace, let go," Jack said. "They have to help us!"

"Do you have proof?" I asked.

"No," he spat.

I dragged him out the door and down the steps. "Then this is a waste of time. They're not going to believe you."

Huffing, he crossed his arms and sat on the bottom step. "I can't believe that didn't work. What are we going to do now?"

"I don't know." I leaned against the stone banister and looked out over the city.

"We have to get home," Jack said, as if I didn't already know that. "Ace, how are we supposed to get there?"

I shrugged, about to tell him "I don't know" again, but my eyes landed on the steamcycles. "Actually, I do have one idea. But you're not going to like it."

CHAPTER 26

Lesson learned. If Ace said I wouldn't like an idea, assume he was right and move on to the next one.

"We're going to get caught," I hissed.

We'd gone down to the end of the block, and now I stood in front of him on the sidewalk, blocking him from view while he tried to make a steamcycle start without the key.

Metal clanged behind me. I smiled and waved at a gentleman walking his dog.

"Ace," I hissed again.

"What?" he hissed back.

I glanced at the guard house down the block. It was way too close for comfort for what we were doing. "Are you sure you know how to do this?"

"I've got a pretty good idea," he said.

"Pretty good?" I repeated.

Another clang, and he swore. "This was Malik's thing, not mine. But I've watched him do it a dozen times."

"That doesn't inspire confidence," I told him. How did I let him talk me into this?

'Just take a steamcycle to fly ourselves,' he'd said. 'We don't need an escort, we'll be fine,' he'd said.

I was having so many second thoughts about this plan. "Do you even know how to fly this thing?"

"Yes. That's the -ow!- easy part."

I had to take his word for it, even though the longer it took for him to start the cycle, the less faith I had that we could pull this off. A guard was going to walk by and see us any minute. We'd be arrested, and my parents would never find us.

Although, if that happened, I could probably transport us out of the cell, so being arrested might not be the worst thing in the world. Just a major inconvenience on a stack of other major inconveniences this week had become.

The steamcycle hummed to life, and Ace crowed. "Woo, there we go!"

I spun on my heel. The steamcycle hovered half a foot off the ground, kicking a circle of dust up beneath it. Ace climbed into the pilot seat and held a hand out to help me up.

That was when people started to notice.

"Hey, what are you kids doing?" a pair of businessmen asked us.

"Come on, we've got to move!" Ace said.

I swallowed my doubts and took his hand, hopping up behind him. I'd only been in steamcars before, and the open air around us made me nervous.

"Hang on tight!" Ace said, pulling a lever that took us straight up.

I wrapped my arms around his skinny waist and squeezed my knees around the seat. This was so much worse than riding a horse.

Beneath us, guards started pouring out the doors and shouted at us to stop and get down.

Ace ignored them and pushed another lever. The steamcycle shot forward.

There were basic rules for piloting steamcars and steamcycles. Stay over the roads, and never fly above the rooftops. Most models weren't capable of lifting that high anyway. Pilots should stop at all intersections and look both ways before continuing. Speed should be limited to avoid nasty collisions.

Ace had apparently never heard any of these rules in his life.

We went over rooftops, and even over other pilots. He never slowed down at all, let alone to check both ways at an intersection.

"We're going to die," I muttered, finally burying my face in his back so I didn't have to see all the close calls when he turned a corner and narrowly avoided another steamcar.

"Relax," he said. "I need you to tell me which way the palace is. And possibly create a smokescreen if the guards catch up to us."

"We should have gotten a map first," I grumbled. We had no idea what city this was or where in the kingdom we were, and therefore nothing to base our heading on. "Find a landmark or a river or something."

"Got it!" he said, and dived down to go under a slower steamcar.

He was going to kill us. Worst idea ever.

We gained altitude, and then banked sharply to the left. "Ace!"

"Calm down!" he said, straightening us out. "Oh, there's the river!"

I peeked out over his shoulder. True enough, a few miles ahead of us was the river. Judging by the width, I assumed it was the Frimare River. It was the only river in all of Wingomia that large.

Multiple bells started clanging behind us. I twisted back to see several guards on their own steamcycles racing to catch up and stop us.

"Ace?" I called.

"Distract them!" he said.

"How?"

"Use magic!"

Right. Of course. I fumbled for my watch, desperate for an idea to give us an advantage. It would have to be something subtle so I didn't blow the royal family secret. And I didn't want to hurt anyone below us or cause any of the guards to crash, which only left a few options.

We'd need to go up, and we had to outrace the guards.

I looked longingly at the ground. The nice, safe ground, that was about to be even farther away. "Brace yourself," I warned Ace.

I used a levitation spell on the cycle, lifting us far beyond the legal limits.

Ace took advantage immediately and leaned forward for more speed. I increased our acceleration and hid my face behind his back, trusting that Ace wouldn't let us crash.

"Woo! This is amazing!" Ace crowed.

At least he was having fun.

We outpaced the guards in no time. They pushed their cycles to reach the same altitude, but it just wasn't physically possible for them. Without any knowledge of magic, they'd assume we got lucky and found the one cycle that could push these heights.

A few minutes later, we reached the river.

"What now?" Ace asked.

The Frimare River flowed south from the Spodale mountains. Chiari was along this river in the middle of the kingdom. All we had to do was follow the river, and we'd eventually reach our destination.

But should we head north or south? How was I supposed to know where exactly we were in the kingdom?

The cycle slowed down. "Jack?" Ace asked.

When we boarded Captain Ryan's ship, we were in the southern half of the kingdom. We hadn't reached the capitol yet when Ace and I sabotaged the ship. I didn't try to transport us very far when we bailed. The likelihood that we were still in the southern half of the kingdom was pretty high.

"Go upstream," I told him.

Nodding, he dived down towards the river to orient us.

A furry tail dragged across my nose. "What the-" I almost threw

180

myself off the back of the cycle.

Ace caught my arm when it loosened around his waist.

Sel perched on his shoulder. "I wouldn't get too close to the water if I were you."

"Why not?" Ace asked.

Sel climbed onto his head and curled up, looking back at me over his bushy tail. "Never know what lurks in the depths."

"Where did you come from?" I asked. My heart still pounded against my chest.

Sel grinned. "How do you know I ever left?"

The fact that I didn't greatly disturbed me. I didn't know how Ace handled Sel's random coming and goings so calmly.

"Hey, Jack?" Ace asked, peering over the side of the cycle.

"Yeah?"

"What gigantic things live in the river?"

Dread filled my stomach. I peered over the side. There was a ginormous shadow under us, far too large to be caused by us or any fish that I knew of living in this river.

"Stay out of the water," Sel chirped, and then bounded off into the air. He dived into an invisible hole and disappeared.

"Take us up higher," I told Ace.

Before we could go even a foot higher, a wave of water shot into the sky in front of us.

Ace turned sharply, but it was too late. We slammed sideways into the water and lost all sense of direction.

CHAPTER 27

The number of times I'd almost drowned was getting way too high.

We crashed into the wave, and I lost my grip on the steamcycle. Jack's arms disappeared from my waist, and I floundered in the water. I didn't even know which way was up. Should I be going up, or should I go sideways? Was I sinking or floating?

Where was the sky? I needed to breathe.

I cracked open my eyes in the hope that I could find my way out of the water, but all I saw was murky darkness, and the water stung my eyes.

Something brushed past my leg. Something big.

All I could make out around me were dark shapes. It all looked like one big tangled shadow writhing around. The polished bronze of the steamcycle glinted in the light, and then it was swallowed by the darkness.

So much for our ride back home.

My chest ached with the need to breathe. I kicked out, hoping whatever direction I went in was the right one.

The water gave way over my head, and I breathed in deep gulps of air. If I never went swimming again, it would be too soon.

"Ace!" Jack yelled off to my right. He swung his arms over his head in large strokes to swim towards me. The surface of the water was rough and choppy, waves surging between us and blocking each other from view.

I got a face full of water and sank beneath the surface again. Panic flooded my body. This was so much worse than when I jumped into the river to escape the guards or when Jack and I fell into that lake. Both times, the water had been relatively calm. Now, it felt like the river was alive around us, and it felt particularly deadly today.

I broke the surface again, coughing the muddy water out of my mouth. "Jack!" I didn't care where his transportation spell put us this time, we needed to get out of here.

"I'm -ah!- coming!"

I twisted in the water to face him again, my head ducking under for a brief moment. Water was the worst. I belonged on solid ground, in between lots of sturdy buildings, with no large bodies of water in sight.

Something brushed past my leg again. "What was that?" I demanded, yanking my knees up.

"Just hang on!" Jack said.

He was still ten feet away at least, and the dark shape we'd spotted in the air was directly under me.

"Jack!"

"Almost there!"

The next pass didn't just brush past my leg. It wrapped around my ankle.

My heartrate spiked. "Do some-" It pulled me under. Water flooded my mouth.

We kept sinking.

I still couldn't get a good look at it. Some kind of tentacle was around my ankle, and what looked like seven eyes at least stared back at me in the murky darkness. Another tentacle drifted up and wrapped around my arm, slimy and sticky at the same time.

Oh, king's beard, I was in trouble. I couldn't pry either tentacle off or kick myself free, and I was already out of air. Where was

Jack? Didn't he have some kind of spell that could help?

I needed to breathe. I was going to drown before this thing stopped dragging me around and ate me or whatever it wanted to do.

I've never wanted to be above water so much in my life. I'd even take free falling through the sky again, anything to get me away from this…this thing.

There was a tug in the back of my mind, and I opened my mouth to breathe even though there'd be no air.

The world blurred around me, and I was weightless, like Jack did his transportation spell.

Oh, thank the *gods*. I didn't even believe in them, but I was willing to start. Especially since, once again, I was free falling.

This was also happening too much lately.

The river was below me. It wouldn't be as bad as when Jack and I did it before, I wasn't quite so high. But it would still be painful.

"What do you have against the ground?" I asked Jack, my voice ripped away in the wind.

Jack didn't answer.

Jack was not in the sky with me.

He was still in the river, staring up at me with his mouth wide open. Why did he look so surprised? Wasn't he the one that sent me up here? I didn't think his magic worked without him, but it got me out of the water and away from that creature, and it wasn't like I knew that much about his magic anyway.

He started laughing, grinning from ear to ear. "Way to go, Ace!"

"What?" I asked, and then I hit the water. Still not a pleasant experience.

I sank pretty far, but this time Jack grabbed my arm and dragged me back up.

"I knew it!" Jack crowed. "This proves you're my brother!"

"*What?*" I demanded, coughing up water.

Jack kept his hands on my shoulders. "You used magic! On your

184

own! That means you have to be a member of the royal family! You are Alex!"

I…

What?

"No, I didn't! There's no way!" I said. "It had to be you!"

He shook his head. "It wasn't me! I couldn't get to you; you were too far down!"

Tentacles curled around my ankle again. The glee faded from Jack's face in an instant, a result of this creature grabbing him, too.

"Not again," I muttered, thrashing my foot to try and break free.

"Hang on!"

The weightless feeling returned, and my vision went out of focus. When everything was back to rights, we were crashing through branches.

If he put us back in the mountains again, I might have to kill him myself.

My stomach collided with a thick branch, and I curled up around it. Jack continued to fall to the ground, landing in a bush with a bunch of broken twigs.

Neither of us moved at first. Then he started to crawl out of the bush, and I slowly unhooked myself from the branch and tried to lower myself gently to the ground.

My hands slipped off the branch and I landed on my back. "Why does your magic do this?" I demanded.

"I don't know," he groaned.

"Just tell me we're not in the mountains again," I said, shutting my eyes and letting myself lie there.

"Ugh, hang on." He pushed himself to his feet and stumbled around for a minute, pausing against a tree. "Huh, the river's right there. We just went to the bank, I guess."

What a relief. I started pushing myself up, cataloguing all the new bruises. My sleeve and the bottom of my pant leg were torn, and the skin was red and itchy.

Jack swore and stumbled back, tripping over a root and falling.

"What?" I asked.

He pointed a shaky finger towards the river. "The thing. It's… It's looking for us."

Back on guard, I jumped to my feet and looked past the tree he'd been standing at.

"What the hell is that?" I asked, watching as some creature made of scales, tentacles, and too many eyes swam up the river.

"It has to be another demon," Jack said. "Which means we're in big trouble. They're nearly impossible to kill."

"So, we should run?" I asked.

He got to his feet. "Yeah, we should run. As fast as we can."

I didn't need to be told twice. We stomped through the underbrush, forging our way between the trees and following the river as much as we could. We didn't want to be visible to that demon, but we didn't want to get lost again, either.

Was it possible to be lost when you didn't know where you were in the first place?

The demon kept swimming upstream after us, until it came upon another ship. That made Jack stop running and watch.

I tugged on his arm. "Come on, there's nothing we can do."

"I could at least tell them where it's vulnerable."

Rifles fired in the distance, and we could hear distant shouting of the sailors. "That is not a place you want to drop in unexpectedly," I told Jack.

The demon snapped one of the masts off and sent it crashing into the river.

"I have to help," Jack said. "That demon is more than they can handle."

"It's more than you can handle, too," I said. "That's why we were running, remember?"

186

"They have real weapons!" He pointed at the ship. "I just need to tell them how to use them!"

The demon screeched, waving a flaming tentacle through the air and dunking it under water.

"I think they're figuring it out," I stated, tugging on his arm again. "Come on, this is our chance to get away."

"Yeah, but…" Jack looked between me and the ship. He set his shoulders back. "I can't just leave them."

"Why not?" I asked. "It's not like we know them."

"That doesn't matter," he spat. "They're citizens of my kingdom, and I have to protect them. Are you coming or not?"

I threw my head back and groaned. If we got separated, there was no guarantee we'd meet up again. And whether we liked each other or not, our odds of survival were better together than apart.

"Can't you help from here?" I asked.

He frowned and stared at the battle, considering. "I don't think my magic can reach that far."

More fire exploded over the demon's head, and another loud shriek pierced the air.

Jack checked his pocket watch. The single hand was on the six, and he frowned. "I don't have enough to transport us both over there and back."

It would be a one-way trip into the middle of a battle. "This is insane, you know that, right?"

"Yeah, I know. But you're coming, right?"

"We better not die, got it?"

Grinning, he grabbed my arm. "Got it."

One last round of weightlessness, and then we dropped onto the deck of the ship.

CHAPTER 28

The ship was absolute chaos. Our presence wasn't even noticed while the sailors ran around with rifles and sabers.

It took a cabin boy carrying extra guns literally running into us for anyone to pay attention to us.

The cabin boy dropped the rifles, and Ace and I bent down to help pick them up while the boy apologized.

"Sorry, I'll get these to the men right awa—hey, you're not part of the crew," the boy said.

"Nope, we're not," I agreed. "But I know how to help. Who's in charge?"

"How'd you get on board?" the boy asked, which was a fair question, I supposed.

"You want to argue, or do you want to kill the monster?" Ace asked.

The cabin boy glanced at the monster. "The captain is at the bow, this way." Gathering up the rifles, he led us to the front of the ship where most sailors were battling the demon. They were quick to notice the replacement rifles, already loaded, and grabbed them from the cabin boy.

"Captain!" I yelled, getting the attention of a man in a gold ascot.

He had thick, curly black hair pulled back in a ball pony-tail and a well-trimmed beard. He fired off one more shot and then backed up to check who called for him, dark brown eyes narrowing when he spotted us. "How'd you get on my ship?"

I took a page out of Ace's book and ignored the question to focus on the bigger issue. "This thing's weak spot is internal. Aim for the eyes and the mouth!"

The captain glanced at the demon curiously. "We've hit an eye already, but we can't find a mouth to aim for it."

A tentacle slid over the deck, breaking the rails. Attempts to shoot the tentacle or slice it proved ineffective, and the ship creaked.

"If you've got anything more helpful, now would be the time," the captain said, taking a loaded gun from the cabin boy and firing.

That was about all the useful information I had. Ace and I stood there, in the way and useless, while the ship pitched back and forth. There had to be something else I could do before this demon broke the ship in half.

Another creak, and the ship rocked violently under our feet. A sailor stumbled over the tentacle, dropping his gun. It slid off the slimy limb and clattered to the deck.

Steam hissed into the air. The tentacle recoiled, springing back over the deck and whipping over the rail, retreating to the waves.

I looked at the gun. It was a typical bronze rifle, but something about the weapon was toxic to the demon.

That was exactly what we needed. "Did you see that?" I asked.

"See what?" Ace asked, arms flailing to keep his balance.

"It doesn't like guns," I said.

"Are we fighting the same monster?" the captain asked, back to me while he aimed for the demon's eyes.

"Not the bullets, the gun itself," I said, snatching one from the cabin boy.

"Wait, that one's not loaded!" the cabin boy yelled.

I approached the rail where another tentacle waved soldiers aside.

"Jack! What are you doing?" Ace yelled.

Holding the butt of the rifle like a saber, I swung at the tentacle. Its flesh steamed and bubbled where I slashed it, and the tip of the tentacle curled up as the appendage pulled away from the ship.

I turned back to Ace and the captain, triumphant. "It doesn't like guns!" I repeated.

The captain blinked and shook his head. "Men!" He raised his rifle and approached the bow where more tentacles wrapped around the rail and threatened to break the ship. "Use the guns as swords!"

Taking hold of a rope reaching up to the mast, he jumped on the railing and demonstrated, sending another tentacle back below the water.

"Come on, we're not beaten yet!" he shouted.

With a loud cry, the sailors rushed the bow. Tentacles were beaten back, slowly releasing the ship one sucker at a time.

The sailors couldn't kill the demon, but they did force it to retreat to deeper water, sinking far enough that we couldn't see it.

We waited around the rail in silence, wary of a surprise return.

Five minutes passed, then ten.

It did not come back.

I melted with relief, body trembling with the leftover adrenaline.

"Mister Springer, get us out of here," the captain ordered.

A man towards the back of the ship jumped to attention, shouting more orders for sails to be lowered and the broken wood cleaned up.

Then the captain turned to me and Ace. "Now then. How did you two get on my ship, and what else do you know about that monster?"

My mind was blank. I had no believable answer for him, and the truth was out of the question.

190

Thankfully, these were the exact conditions Ace thrived in.

"We were stowaways, sir," Ace said. "Been on the run from the man controlling beasts like this for days."

The captain grimaced. It was unclear what part of Ace's lie bothered him more: the idea he'd had stowaways, or the idea of a man being able to control a monster like that.

"There are more beasts like that, then?" the captain asked.

"Yes," I said. "We don't know how many or where they are, but they're out there."

"And they're after the two of you?" he asked, hints of suspicion and disbelief starting to color his voice.

I shared a glance with Ace. "More or less."

He nodded and crossed his arms. "That's a lot of effort to track down two boys."

I did my best to control my face while I internally panicked. What should I tell him? How did I answer something like that?

"And the full story is none of your business," Ace stated. "If you could drop us off on the bank, we'll figure things out ourselves."

"Now hold on," the captain said. "If there are more creatures like that out there, we need to warn people how to fight them."

He wasn't wrong. That tentacle demon was a long way from the forest. How many others were wandering the kingdom? How many people would die because they didn't know their weakness?

Was that weakness even universal? What if it was unique to this demon alone?

"You can handle that while we keep ourselves alive," Ace said.

"Or we could all go to Chiari," I suggested, hope fluttering in the back of my mind. "The capitol is the best way to get news out fast."

The captain's face twisted and he looked over his ship. "Our main mast is broken. We need to repair that before sailing anywhere."

191

My hope did not get very far. "How long will that take?"

"Two or three days, depending on the nearest town and the supplies available."

Was it worth it to stay put for a few days if he could give us a ride to the capitol? Or were we better off trying to walk?

Ace looked to me to decide.

I was reasonably sure we could trust this ship not to try and attack the palace if they realized who I was, and having a ship full of people to help if another demon showed up sounded like a good idea. "Would it be possible for you to take us to Chiari, then, so we can warn people about the demons?"

He swayed his head from side to side. "We still need to deliver a shipment down south. The delay to fix the mast is already putting us behind a few days, we can't afford two more to go back up north."

"That's fine, we'll figure out our own ride," Ace said. "Just get us to land."

"I don't know how comfortable I am leaving two kids on their own with monsters hunting them," he said.

"We can handle ourselves," Ace said. "Don't lose sleep over us."

My face did not reflect the confidence that Ace felt at this proclamation. We'd barely survived the last few days on our own. We had no plan for shelter or dinner tonight, let alone for the next few days.

The captain raised a brow at us. "How about a compromise? You come with us to the nearest town, and I ensure you have a ride and protection back to the capitol?"

It would mean backtracking, but protection might be worth it.

I shared a look with Ace.

He shook his head. "We don't know if we can trust him. It could end up like the last captain."

The thought of Captain Ryan made my mood sour. Ace had a

point. I'd been too quick to trust Ryan, and we'd ended up in even more trouble.

"I think you boys misunderstand me," the captain said. "You leaving on your own isn't an option. Not when monsters like this are out hunting you. I'd never sleep at night if I didn't know you two were okay."

"Not our problem," Ace snapped.

"Well, unless you plan on swimming to shore, you're stuck on board until we dock regardless," the captain said.

Ace pressed his mouth shut and glared at the water behind us. Even if he did know how to swim, neither of us would risk it right now with that demon swimming about.

"Then we'll stay on board until you dock at the next town, and we'll revisit this discussion then," I suggested. "Does that sound fair to everyone?"

Whether or not it was fair didn't matter. It was the only option.

"Well, now that that's sorted. What are your names?" the captain asked.

"I'm…Jack, and this is Ace." I tripped over my introduction, so used to announcing myself with my title. It was better to keep that detail a secret, though, until we knew for sure this crew was trustworthy.

He nodded. "I'm Captain Lafiyet. Welcome to the *W.S. Ekonaor.*"

CHAPTER 29

The difference between Lafiyet's ship and Ryan's was like night and day. Ryan had been content to let me and Jack wander around as passengers, partially because I'd been sick, and partially to keep us from figuring out they were actually Chimers before we reached Chiari.

Lafiyet's belief was that you had to work to eat. Jack and I had to help clean up the broken rails and the fallen mast, saving what could still be used.

He treated us fairly, though, so I couldn't complain. And being surrounded by all the crewmen kept Jack from bothering me about his stupid Alex theory.

There was no way I'd used magic myself. I didn't have one of those fancy watches he carried, and I didn't have the first clue how magic worked. Jack had to have done the spell somehow.

Jack would only let me avoid this conversation for so long, though, and after we'd eaten our share of dinner and were sent up to scrub the deck with the cabin boy, he deliberately pushed me to the far side of the ship from the boy so we could talk while we worked.

"I can't believe I didn't think to have you try casting a spell yourself before, we could have answered this question days ago if we'd known!" Jack said.

I leaned my weight into the brush and scrubbed. "I'm not your brother."

"Yes, you are. You used magic, you have to be related to me somehow!" He was doing a lot more talking than scrubbing, and he was kneeling in a puddle.

"Says who?" I demanded. "Is Dr. Carl related to you?"

He frowned and put his head down. "I don't know. I have to ask Mother if she had a sibling I didn't know about, or a cousin or something."

I crawled forward on my knees and scrubbed at the deck. Thick sludge coated the wood from where the tentacles had dripped steaming flesh. "Or, maybe magic isn't that special. Maybe other people can use it, too."

He hummed and idly pushed his scrub brush back and forth over the same spot. "I don't think that's likely. If it were possible for another family to use magic, they would have done it by now, don't you think? Besides, we look too much alike."

"We do not," I disagreed. Not that I'd seen myself in a mirror that often, but I could guarantee my face wasn't as round as his. It was impossible to tell if our noses were the same since mine had been broken a few times, but our hair was definitely different.

"Do too," he chirped.

"Will you drop this, already?" I asked, scrubbing harder at the sludge. Now that it had dried, it did not want to come off the deck. "I didn't use magic, and I'm not your brother."

"Well, I didn't use magic, either, so how did you get away from the demon?" Jack demanded.

"I don't know," I admitted. "But I couldn't have done it. I don't know the first thing about using magic."

"A lot of magic is instinctual," he said. "If you want something badly enough, and can picture it clearly enough...then you can make it."

195

"Then I definitely don't have magic," I stated, scrubbing faster and faster. "Because I imagined full course dinners my entire life and it never appeared. I wanted a safe home, and a family that cared for me, and magic never did a damn thing." Bristles broke off the brush. "I had to work for every scrap I ever got."

My food was stolen or trash no one else wanted. My home was a collapsing house abandoned by everyone else. My family were a trio of kids society turned their backs on. If magic were that easy to use, I'd be living a completely different life.

Jack was quiet. "Sometimes I think that's the way you want it."

I whipped my head around to stare at him in open-mouthed shock. "What?"

He shrugged. "You have the perfect chance to jump into a royal family, where you'd be well taken care of and never have to worry again. But you won't even consider it. For some insane reason, you *want* to go back to living on the streets. You complain, but I think you like it."

I didn't even have a response to that. Of all the crazy things he'd ever said…how could he think I *liked* living like that? "You think I enjoy starving every day? Freezing in the winter and boiling in the summer?"

He looked down and started scrubbing at the deck. "I think part of you likes the thrill and the challenge. Maybe you never accidentally used magic to manifest a three-course meal because you were more interested in seeing if you could make your own dinner with your own hands."

His reasoning made a twisted kind of sense, and I hated that a little bit. "You're saying I made my life harder on purpose."

"Not on purpose," he corrected. "You didn't know magic was an option, so you thought your only choice was to put dinner on the table yourself. And you rose to that challenge. You're scarily good at it, actually."

"You have to be if you want to survive," I said.

196

He nodded. "I know. But you don't just survive. You thrive on the streets in a way most people can't. Anyone else in your position would be jumping at the chance to be considered a prince. Not you, though. You would actually prefer to go back to that life."

Of course I would. My friends were in that life. Everything I knew, everything I was. It was all waiting for me on the streets of Gallen, not in some palace in Chiari with people I'd never met.

"It's my life," I said, leaning back over the deck to scrub. "It's all I have, and you can't take that away from me."

With a heavy sigh, he gave up trying to convince me otherwise. We finished scrubbing the deck in silence.

The *Ekonaor* crawled through the river. The damage from the demon attack meant we couldn't sail at top speed, and it was going to take us all night to reach the next town. There weren't any extra beds, but some of the sailors handed over some extra blankets for us to curl up on the floor if we wanted.

I didn't want to risk more nightmares, so I didn't bother, choosing instead to spend the night on deck, leaning over the rail. Jack stayed below to try and sleep.

There were a few sailors out on deck to keep watch, mostly chatting with themselves up by the helm. They made no move to approach me, and I had no interest to talk to them.

I had enough thoughts circling in my head already.

Jack was wrong. I didn't want my life to be this hard all the time. Eventually, I wanted a real home I didn't have to fix every day, that didn't leak when it rained. A place I could store food for more than a couple days, so I wouldn't have to worry about where my next meal came from. I wanted a place where I'd be safe, and where my friends could be happy.

And if I could open that place up to other kids like me, that would be pretty great.

But this wasn't something I could have right now. I didn't have the money, and I was too well known in Gallen. No one would take me seriously if I tried to hold down a real job. So, all those dreams were shoved to the back of my mind while I worried about getting through the day.

I flexed my hand. My life would have been so easy with Jack's magic. I could have levitated wallets out of people's pockets, or just built a safe home for my friends and I. Magic could have made almost everything we did so much easier.

If I'd had it the whole time and never known…

Even just knowing a week ago, when I was back at the orphanage with Sara and Papa…

I clenched my fist. Jack's magic could have saved Sara. We could have transported out of the yard, or I could have fought Papa off better. Sara would have lived.

Sara would have lived.

I dug the heel of my hand into my eye. There was no way I had magic. I wouldn't be able to live with the knowledge that I could have saved her with it.

This whole thing was ridiculous. The sooner this little adventure was over and Jack was back in the palace while I went back to Base, the better.

CHAPTER 30

I didn't sleep much on the *Ekonaor*, and as far as I could tell, Ace didn't sleep at all.

We reached port early in the morning anyway, just after dawn, and Captain Lafiyet roused the whole crew to help with docking. Once the process was underway, he left the first mate in charge and turned to me and Ace again.

"Alright, boys. Looks like the *Ekonaor* will be docked here for two days to repair the mast."

That wasn't terrible, but it was time we could be using to travel home.

"Chiari is about a day's ride from here on the river," Lafiyet continued. "We find a quick skimmer in the next two hours, we can make it there by sunset. Find a place to spend the night, and then we can report that monster attack to the palace in the morning."

"With the right timing, you could be back here in two days, when repairs are done," I realized.

Lafiyet nodded. "Exactly. I trust my men to get the ship fixed up right. I don't trust you two to make it to Chiari on your own."

I scowled, unable to argue with his assessment. Ace and I hadn't exactly been making fantastic progress on our own. The number of times we'd almost died was concerning. It should be easier now

199

that we were closer, but somehow, I was more nervous about our chances. Especially when he'd barely talked to me since last night.

"Why can't you tell the guards here about the attack?" Ace asked. "Why do you have to come to Chiari with us?"

"I already sent a man with a message to the local guardhouse," Lafiyet said. "But if there are monsters all over the kingdom, we need the King's resources. I just hope the palace takes us seriously and grants us an audience quickly."

I nodded. This was exactly the kind of thing the air force would be good for. "We can go directly to the king, that won't be a problem."

"Won't be…what?" Lafiyet asked. "You're saying you can get in to see the king without a fuss?"

I blinked. "Oh, um."

Ace sighed. "His dad works at the palace. He can get in."

That wasn't a lie, but it felt like it was.

Lafiyet eyed us, slowly nodding. "Right. Well, then, there's no time to waste. Let's go find a skimmer willing to take us."

Ace and I followed after him, exploring each pier.

The docks thrived with activity, even this early in the morning. Cargo was loaded onto waiting ships. Fishermen inspected their nets and called for lazy crew members to hurry up.

I watched one ship toss ropes from the dock to the men on deck to cast off. Wind caught the sails, and it slowly pulled away from the pier.

Ace grabbed my sleeve and tugged me along. "Come on, Lafiyet is talking with someone."

Reluctantly, I turned away from the ship and scanned the docks again. Lafiyet was ahead of us, talking with a gruff older woman in front of a skimmer.

Skimmers were small boats meant more for racing than cargo, but they were often used to make small rush deliveries. This one

200

would barely fit the four of us, but it looked sturdy.

I peered at the little craft, trying to read the name painted on the bow. The morning sun cast it in shadow, though, and I couldn't make it out.

"I've already got a job today," the woman said.

"This is more important," Lafiyet insisted.

"Look, buddy, I ain't some pleasure ship for you and your brats."

"We're not looking for a joyride," Lafiyet argued. "It's imperative we get to Chiari as soon as possible."

The shadows on the side of the skimmer jumped. Ace and I both glanced over. Lafiyet and the new captain were too busy arguing to notice.

A gap formed in the middle of the shadow, a crescent moon on its side.

Or, a wide smile.

Ace swore.

"So, you see the grinning shadow, too?" I asked him.

"Yeah," he said, distracted. He was already scouting the docks. "Last time I saw one was a few days before I met Dr. Carl."

Ice ran down my back. "How did he find us?"

The shadow slid off the skimmer, onto the water, and then over the dock to join with a larger shadow at the entrance of the pier.

"Questions later," Ace said. "We need to go."

A good idea in theory, but the only thing behind us was the river and ships we couldn't sail by ourselves.

In front of us, Dr. Carl rose out of the shadow.

A passing sailor stopped in his tracks, eyeing Dr. Carl up and down. Blinking, he shook his head and kept walking, dismissing everything he'd just seen.

Dr. Carl stepped towards us.

Ace swore again and backed up. "Now what?"

"I don't know," I admitted. Should we fight? We were bound to start throwing spells, and I didn't think the whole port would ignore that as easily as the sailor dismissed Dr. Carl's arrival.

But there was nowhere to run, and Dr. Carl didn't look very chatty.

Lafiyet happened to glance at us and noticed our faces. Brows scrunching together, he followed our gazes and spotted Dr. Carl. "Is that the man responsible for the monsters?"

"Yes," Ace said with no hesitation.

Lafiyet drew his saber. "Then maybe we can end this right here."

"What are you doing?" the female captain asked.

Dr. Carl quirked a brow at Lafiyet and then waved his hand, sending both captains flying into the river.

I had flashbacks of Dr. Carl doing the same to Lucas, and my heart ached. Lucas had deserved so much better than that.

"No more games, children. You're coming with me," Dr. Carl said.

"Like hell," Ace snarled, grabbing onto my sleeve. "Get us out of here, Jack."

Dr. Carl lunged, shadows bursting out around his shoulders like extra arms to cage us in.

I hesitated.

If I transported us now, we'd end up who knew where in the kingdom. It could take us days to get back to the river again. We were so close to Chiari right now; I couldn't stand the thought of giving that up.

If I didn't, Dr. Carl would capture us.

"Jack!" Ace yelled.

Shadows cut off any escape route we might have had on foot.

There was no choice. I had to transport us. But maybe I didn't have to risk our progress.

I grabbed my watch and Ace's hand, focusing on a point on the docks beyond the pier, on the other side of Dr. Carl.

Wood blended into water, and sound warped and twisted around us. My stomach lurched as the world righted itself, ten feet over a pyramid of barrels.

"Why?" Ace demanded, right before we crashed into the barrels. Some went rolling down the docks. A few broke under us, spilling fruit all over the planks.

"Where the bloody hell did you come from?" a sailor asked, standing over us.

"Sorry," I said, getting up as fast as I could. I slipped on a pear and fell back down, squishing plums beneath me.

Lovely. The dirt and river water weren't bad enough, now I'd be covered in sticky juice, too.

Ace groaned and climbed to his feet. "I meant get us out of town!"

"I didn't want to risk getting lost again," I said.

"Because dealing with him is such a better option?" Ace asked, pointing at Dr. Carl running up the pier towards us.

"I imagined this being much quieter," I admitted. I hadn't anticipated crushing a bunch of barrels and causing a scene to immediately give away our location.

"Look at this mess!" the sailor said. "Who's going to pay for all this ruined fruit?"

I winced. "I'm really sorry—"

"Run!" Ace yelled. He grabbed my wrist to pull me away, weaving through the small crowd starting to gather.

"Seize them!" Dr. Carl yelled. "They're thieves!"

Ace swore, loudly and colorfully.

The next thing I knew, a bunch of hands reached out for us.

203

Sailors apparently really hated thieves. "He's lying!" I yelled, knocking aside someone's hand.

"They don't care," Ace said, ducking down and crawling through someone's legs. He let go of my wrist, and the separation sent panic down my throat. "Stay close!"

I tried to follow his route as best I could, but he bobbed and weaved through the men like a dance. Without breaking his stride, he jumped up on a barrel and over their heads, rolling when he hit the ground and popping back up like he'd never stopped.

There was no chance of me replicating his graceful stride. I wasn't nearly so agile or quick. The only way I could avoid capture was magic.

I didn't want to be obvious about using it, though, so I limited myself to my levitation spell, keeping people's hands just out of reach so I could slip by.

It was nerve wracking to work our way through the crowd. Even after we were through the worst of it and could flat out run, my heart beat over time.

"You can't run forever!" Dr. Carl yelled behind us, lost somewhere in the crowd.

"He's got a point," Ace turned back to me. "Where are we going?"

"Find somewhere quiet where we can catch our breath," I said, gasping for air. It didn't matter how big the stitch in my side grew, stopping wasn't an option.

There was a flash of green and gold, and then Ace made a sharp turn up a street. I skidded on the cobblestones to make the same turn, getting a glimpse of Dr. Carl coming up the street behind us fast.

I followed Ace down the street and around another corner. Away from the docks, the town wasn't so busy this early in the day. There wasn't anyone to avoid, no one jumping out to try and cut us off.

Ace turned down an alley, aiming for a stack of crates. He bounded up them like a set of stairs, jumping from the highest one and catching the edge of the roof above, effortlessly hauling himself up.

Stopping in front of the crates, I looked up at him in disbelief. He was skinnier than a twig, where did he hide the muscles to do that? I had no breath to call up to him and ask him to slow down, to tell him that I couldn't follow this kind of path.

His face peeked over the edge. "Just use your watch!"

Oh, that was a good idea. I used another levitation spell to join him on the roof, and not a moment too soon.

Once we were out of sight, Dr. Carl rounded the alleyway. He paused when he didn't find us, and shadows roamed over the walls ahead of him.

Ace tugged my arm, dragging me away from the edge. We carefully crept over the roof. He made it look easy, barely even checking where he put his feet. I almost lost my balance every other step, and every minor slip was another mini heart attack.

But we didn't see Dr. Carl again, or any of his shadow scouts. "The roof was a good idea," I told him.

He nodded, scanning the surrounding roofs to plan our next step. "People rarely think to look up."

It certainly wouldn't be my first guess. No matter how many times I watched him, I still didn't understand how he climbed up here.

The houses weren't all the same height, and we took a break on a lower house so we could lean against the siding of the house next to it.

"We'll lay low here for a while," Ace said, putting his hands behind his head and making himself comfortable.

I gave up on being comfortable days ago. "We should go find Lafiyet," I argued. "Maybe it's not too late for him to escort us to Chiari."

"Dr. Carl probably has those weird shadows looking for us all over the city," Ace said. "He knows we're close."

I frowned. "I still don't understand what he wants with us in the first place."

He shrugged. "Does it matter?"

"Kind of," I said. "What if he has accomplices? Or there's a huge scheme that involves us?"

"Then we don't get caught, and whatever he's planning won't work. Which, again, does not require knowing his master plan."

There wasn't any point arguing more about it, but I didn't agree with him. What if he wasn't the only one who wanted us?

And how badly did he want to capture us? What lengths was he willing to go to?

I hugged my knees to my chest. "The sooner we're home where he can't reach us, the better."

"Well, if you want to make it there, we need to be smart about this," Ace said.

Sighing, I put my head on my knees. "I know. Doesn't mean I have to like it."

He snorted. "Welcome to the real world."

CHAPTER 31

We stayed on the roof for a few more hours, until Jack's hunger forced us down to hunt down some food. He wasn't used to eating as little as I did some days, but he'd been pretty good at not complaining all the time.

He still wanted to go back to the docks, but that sounded like the worst possible place for us to go. Dr. Carl had to know we were trying to take a ship up the river. He'd be watching for us there.

We'd be better off risking Jack's transport spell. Even if we ended up lost again, it was better than being anywhere near Dr. Carl and his secret plans.

Jack refused to consider it, though.

A small, traitorous voice in my head whispered that I might be able to do it. There was a chance I'd done it before, so there was a chance I could do it again and force Jack to leave this port and go somewhere safe.

That voice was insane and I kicked it out of my head.

While Jack and I debated on our next move, I nabbed two newsboy caps for us, and slowly led him farther away from the river. He didn't seem to have any idea where we were in town, which made it easy to guide him where I wanted.

He didn't say anything about my pickpocketing along the way, either, too grateful for the bread and fruit it allowed us to buy.

We ate it all while we walked.

"Can't we get meat or something?" Jack asked.

"The only precooked meat is in the markets, and there are too many people around," I explained. "And we have no way of cooking uncooked meat."

Sighing, he accepted that and continued following me through the city. I didn't have a destination in mind, but I didn't want to sit still, either. So, we wandered as the sun rose higher and higher, eventually sinking again.

"You know, I used to love the days I could leave the palace and visit some random town," Jack said in the late afternoon, when dark clouds rolled over the sky. "I felt like I'd never see enough of a place before I had to go home."

"I'm guessing you've seen enough."

"I just want to go home," he said. "I'm tired, and hungry, and I feel like I'll never be clean again. My feet hurt, I'm cold, and I don't want to argue with you about every little thing anymore."

We stopped walking, and the first drops of rain started to fall.

He stared at the ground, lower lip trembling.

I rubbed the back of my neck. What could I tell him to make him feel better?

Everything would be okay? I couldn't promise that, and it would be nothing but words.

I couldn't tell him things could be worse, that never did anything to help anyone's mood.

There wasn't a way to fix anything, either. It was only early spring, so the weather was still chilly, and it would stay that way for weeks, yet. Food was an ongoing issue, and good sleep was hard to come by.

"What do you want to hear right now?" I finally asked.

"I want you to tell me we're doing everything possible to get home," he said, dragging his sleeve over his eyes.

"Of course we are," I said. "I'm not enjoying this anymore than you are."

"Then could you act like it?" he snapped, glaring at me.

"What does that mean?" I snapped back.

"You jump around like this is all normal, and you're...I don't know, it's like you're at home, out here." He gestured broadly to the town around us, nearly smacking a man in the face.

"This is normal, to me," I reminded him. "And yeah, maybe I've been excited that I can pickpocket so easily here, but that's only because no one recognizes me and I can get close enough to them. It's not like I want to live by hurting others. I just don't have a choice. Right now, neither do you."

"There has to be another way. Aren't there shelters?"

I laughed. Shelters were overcrowded and barely better than sleeping in the middle of the road.

"Please," Jack said. "Can't we go find one for the night?"

I crossed my arms. "It's not a pretty picture. You still want to see?"

He set his shoulders back and nodded.

Maybe it would be good to show him. "Alright, but we'll need to eat before we get there."

"Why? The whole point is they're supposed to have food for you," he said.

"You'll see."

I risked the busier markets so we could buy some meat pies, something a little more filling than fruit and bread. The slight drizzle had already sent a lot of people inside, so it wasn't as crowded as it could have been.

Then, I looked for a shelter. Most were attached to churches, which made them easy to find from the roofs. All churches had the same sun symbol at the top of a steepled roof.

We got there just before sunset. The church itself was clean, with freshly painted bricks. The shelter, on the other hand, had chipped bricks and a boarded-up window.

Jack frowned as we approached the shelter, clearly noting the differences.

A faded green door was propped open, and we stepped inside. A middle-aged woman greeted us beside a small desk, holding a journal and a fountain pen. She had dark brown hair pinned up neatly on her head, and soft brown eyes. A green bow was pinned to her dress.

"Welcome! My name is Julia. Are you looking for a place to stay?"

"Yes, if that's alright," Jack said.

"Of course! We never turn anyone away," Julia said. "We'll find room for you somewhere. What can I call you both?"

"Ace and Jack," I replied.

She wrote our names in her journal. "And are you boys hungry? Dinner isn't over yet if you'd like to grab something."

"We ate already," I said, stomping on Jack's foot to keep him quiet.

The meat pies had been good, but we could always use more food. This just wasn't the place.

Julia looked a little relieved as she wrote that down, too. "Alright, then. There should be some space for you in room number three. Odd numbers are on the right side of the hall. If you can't find space, find one of the workers, okay? They're wearing green bows like me."

"We will," I said.

"Good. The big doors all the way at the end is the community room. That's where everyone will be eating. Feel free to join them,

210

even if you don't eat."

"Thanks," I said, pushing Jack along.

This place made my skin crawl. It wasn't the orphanage, but anything where people and beds were crammed into a room reminded me of that place.

"What's that smell?" Jack whispered.

"Old building mixed with too many people," I responded just as quietly. We didn't know how thin these walls were or who could hear us and take offense.

Room three was a windowless room with bunk beds sticking out from the walls. From a quick glance, it looked like every bunk was already taken, but some bare floor on the far end of the room looked free.

"Come on," I said, leading Jack over to it.

The men in the bunks eyed us, some offering polite smiles and nods. A man missing a hand waved his wrist at us.

Jack flinched beside me, and the man hid the stump under his blanket.

That man wasn't the only one missing a limb. One curled up on his side near us was missing an eye, and half of his head was wrapped in heavy bandages.

Not all the injuries were visible, though. There was an older man near the door holding a gibberish conversation with his neighbor, who just smiled and nodded at anything the first one said.

Jack and I claimed the bare patch of floor and leaned back against the wall. "What happened to everyone?" he asked.

I shrugged. "Work accidents, probably."

He looked over the room in horror. "Work accidents? Are commoner jobs that unsafe?"

"Some of them," I said.

He opened and closed his mouth, but couldn't come up with

anything to say.

"Go talk to them," I said. "Find out their stories."

Determination settled over his face, and he climbed back up to his feet and approached the closest person, a middle-aged man with crutches beside his bed and an empty space where his left leg should be.

I crossed my arms and watched. Jack was going to learn about a whole new world.

CHAPTER 32

"Mind if I sit here?" I asked, gesturing to the edge of the man's bed.

He looked up from the book he'd been reading. "Why?"

"I wanted to ask you something," I said carefully. It was weird to ask for his life story, but I needed to know if Ace was right. Were all these people hurt at work? There were supposed to be regulations to prevent this sort of thing. Were they not enough? Were they too late?

"What?" the man asked, narrowing his eyes in suspicion.

"I just wanted to know what happened to you," I admitted. Lying was an art I hadn't mastered, and if the guy was going to be mad at me either way, I should at least be honest.

He raised a brow. "You want to know why I've only got one leg?"

"Yeah, and how you ended up here."

He shut his book, fire burning in his eyes.

Oh no, I definitely made him mad. Time to go. "Never mind, you don't have to tell me-"

"Sit down. I'll tell you how I lost my dang leg at the bloody steel mill."

He didn't wait for me to sit before launching into the bribes given to the safety inspectors so the outdated equipment in the mill didn't have to be replaced. Of how the old machines were finnicky on the best of days, and when he kicked one to start it up again, it released a burst of melted steel all over his leg. The burns had been bad enough, but then they were poorly treated and grew infected, until he had to either lose his leg or lose his life.

"Can't hold down a job when you can't stand," he said. "Can't pay bills without a job. Been here for months."

There was a gaping hole where my stomach used to be. "That's awful," I said.

A man across the room piped up. "You think that's bad? You should hear how I lost my hand at the logging factory!"

He launched into his own tale, which sparked someone else to rant about how they got hurt, and the chain continued with everyone trying to one up each other. I listened to every tale of bribes and faulty equipment with growing horror.

Was this what life outside the palace was really like? Were people really suffering this much?

I stumbled back to the spot Ace and I had claimed in a daze, sliding down against the wall until collapsing on the floor. My head spun. "How did this happen?" I asked.

None of this even touched on what happened to some of the men in here who didn't seem able to talk at all, who seemed to be living in their own little world. I didn't know how to approach any of them, and I wasn't sure I wanted to. What I'd already learned was bad enough.

Ace gave me a long look. "I tried to warn you. It's…hard, here."

No kidding. The room felt like an abyss of bad luck.

And this was just one room, in one shelter. How many people in the kingdom had similar stories?

From the way Ace had brought it up, I'd known it would be unpleasant. I still hadn't been prepared for how bad.

"There's one more thing you should see," Ace said, standing and holding out a hand.

I eyed his hand warily. "I'm not going to like what you show me, am I?"

He shook his head. "This is why we aren't eating here."

I inhaled and tried to find the motivation to take his hand and stand up. How much worse could this place get?

Ace waited patiently until I finally accepted his hand, and then he led me out back into the hall and to the large doors of the community room.

Long tables and benches filled the room. People were scattered among them, some in groups, some by themselves. Women with children shared plates of food between them. An older man spoon fed broth to an old woman with no teeth.

Ace bypassed the center of the room to where the serving tables were. Workers with green ribbons handed out rolls and bowls of soup that looked like nothing but broth. Small portions of some kind of grayish meat loaf were served with mushy corn.

I was very glad Ace made us eat before we came. Nothing on this table was appetizing, and seeing how many people were here, with no other options for food…it wouldn't be right to take any when we didn't have to.

"Is this all they have?" I asked.

"Yeah," Ace said. "Even getting this much is a struggle sometimes."

I shook my head. "This is all wrong. Why is it like this?"

"Because you palace people never come to places like this," he said. "You have no idea what the rest of us have to go through."

That had never been more obvious than right now. "I swear I'm going to change all this when we get back. Will you help me?"

He did a double-take. "What?"

"Help me fix this, make it right. You understand it all better than

215

I do."

He blinked. "Uh."

I genuinely wanted his help, but it also occurred to me that this could be another way to get my brother to willingly stick around the palace while he kept denying he was my brother.

"Think about it," I offered. "I'm going to go lie down and pretend I don't exist for the rest of the night."

He followed me back to our room. Two blankets had been left in the little bare floor we'd claimed for the night, and I thanked the room at large before taking one and hiding under it.

If this was the kind of shelter people had when there were no other options, it was no wonder they preferred to stay on the streets or turned to crime. No wonder they cried for revolution.

Ace's way of life made a lot more sense, too. He took care of himself and his friends so no one else had to. It might not be a good life, but it was his and he'd built it. I was starting to understand that a little more.

It was a long time before I was able to fall asleep.

Conversely, it felt like no time at all before someone kicked me awake, and I heard Ace gasping for air beside me.

He must have had another nightmare.

The room was dimmer, but some lights must stay on all night because I could see him sitting up and trembling.

"Ace?" I asked.

He jumped to his feet and hurried from the room without a word.

Groaning, I got up to follow him. I knew nightmares weren't his fault, but couldn't he at least stay inside when he woke up?

I dragged my hand over my face and chased him down the hall back to the front doors. Two men sat beside them like guards, quietly chatting, but they looked up when Ace barreled past them and slipped right out into the street.

"Wait, are you coming back?" one of them asked after him.

"Probably not," I said, even though it pained me to give up on sleep for the rest of the night. "We're Jack and Ace."

Nodding, they let me out to check on Ace.

For a second, I didn't see him.

My heart jumped into my throat. He could disappear on these streets and I'd never see him again. I'd be all alone out here, completely clueless to how anything worked.

Then I spotted him hauling himself up onto a roof down the block, and I let out a sigh of relief.

I used levitation to follow him up there again. He'd perched himself at the very top of the roof and sat down, looking up at the stars.

"So, is this just a thing with you?" I asked, taking a seat beside him. I yawned so hard my jaw popped.

"I'm sorry, go back inside," he said. Something in his voice sounded off. More fragile, almost.

Humming, I shook my head. "Already told them we wouldn't be back."

"This is my problem; you don't need to worry. I know you're tired, and it's cold out."

With the lack of sun, it was downright freezing out here, but I didn't bring it up. "I am exhausted," I corrected, and let my head fall onto his shoulder. It wasn't something I would have done if I'd been more awake, but he didn't react so I didn't move. "But we're in this together, and I'm not leaving you alone. I'm here if you want to talk about it. Or if you want a distraction, I can come up with something. Or if you want to sit in silence, that's fine, too."

He didn't say anything for a while, so I assumed he chose silence and let my eyes slip shut. It was too cold to worry about drifting to sleep and falling off the roof.

"Can you distract me?" he quietly asked.

"Sure." The first thing that came to my mind was Miranda, one of the noble girls around my age. We exchanged letters a lot, discussing everything from what we had for breakfast to politics. She would tell me about her garden, and I'd tell her about my fencing lessons with Lucas or my latest painting.

So, I told Ace about her, and then about some of the other noble kids, until the sun came up and the town started to wake and our stomachs growled.

"Thanks," Ace said.

"You're welcome," I replied. "Think we can find some breakfast?"

He nodded. "And then I'll find another steamcycle to steal."

Our ride with Lafiyet was probably long gone, so this was the next best thing. "Sounds good."

It would be slower than a skimmer on the river, but any progress was good progress, and I was learning that beggars couldn't be choosers.

CHAPTER 33

The last time I'd been this tired, it was because I'd been ridiculously sick. Granted, that was only a week ago, but I hadn't slept properly since then and it felt like Damon had latched onto every individual limb.

I couldn't sleep without dreaming of Sara, though. Waking up from those nightmares was worse than not sleeping at all.

Jack's distractions afterwards helped pull me out of my head, but I still wouldn't risk sleeping. It didn't matter how tired I was, I didn't want to have that nightmare again.

Better to keep moving, keep my thoughts elsewhere.

The steamcycle was easy to steal this time, and we blended in with morning traffic. I flew us back to the river, and then north over the banks.

Jack was tired, too, and didn't even blink at my reckless speed. He kept his face buried in my shoulder. If I couldn't feel how he tensed with every turn, I'd worry he'd fallen asleep.

He desperately needed it. As poorly as I'd been sleeping, he hadn't been faring much better, too busy trying to help me. Guilt threatened to eat away at me over that, too, but I tried to push him away every time. He chose to stay anyway. I didn't need him to calm me down, I'd manage if I had to. Just because he helped didn't mean

I'd be lost without him. So, if he wanted to lose sleep for no good reason, that was his decision.

A wind current pushed us to the side, out over the water. I adjusted until we were over land again. That demon wasn't surprising me a second time.

This was almost peaceful. We were the only steamcycle around. They weren't meant for long distances like this, and we'd have to land soon to refill the tank with fresh water once we burned through what we had. Most people preferred to fly over the roads, anyway, so the only other crafts we saw were larger airships flying well above our altitude.

That meant we more or less had the sky to ourselves. No guards chasing us, no shadows coming to life.

I could almost relax.

It was a weird feeling.

Sel's weight settling into my lap felt more normal.

I glanced down at the green fox. He licked a paw and washed his face. "Can I help you?" I asked.

"Hmm?" Jack hummed, lifting his face from my shoulder.

"Copper is very good metal," Sel said.

Jack flinched behind me, arms tightening around my stomach. "Where did you come from?"

We asked almost every time we saw Sel, but he never answered. Now was no different.

"Even bronze and brass are damaging, but copper is the best weapon," Sel said.

"Weapon?" I asked.

"Why are you giving us a metal lesson?" Jack peered over my shoulder.

Sel jumped onto the windshield of the cycle, blocking my sight. Good thing we weren't in town, or that would have been terrifying.

220

His grin stretched unnaturally across his face. "Why indeed, princeling? Why indeed?"

A bloodcurdling shriek below us sent birds fleeing to the sky around us.

Jack's arms tightened even more around my stomach.

"What the hell was that?" I demanded. My knowledge of wild animals was limited, since I'd never left the city before now, but that didn't sound like a normal animal.

"Please don't let that be what I think it was," Jack said.

"What will you do?" Sel asked. He jumped from the windshield to my head, and then up into the air, where he disappeared.

"That was weird, even for him," I said. "But what do you think that thing is?"

"It sounded like a demon I fought a few weeks ago. I killed that one by shooting a gun in its mouth."

"Not another demon," I groaned. "Are they actually targeting us? I was lying when I said that!"

"I don't know," Jack said.

Another screech pierced the air, this one closer.

"These woods aren't that small," Jack muttered. "We have to take care of it."

"Because that's worked so well for us in the past," I stated. "Let's just keep flying."

He tugged on my arm, causing the cycle to swerve. "People could get hurt. They could be killed. We're two of only a handful of people who know about these things."

"So let the other handful do something about it," I argued, straightening us out.

"I can't do that, Ace. I'll jump off the steamcycle if I have to."

And then I'd have a steamcycle to myself to get back to Gallen. "That's not the threat you think it is."

He muttered something I couldn't hear with the wind. "Would you just take us down lower?"

"Do you have a plan?" I demanded. "Can you make a gun to shoot in the thing's mouth?"

"No, I don't know them well enough to recreate them. If I knew why the rifles the other day were so effective, I could at least make the shape---wait, the copper!"

"What?"

"The copper was the weapon!" Jack said.

I blinked. "Did Sel infect you with some weird copper thing? What are you talking about?"

"No, he was giving us a hint!" Jack said. He pulled his arms back, and something glimmered behind me while he cast some spell.

"Copper was a hint?" I asked.

He took a second to answer, finishing whatever spell he'd been doing, now brandishing two long swords in gleaming copper. "He said copper is the best weapon. He must have meant against demons! The rifles weren't true copper, probably brass or bronze, which he said are also effective."

One of the swords was pushed into my hands. "Wait, I don't know how to use this!" I'd never held a sword in my life.

"I've only used rapiers before, but I think long side slashes will be more effective," Jack said. "Take us lower, we can beat this thing."

My head was spinning. Rapiers? Long slashes? I had no idea what he was talking about. And he thought we could beat this? "This is a terrible idea."

"No, we can do it," he insisted.

"You want us to willingly face off against a demon?" I clarified.

"Yes."

It was hard to argue with that confidence. "Alright. If this kills us, I'm murdering your ghost."

I brought us closer to the trees, but we didn't have to go far.

The demon met us in the air. Black wings gleamed in the sunlight, shining like polished metal. A long tail snaked through the air behind it, the end tipped in iron spikes. Six legs climbed the air currents like stepping stones. Its snout curled over iron teeth, and eight red eyes glared at us. There were horns on its head, talons on all six feet…even the tips of its wings were sharp and lethal.

Sweat loosened my grip on the sword. This was the thing Jack wanted to fight?

"Still want to do this?" I asked.

"I'm a little less enthusiastic, but yes, we can do this."

We were absolutely going to die.

But it was too late to try and run away. The demon came after us with another loud shriek.

I swerved to the side and pushed the altitude lever, causing us to drop rapidly. Flapping wings almost took our heads off.

The demon flipped in the air and took another swipe at our left side. Neither of us were left-handed, and the swords were on our right. Jack couldn't get his arm up over my head in time, and we leaned so far to the right we rolled the cycle through the air.

I dropped my sword altogether trying to get us back under control. "'Fight the demon,' he said, 'we can do it,' he said." I muttered under my breath while pulling and pushing levers, trying desperately to keep us from crashing. "Turns out he can lie!"

"New strategy," Jack said. "You pilot, I'll try and fight."

"You better do more than try!" I braked hard and yanked back on the steering wheel, almost accidentally throwing Jack off the back end, and the demon sailed past right in front of us. Its tail clipped the front end of the steamcycle, denting one of the pipes.

"Get me close to it," he said. He stood on the foot rests, left hand curled in the collar of my shirt to keep his balance.

"We're going to die," I stated, but did as he asked.

The demon made another pass. I dove under it, skimming the branches. Jack dragged the sword under its belly. The skin hissed and bubbled, and gold blood poured out.

"There, see, we can do this," Jack said.

Screeching, the demon twisted and dived for us, jaws snapping shut inches behind the tail pipes.

I swore and pushed down on the accelerator.

The next snap caught the tail pipe and ripped it free. We went spinning, and Jack got a good slash in on the demon's mouth while I fixed our flight and gained some more altitude.

"Could you do this a little faster?" I asked. A low whining noise vibrated through the cycle, and the side the tail pipe was ripped off of shook more than the other.

"You want to switch places?" Jack demanded.

"You don't know how to fly!" I snapped. Not to mention I had no desire to be any closer to this thing's teeth than I needed to be.

"Go left!" He pushed me left, jerking my hands to the side and forcing us to bank sharply.

We screamed and flipped, losing altitude. The demon's wing slashed over us. We felt the wind.

The highest branches of the forest brushed the bottom of the steamcycle. I was running out of room to duck these attacks. "I need your levitation spell again!"

Grunting, he batted aside the demon's tail. It sounded like a hammer and anvil from a blacksmith's forge. "A little busy!"

I pulled back on the altitude lever, getting the cycle as high as I could without his magic. There were a couple more clangs of metal, and Jack shifted around so much, I worried he'd fall off the cycle.

Anytime he called out a direction, I followed it, no questions asked. He was the one keeping an eye on the demon while I made sure we didn't plummet out of the sky, so if he said "Right!" I was

224

going right. He also called out directions to give himself an opening to strike back. Bleeding yellow slashes decorated the demon, now, but it wasn't any closer to slowing down.

"I thought you were going to kill it," I said.

"I'm trying," Jack said. "I can't cut it deep enough to really hurt it."

"Then make a bigger sword!" I yelled. He made that one, he could make a weapon better suited to this fight.

"I---wait, I have an idea," Jack said.

The cycle sputtered and we dropped a few feet. Swearing, I eased back the accelerator. We'd burned through almost all the water in the tank. "Whatever it is, do it fast!"

He hung onto my shoulder and twisted in his seat. Then, he hurled the sword back at the demon.

"Are you insane?" I demanded. That better not have been his only idea.

Jack didn't answer me.

And the sword didn't fall harmlessly to the trees below. It curved upward, stabbing the demon in the stomach.

Snarling, the demon curled inwards to protect itself and ripped the sword free.

It spun a few times in the air, and then came back up to pierce through one of its wings. Then, like a sewing needle, the sword flipped back over and made another hole in the demon's wing.

My mouth dropped.

"Can't believe I didn't think of this sooner," Jack muttered.

"I'm smacking you once we're back on the ground," I warned him. Now we didn't have to get so close to the demon for Jack to land any hits, and he was able to keep the thing back.

It was still slow going though. The demon was big, and even though Jack was able to stab some vital areas, it took a few minutes

225

before it finally started to lose altitude.

"Just die already!" Jack yelled, and sent the sword straight through the demon's mouth and up into its head.

It hovered in the air for a moment, and then the whole thing melted into black goop, raining on the trees below.

For a second, we held our breath, as if the demon might pull itself back together and attack again. Nothing happened, though. No roaring demon, no deadly wingbeats.

It was over.

Jack collapsed onto the seat behind me, panting. "That…takes care…of that."

I shook my head. "Alright then." My heart pounded in my chest, and my hands shook on the pilot wheel.

The cycle jerked again, dropping another few feet. This time, I couldn't coax it back up. My heartrate skyrocketed again.

"What are you doing?" Jack asked.

I pushed and pulled levers uselessly. "We're out of fuel, we're going down."

He clutched my shoulder. "We're way too high!"

No kidding. I threw my hands up. "What do you expect me to do about it?"

"I don't have any magic left!" he said.

How was he always out of magic when we were about to die? How did this keep happening?

The trees raced up to meet us. There was no way to control this landing in a way that wouldn't hurt.

Jack pulled back on my arm. "We need to teleport if we don't want to die."

"Then do it!" I yelled.

"I need your help!" he snapped. "Just don't overthink it and concentrate on anywhere but here!"

226

I could focus on being anywhere else with no problem. Falling to our deaths was the last place in the world I wanted to be right now. I would even rather be back with Dr. Carl and whatever crazy scheme he had. I'd rather be shipped off to the air force.

Mostly, I wanted to be home, in Gallen, with Jade, Malik, and Damon. They must be so worried about me.

Jack grabbed me and jumped off the cycle, letting it plummet towards the trees while that weightless feeling overtook us.

My gaze landed on an air ship in the distance just as the sky blurred around us.

CHAPTER 34

When the world settled around us, we were still falling.

We crashed into some kind of canvas sheet, and slid until falling through open air again. It was only a short fall this time before we landed on a solid wood floor.

Not a floor, I realized, feeling the vibrations under my hand. A deck. We'd transported right onto a ship.

It was too much to hope we'd found Captain Lafiyet again, but that didn't stop me from looking up in excitement.

The crewmen did look familiar. The few gathered on deck, working to repair a broken railing, stared slack jawed at us. One pointed up at the sails we'd come from, silent questions forming in his mouth.

"The brats are back," another one said.

The sailor beside him dropped the wooden beam. "Get them."

"Wait, hold on!" I said, throwing my hands up.

Beside me, Ace swore and scrambled to his feet.

The men rushed us. We kicked and punched, and Ace was slippery enough to keep squirming out of their grasp, but there was nowhere for him to go.

It didn't take long at all for both of us to be pinned to the deck.

If I were a different person, I'd be more offended that Ace had three men holding him down while it only took one to keep me in place.

A man walked up the deck towards us. All I could see were his boots, taking their sweet time to stop in front of us. He squatted to look in my face.

"King's beard," I swore.

It was a ship Ace and I had been on, alright. But it was Captain Ryan's ship.

Ryan grinned. "It's good to see you boys again, too. We were hoping we might catch you again, since we knew where you were heading."

I hadn't even considered that Ryan might come after us. I thought we'd knocked him out of the picture when we made his ship crash, but we must not have done as much damage as we thought.

"Let us go, you—" Ace's swearing was cut off by the sailor pressing his face into the deck.

Captain Ryan didn't even glance at him. "I do have one question, though."

Well, this ought to be good.

"How did you get on the ship?" he asked. "I know you weren't stowing away anywhere, and we're up too high for you to have randomly climbed aboard."

The blood rushed from my face. Of all the questions, that was one I couldn't answer. Even if I was any good at lying, what would be believable?

Ryan grinned. "Why don't I tell you what I think?"

"No one cares what you think," Ace spat.

Again, Ryan ignored him. "See, I heard an interesting story from Lord Basil. He says this whole kingdom used to be overflowing with magic, but these days only the royal family has any."

Who was Lord Basil? How did he know any of this?

Ryan pointed up at the sails. "You appearing just now? That pretty much confirms it. Even the way you survived the other day had to be because of magic, wasn't it?"

I didn't answer. I didn't have to.

Nodding, Ryan spit on the deck in front of my face. "Your pathetic family is even greedier than I thought you were. I can't wait until you're all dead and Lord Basil rules in your place. He promised to bring magic back to the kingdom for the rest of us, so we can all make our own lives a little easier. He won't hide it away like you do."

My head spun. It sounded like Lord Basil was some kind of leader to the Chimers. They planned to put him in charge once my family was out of the way. And he wanted to bring magic back to the kingdom. Was that even possible? Or was that an empty promise he'd made to get everyone to support him?

It didn't really matter. What mattered was that he knew about magic in the first place.

"Wait, wait, king's beard," Ace said. "They're talking about Dr. Carl. Jack! They're talking about Dr. Carl!"

My neck would have snapped if I'd been able to look back at him. "What?"

"Someone called him Lord Basil while I was there, he must use more than one name!" Ace said.

"So, you know him as a doctor," Ryan said. "Yes, he spends a lot of time offering his knowledge to the commoners who can't afford traditional doctors."

What a brilliant way to find his followers. He helps those most likely to already have a grudge against the king and recruits them, and word of him spreads through the lower class, far away from the palace ears. No wonder it felt like the Chimers rose out of nowhere. They built themselves in the poor parts of town no one wanted to look at.

230

This explained some of what Dr. Carl wanted with us, at least. He was part of the revolutionary efforts and probably wanted to ransom us against my parents.

I still didn't know if he really wanted to try and bring magic back, or if he could, but I'd worry about that later.

"Well, you don't need to worry about what to call him or what he plans to do," Ryan said, standing up again. "You'll be dead by the end of the week."

I sucked in a breath. They still planned to attack Chiari.

And if they had Dr. Carl and his magic on their side, they stood a stronger chance of succeeding than I wanted to admit.

"Lock them up!" Ryan ordered. "Separately."

Ace and I were dragged to our feet amidst the jeers of the men. I was tied to the mast where Ryan could keep an eye on me, and Ace was taken kicking and screaming below deck.

We'd been in a lot of close calls over the last few days. Even ten minutes ago was cutting it close.

But this? Tied to the mast with no magic and no Ace…this felt like the grimmest situation we'd been in.

And flying all the way up here meant there was no one coming to save us.

My arms went numb against the ropes after twenty minutes. I couldn't wiggle free or reach the knot, and I gave up on it pretty quickly. Someone had their eye on me at all times, and when I started squirming too much, a knife impaled the mast inches from my head.

Considering this was a moving ship, I was lucky they hadn't hit me. I resigned myself to waiting for a better opportunity. If I waited a few hours, claiming I needed a water closet might work. And by then, some of my magic would have recharged. I'd stand a better chance with that.

I just hoped Ace could hold out that long. They didn't seem to have any interest in him, which meant Dr. Carl—Basil, whatever his

231

name was— hadn't told them that the long-lost missing prince was also in the picture.

Whether or not Ace believed it, we only teleported to this ship because of his magic ability. I was wiped out after fighting that demon and couldn't have casted the simplest of levitation spells. But wherever he stored his energy, it was usable. It allowed me to cast the spell and fuel it with his magic instead of my own.

There was absolutely no doubt: Ace was Prince Alex.

This was going to be huge if we lived long enough to tell anyone about it.

Waiting for a better moment wasn't the most exciting thing in the world. Most of the sailors were content to ignore me, and the ones that seemed to have a personal grudge against my family were kept away. I assumed Captain Ryan wanted me presentable, or at the very least recognizable, when we arrived, and I was in rough enough shape as it was without anyone throwing any punches.

This didn't leave me with much in the way of entertainment, though, and I was so exhausted I fell asleep.

Not a deep sleep, and not for very long. My neck was at a weird angle and protested when I woke up. At this point, there wasn't a part of my body that wasn't uncomfortable for some reason.

But, as terrible as this situation was, we were that much closer to Chiari, to home. Returning as a captive wasn't exactly how I imagined seeing my parents again, but it was better than nothing. If I could time it right, maybe Ace and I could escape right before we arrived.

This meant more uncomfortable waiting. I had a coughing fit around dusk, and a sailor took pity on me and gave me a cup of water.

It helped a little, but it also awakened the hunger pangs in my stomach, which were becoming an old friend after so many days. Food, however, was not part of the sailor's generosity.

"Make sure Ace gets water, too, please," I asked when he turned away.

He glared back at me.

"I know you don't like me, but he's not royal." I winced saying it, since he technically was, even if I was the only one who knew it. "He got caught up in my mess." My face was doing something weird. I wanted to look earnest and pleading, but it probably looked more desperate than anything else.

Let this be the one lie in my life that anyone believes. Let me be able to do this one thing for Ace.

The man snorted and took a cup of water below deck.

I let out a sigh of relief.

That was the only exciting thing to happen for hours. I tried once to claim I needed a water closet, which got me untied from the mast and personally escorted to a bucket with a knife at my neck, and lost me my dignity when I then had to use the bucket.

Worse, the sailor noticed me toying with my watch on the way back, and snatched it from my grasp.

"Fancy heirloom?" he asked, opening the face. He held it out of my reach when I made a move for it.

My heart pounded. I needed that watch back. "Yes? And..." What could I tell him to make him think it was worthless? "And it's broken, so it's useless to you, so give it back, please?" I bit my lip.

He did not believe me. Pocketing the watch, he tied me to the mast again and brought it to the captain.

Ryan couldn't have known what it was, but he kept it anyway, taking whatever magic I'd stored up and leaving me defenseless.

I hoped Ace was having a better time.

CHAPTER 35

The ship had its own brig, and I was literally tossed through the air inside. Metal bars clanged shut, and keys jingled as the lock turned.

I was still trying to get my bearings. The brig was small, barely large enough for a grown man to lie down. A bucket in the corner was meant for any private needs, so the only reason anyone would unlock this cell door was if they wanted me for something.

I stood up and gripped the bars. I'd been thrown in cells before, when I was younger and not so good at avoiding the guards. Back then, I'd been small enough to slip through the bars when they weren't looking. Even now, depending on the cell, there was a good chance I could squeeze through.

These were too narrow even for me.

"Don't try anything," a sailor said, setting a chair down across from me and dropping into it. The keys dangled from his belt.

"I take it you're my watchdog?" I asked.

"For now," he said. "After the havoc you two caused last time, we're not taking any chances. Lord Basil wasn't too pleased when we asked him to come repair what you'd done, but we promised to catch you again to make up for it."

That explained why the man had been at that port town Jack

and I went to with Lafiyet. He'd already known we were in the area. Though, how they'd even contacted him was still a mystery.

"Look, we only did what we had to do," I said. "You want to kill Jack's family, of course he took it a little personally."

"Those royals would slaughter all of us without a second thought if we let them," the man snapped. "They don't care if we live or die, why should we care about them?"

"I get it," I said. "Believe me, I get it. I'm a street rat. I've fought and stolen for everything I've ever had. But there are a lot of other people that are going to die if you go through with this."

"I know," the man said, dropping his gaze to the floor. "But we can't bring about real change without doing this. That's just the price we have to pay."

I didn't know what else to say to try and make him change his mind. I wasn't good with words like that, not the way Jack was. My method involved a lot more shaking shoulders and slapping sense into them. With that off the table, my mind was coming up empty.

"Please, just let me go. I got caught up in this by mistake."

He snorted. "And where are you going to go? Going to jump overboard?"

That was a valid point.

"No, you're staying right there where you can't cause any harm."

With that, he crossed his arms and leaned his head back against the wall, settling in for a nap.

I made one attempt to squeeze through the bars anyway, and he pulled out a pistol and rested it across his thighs.

I gave up and sat down in my cell, trying to think of something else.

At least we were still on our way to Chiari. The circumstances might not be great, but we would ultimately get where we wanted to go. And maybe on the ship we wouldn't run into anymore demons. Or, if we did, Jack and I wouldn't have to deal with them. Hopefully.

Not likely, we were the only ones who knew how to fight them. Well, Jack did, and he was unable to keep his nose out of it.

I was just going to hope we didn't run into any at all.

Sliding back into a corner, I made myself comfortable and settled in to pass the time. I couldn't get out right now, but an opportunity always presented itself eventually. And if I was quiet and not causing problems, it usually meant whoever was watching me relaxed and let their guard down. I just needed to wait for that moment.

And have a plan by then, but I'd figure something out.

It would be super convenient if I did have magic like Jack right now. Then I could transport to the other side of the bars, or levitate the keys over here. Or I could have made the bars disappear altogether, or any number of other things. The possibilities were endless.

But magic was Jack's thing. The voice in the back of my mind whispering it might be mine, too, if Jack was right and I was his missing brother, could go back to wherever it came from.

I was nothing more than a half-starved street rat, with a handful of bizarre skills that were useless to most people. I couldn't even fit through these bars—

My eyes narrowed at the last bars, all the way to the side against the next cell. The gap was a little larger than the others. I might....

Yeah. I might be able to squeeze through there. All I needed now was something to distract my watchdog so I could try.

Until then, I settled in to wait. Exhaustion meant I dozed whether I wanted to or not, but it was a light, dreamless sleep.

Someone came down with water a few hours later, wordlessly passing it to me through the bars. They didn't have food, and I didn't ask for any. I did take the water, though, and then I went back to sitting quietly in the corner.

My watchdog traded shifts with another sailor, this one whittling away at a scrap of wood to keep himself busy.

"Where are Petra and Sammy?" I asked.

236

The crewman glanced up at me. "Stayed behind in the last town. Captain didn't want Sammy anywhere near the mess you two were going to cause us."

That was fair. At least they were okay. I'd been getting worried that they'd been hurt when the ship crashed since I hadn't seen them.

We didn't speak again for the rest of the night, not until the ship groaned around us and we were thrown forward.

"What was that?" I asked.

"We're slowing down," the sailor said, pocketing his knife and tossing the last splinters onto his little pile of shavings. "We must be over Chiari."

We were here.

"What happens now?" I asked.

"Now we find out how much a prince is worth to his soulless parents." The man grinned, all teeth.

I gripped the bars. I didn't like the King and Queen either. Most of the terrible things that happened in my life were a result of them somehow. But I couldn't help being offended on Jack's behalf. He talked about them like they were the best parents in the kingdom, like they were personally responsible for every good thing that existed.

And considering how disconnected Jack was from how everything in the kingdom worked, maybe his parents had the same problem. Maybe…maybe they just genuinely didn't know how bad it was, and once they did, they'd want to fix it.

It occurred to me that if I was Jack's missing brother, that meant his parents would be my parents.

My knuckles whitened around the bars. Pressure squeezed my chest until I couldn't breathe.

Parents.

I…might have parents.

And they might be the king and queen.

I physically shook myself. That was not a line of thinking I was at all ready for. The whole concept could go in a box and be thrown off this cursed ship.

Gunshots interrupted my thoughts. The man watching me jumped up and took a few steps towards the stairs, then glanced back at me and pulled a face.

"Go on, I'm not going anywhere," I said.

He did not leave, but his back was to me while he stayed ready for anyone who might wander down this far.

It would have to do. I crouched down next to the bars and pushed my head through. The act crushed my nose and my ears, and took a few seconds, but I managed and started wiggling my shoulders after.

My watchdog chose the wrong moment to look back at me. "Hey! You little—"

Panic flooding my body, I yanked myself back into the cell. Or, tried to, anyway. Getting my head out had been a careful procedure. I couldn't undo it recklessly, and not with a sailor about to stomp on my face.

He raised his boot, and I slammed my chin against the bars trying to yank my head out of the way.

Then…I didn't know what happened. One second, I was flailing on the floor, trying to not get crushed by this man's heel. The next, I was falling on top of him.

CHAPTER 36

I was given more water and some bread in the morning. It didn't even take the edge off my hunger, but I had a feeling complaining wouldn't go over well.

We were almost to Chiari. The sailors prepped for arrival by loading their rifles, sharpening sabers, and stashing extra weapons around the deck.

They were not anticipating a peaceful welcome.

The higher the sun rose, the more certain I was that people would get hurt today. Not just the crew on this ship, but whoever greeted us in Chiari. These men meant business.

Around mid-morning, Captain Ryan and the first mate joined the helmsman on the top deck. The ship slowed, and sailors scurried into the rigging to furl excess sails and protect them from stray gun fire.

Another hour, and sails from another ship rose beside us, flying a dark blue flag with my family crest in bright silver.

Ropes were sent across to connect the ships, and a gangplank set up across the rails. Ryan met the new captain and his first mate at the rail.

Ryan's first mate stood beside me, knife concealed in his vest but in easy reach.

The new captain carefully crossed the gangplank, keeping

hold of a rope from his ship while on the boards. "Good morning!" he greeted. He had a clean-shaven face and dark hair, and barely looked older than me. He and the rest of his crew all wore dark blue guard uniforms, but he had the gold trimmings on his shoulders to designate his rank.

I was surprised to recognize him. That was Captain Wilde, one of the youngest people to ever reach that rank at only twenty years old. I'd been with my father when he was awarded his first ship last year, the *W.S. Tachsif*.

"Morning, Captain," Ryan greeted. "What can I do for you?"

"I'm going to need you to adjust your navigation six degrees west; flying over the palace is prohibited," Wilde said, skipping any pleasantries this sort of thing normally required.

Did he know something was wrong already?

"Ah, I'd love to, but the palace is actually our destination," Ryan said. "I've got business with the king and queen."

Wilde's eyes narrowed. He hadn't looked around the ship yet, otherwise he'd have spotted me. Or had he noticed me before and wanted Ryan to think he hadn't?

"In that case," Wilde said, "you'll need to dock in the river and provide the proper forms."

"You don't understand," Ryan said, stepping back and drawing his pistol. With a sweeping gesture, he drew Wilde's eyes to me. "I need to go directly to the palace, and you're not going to stop me." He aimed the pistol at Wilde's face.

Wilde made eye contact with me, as calm and collected as he'd been the whole time. This turn of events hadn't surprised him even a little.

"I'll give you one chance to surrender now. There won't be another offer of mercy," Wilde said.

Ryan laughed. "I'm not the one who will need it."

Sighing, Wilde cocked his head. "Very well, then. Men! Secure the Prince!"

The man beside me drew his knife and stuck it under my chin.

It was shot out of his hand a moment later by a woman on the other ship, peeking over the rail at the stern.

With the direct threat to me handled, chaos erupted. Men from Wilde's ship threw their own lines and boarded Ryan's ship. The crew met them with steel and gunfire.

Wilde fought Ryan himself with a saber. He'd already cut Ryan's gun hand, and the pistol had fallen out of his grasp and been knocked aside.

Next to me, the first mate cursed and shook out his hand, drawing his saber to meet the man in dark blue racing towards us. It took three moves for the sailor to disarm the first mate, and then he slammed the hilt of his saber into the first mate's temple. The man crumpled to the ground, groaning.

"Your Highness," the sailor greeted, slicing through the ropes. He had dirty blond hair, and a goatee wrapping around his mouth. "Officer Havoc, at your service. I'm going to get you over to our ship."

I shook out my arms. "Thank you, but there's someone else we have to get first. He was taken below deck."

Havoc grimaced. "One of the others can get him, we need to get you somewhere safe."

"I'm not leaving without him," I stated.

Havoc's gaze caught something to the left, and then he pushed me down to the deck. A stray bullet sank into the mast. "Sir, I really insist you leave this ship immediately."

I pushed him off me. "Your orders are to protect the prince, right? Well guess what, there are two princes, and the second one is below deck!"

His mouth dropped open. "That's not…"

"Now are you going to help?" I asked.

Havoc threw his head back and sighed. "Fine. Stay low, stay close, and be quick."

I nodded and picked up the knife that had been shot out of the first mate's hand. It wasn't much, but against actual trained fighters, I didn't stand much of a chance anyway. Better to have a small, easier to use weapon than something that would get torn out of my grasp within seconds.

Sheathing his saber, he brandished a pistol in each hand and led the way to the stairs. Ryan's crew was still attempting to keep Wilde's men from boarding, and most of the fight was happening on the starboard rail. Only a few had scattered around the rest of the deck.

A man charged up the stairs. Havoc didn't hesitate before shooting him in the face.

I made a strangled wheezing sound.

"Don't look at the body," Havoc said, and after making sure no one else was coming, he guided me down the stairs ahead of him.

"Was that necessary?" I asked in a voice too high to be my own. How was he able to kill a man so easily? The kingdom wasn't at war, how would he have practice?

He pushed me along. "Now we know he won't be a threat. Do you know where they took…your brother?"

"I…no, I don't, but…" I glanced back at the body, but Havoc blocked my view.

"They've got to have a brig…it's usually the bottom level, come on."

We ran into a few more hiding crewmen, but the fight never lasted long. Havoc shot to kill, preventing most of the crewmen from even raising their swords in the first place.

When we reached the lowest level, there were sounds of fighting. A man swore, and then Ace burst into the hallway.

242

CHAPTER 37

I didn't know who was more surprised, me, or the guy I'd just flattened. We both cursed up a storm, and I rolled off him onto the floor, no longer locked in the brig.

The brig itself was still locked. The keys were still securely attached to the man's belt.

I had…transported out of the cell.

And there was no sign of Jack anywhere to blame it on.

That meant…

I swallowed.

Looked like I'd have to examine that mental box about my potential parents after all.

"How the *bloody hell*—" the man started, glancing between me and the bars.

Laughing, I bolted for the hall. The brig was located on the second lowest level of the ship with most of the cargo. Jack could be on any one of these levels, or all the way up on deck.

How was I going to find him and get us out of here without getting killed?

A hand wrapped around my arm and dragged me back. I spun with the movement and slammed my fist into his face. He grunted.

I swore loudly and shook out my hand.

"Nice try, kid," he said. Hefting me over his shoulder, he brought me back to the brig and fumbled with his keys.

"Come on, you don't want to be down here, either," I tried. "I won't tell if you won't."

The cell door squeaked open, and he tried to throw me in. I grabbed hold of his coat, and he stumbled in after me. His elbow knocked against my cheek, and we stumbled to the floor. Still swearing, he wrapped his hand around my arm.

I pulled out my wrench and whacked him in the face. It went much better than using my fist had. It also elicited a much louder swear. It did not, however, get him to release my arm. So, I hit him again.

"Son of a-"

I cut him off with another whack. "Let go!"

He caught the next hit and twisted the wrench out of my hands.

I let him take it and then reached down to bite the hand he had on my arm. He finally let go, and I ducked his attempt to hit me with the wrench and scrambled to my feet and out of the cell.

"Get back here!" he shouted.

I slammed the door behind me, but he was too close and caught it before it shut.

By the time he stepped around the door to chase me, I was already disappearing into the rest of the ship. "You little brat, get back here!"

Being chased by someone cursing my name was a familiar feeling. Unfortunately for me, he knew the ship better than I did. I ran down a row of cargo and around a corner, only to find him waiting for me at the other end.

And unfortunately for him, I was smaller, quicker, and more creative. I jumped onto a crate, ducking low because of the ceiling, and then threw myself off feet first right on his head. We crashed

244

to the floor in a pile of limbs again, and I rolled head over heels, popping back up and bursting out into the main hall again.

A man in a dark blue uniform almost shot my head off.

Jack screamed "No!" and latched onto his arm.

I blinked. Where had they come from?

The man chasing me stumbled out after me.

I turned, another swear on my lips, and then a gunshot deafened me.

The man behind me fell over sideways, a red hole in his temple.

Jaw on the floor, I looked at the man with Jack. Jack was still hanging off his arm, but the man had adjusted the angle of his wrist the make the shot.

Jack sighed and let his arm go. "Ace, this is Officer Havoc. Havoc, this is my brother, Ace."

The denial automatically rose in my throat, but…I couldn't deny it anymore. Not when I'd used magic myself, with Jack somewhere else entirely and unaware of what was happening.

Instead, I nodded. "Thanks for the help."

Jack brightened considerably, grinning like Sel.

Havoc reloaded his pistol, dumping the empty shells all over the floor. "Thank me when I get the two of you off this ship. Let's go."

If Jack trusted him, that was good enough for me. There wasn't time to second-guess everything. We both followed him without a word through the ship and up the stairs. Twice, he threw out a hand to stop us while he checked a blind corner, but most of the fighting seemed to be on the deck.

We paused at the bottom of the last staircase, gunshots and steel on steel ringing above us.

"Okay," Havoc said. "Our goal is to grab a line and get to the *Tachsif*. Most people should be distracted with their own fights, but we can't assume that means we'll be in the clear. I want you two to stay low and run as fast as you can to the rail."

It was a simple plan, but it still felt like there was too much that could go wrong.

"Ready?" Havoc asked.

Jack and I nodded.

Then the plan went wrong before it could even start. Someone from Ryan's crew stopped in front of the doorway and glanced down, giving us a double take. If it were me and Havoc, he probably wouldn't have cared.

But his eyes landed on Jack, the critical piece in their plan to attack the palace. "The prince is over here!" he yelled.

Havoc swore and fired up at him, but he only hit the man's shoulder. It wasn't enough to stop him or the two men who came running at his call. He fired again, hitting one of them in the leg, but then they started to fire back. We had to retreat down the hall and find cover.

"Now what?" I asked. We couldn't even get on deck to make a break for it to his ship.

"We can try and force our way through, but I don't like our chances," Havoc said.

"What about the other entrances to the deck?" Jack asked. "They pulled crates through the grates near the bow."

"They latch from the deck," Havoc explained. "And boosting you two up there would be too noticeable."

Jack and I could attempt to transport ourselves to his ship, but I wasn't confident about aiming that spell with other people, and when I went to suggest it to Jack, I noticed the chain for his watch was gone. It looked like that option wasn't on the table, either.

Well, if we couldn't fight our way through and we were trapped below deck, what else *could* we do?

Memories from our last trip aboard Ryan's ship came back to me.

There was a lot we could do down here, actually, especially with Havoc watching our backs.

"We'll sabotage the ship," I said. "They trapped us down here, but we can get to the engine room."

Jack nodded. "Yeah, that'll distract them long enough for us and Captain Wilde's men to get off while they try and save the ship."

"And how do you expect *us* to get off?" Havoc asked. "You'll send everyone running right to us."

"Uh…disguises?" Jack shrugged. "We can steal some clothes from the crew and make it look like we're one of them."

"We've done this before," I said. "We got off just fine then, we can do it again."

Granted, last time we had Jack's magic. But he'd managed to save us before when his watch had been depleted, so I was putting my faith in his ability to repeat that trick.

Footsteps ran down the stairs.

Havoc leaned around the doorway to shoot whoever came down. His aim was incredible, and both men that risked coming down landed in a pile at the base of the stairs. They did not move again.

I breathed in through my nose and forced myself not to look at them for long. My nightmares didn't need any extra fuel.

"Alright, we'll try it your way," Havoc said. He jerked his head back, keeping his gaze trained on the stairs. "Go."

This time I led the way through the ship. I'd lost my wrench, but Havoc and Jack had left a trail of bodies on their way to come get me, and all of them had their own pistols now going to waste. Without thinking too hard about it, I nabbed one.

"You know how to shoot that thing?" Havoc asked.

"I'm not aiming at people, I'm using it on the pipes," I said.

"Oh, good idea," Jack said. "That'll be much harder for them to fix."

I nodded and checked another corner. We didn't run into anyone until we found the engine room guarded by four of Ryan's men.

Havoc jumped in front of us, firing off four shots one after the other. The first crewman fell, but the rest had time to move out of the way. The worst they got were bullets in the arms.

When the crewmen raised their guns to return fire, Havoc elbowed us back around a doorway for cover. He would lean out to aim, but now that he'd lost the element of surprise, it wasn't going as well as his previous victories.

"We need to do something," Jack muttered.

"I'm open to suggestions," Havoc said. He didn't look back at us, too focused on the fire fight.

Ultimately, we needed to get past the guards to reach the engines. There would still be mechanics to get around, but with three of us, we stood a pretty good chance.

It was just getting past these guards that was the problem. Jack's magic would have been helpful; we could have levitated their guns or something to give Havoc an opening.

All I knew how to do was transport, and claiming I knew what I was doing was being generous.

It wasn't the first time I'd been forced to make do with next to nothing. The trick was figuring out the best way to use it.

I tugged on Jack's sleeve. "We can transport behind them."

He shook his head. "Ryan has my watch."

"I'll do it," I said.

He blinked. "What?"

"I did it earlier," I went on.

He cocked his head. "But you don't have a watch, where will you draw the magic from?"

I shrugged. "From wherever I did before, I guess." Now wasn't the time to get into the specifics of how magic worked.

He frowned and considered it.

Havoc leaned back and reloaded his pistol again. "You boys got a plan?"

"Not much of one," I admitted. "But I think I can give you an opening."

"We don't know it will work," Jack added.

A bullet scraped the doorframe next to Havoc.

Grimacing, he snapped the bullet chamber shut with a snap. "Something is better than nothing."

I took a deep breath. "Try not to shoot us."

He snapped his gaze towards us. "Wait, what are you doing?"

Grabbing Jack's arm, I summoned that weightless feeling, imagining us right behind the men in the hallway.

I didn't expect the spell to work, and finding myself in midair was a shock. That was nothing compared to everyone else's surprise, though.

It wasn't a long drop, so Jack and I landed on our feet. I sprang forward and tackled one of the men immediately. Havoc used the distraction to shoot the second one in the neck, and Jack flashed a knife that made the third stumble back. Havoc finished the remaining two off.

My stomach turned unpleasantly. I would definitely be having new nightmares after this.

Havoc helped me back to my feet and pushed us onwards. "I'm not going to ask questions right now, *but I have questions.*"

Jack winced. "That's fair."

I wasn't worried about whatever we chose to tell Havoc later. The priority at the moment was still to bring the ship down.

We were right outside the main engine room, and pipes lined the ceiling leading into it. Jack and I started damaging them while Havoc scouted ahead for the mechanics.

249

I used my stolen gun to shoot the pipes, sending jets of steam hissing into the air. Jack turned knobs until the pipes creaked and groaned. Once we'd done all we could, we followed Havoc into the engine room. Boilers and heavy machinery drowned out the sound of anything else. That made it terrifying to find a mechanic Havoc had already shot since we never heard the gunfire.

It also meant that we startled each other when we found one another again. Havoc nearly shot us, and we tripped over our own feet jumping back.

"Sorry," Havoc said, helping us both back up. He had to yell to be heard. "I took care of all the mechanics."

Then all we had to do now was break things.

CHAPTER 38

We knew we'd done all we could when all the machinery around us silenced at the same time. The ship shook under us, and then pitched forward.

"Get back on deck!" Havoc yelled, making sure we ran ahead of him.

The ship evened out again, but we were still descending way too fast. At most, the helmsman might have found a way to control the fall. This ship would still crash.

And we needed to be off before that happened.

"Officer Collins will keep the *Tachsif* even with this one as long as he can, and Wilde will be looking for us," Havoc said as we hurried up through the lower levels. "Most of this crew will be more worried about saving the ship or saving themselves to care about us."

He was right about that. We only ran into a handful of living crew members while we made our way back up to the deck, and none of them looked twice at us.

The deck was in a frenzy when we finally made it up there. Like Havoc expected, the *Tachsif* was in a controlled descent right along with us, the lines men had used to board Ryan's ship still flapping about wildly in the wind. Most of Wilde's men had gone back over, but Wilde stood on the rail of Ryan's ship, one hand looped around a line to get back to safety. His eyes found us right away.

Havoc pushed us towards him.

"Both of you get across, quickly," Wilde said, choosing to worry about Ace's presence later.

"You first," I nudged Ace ahead of me. He glared back and opened his mouth. "No time to argue! Go!"

With an exasperated sigh, he gave in and took the line Wilde offered him, barely even hesitating before swinging across to the *Tachsif*. A blonde woman greeted him on the other side and tossed the rope back to Wilde, who managed to catch it with ease. A weight attached to the bottom kept it from flapping wildly like the others.

"Your Highness." Wilde offered me the rope.

I took it and climbed up on the rail, and then made the mistake of looking down at the gap between the ships.

That was a long way to fall if I slipped or couldn't hang on.

"Come on, Jack!" Ace said, waving me over.

My palms were sweaty. I looped my hand around the rope to keep them from slipping, and then I told myself to be like Ace and jumped off the rail.

I was on the *Tachsif* in seconds, my stomach lost somewhere between the ships. Warm hands steadied my landing and pulled the rope out of my hands, tossing it back to Wilde and Havoc.

"Nice job," Ace said, leading me away from the rail to make room for the others.

Havoc landed on quick feet, and less than thirty seconds later, Wilde followed, shouting orders to cut the rest of the lines and get out of here.

Havoc and the blonde woman escorted us up to the top deck, each of them keeping a hand on us as the ship pitched and righted itself. Wilde joined us a minute later, one eye tracking Ryan's ship as it plummeted.

It was all Ryan's helmsman could do to keep the ship level. They were dropping fast, already three ship lengths below us.

"Think they can clear the Villa?" Havoc asked.

The bottom of my stomach dropped out. I leaped for the rail, peering over to see where the ship would crash.

We were on the fringe of the Villa, but the ship was dropping right over the last row of nobles' houses before the forest.

"Oh no, no no no no," I muttered.

If they could just sail another fifty feet west, they'd be over the forest. They wouldn't hurt anyone else in the crash.

Ace put a hand on my shoulder. "Tell me what to do. There's some kind of spell that will work, right?"

I took a deep breath to calm down and think. Explaining how levitation worked to Ace would be too complicated, and he wouldn't be able to control such a big target from so far away as a beginner. Not to mention, we didn't have that kind of time.

But I could channel his magic again, the way I'd transported us to Ryan's ship in the first place.

"Don't move," I said. He already had a hand on my shoulder, so using his magic to fuel my spell wasn't hard. It was the same principle as reaching for my watch, only I was using him instead.

Later, I'd ask Mom why Ace didn't need a watch. There wasn't time to worry about it now.

Moving the ship took a lot more mental focus. I wasn't used to levitating anything so big. But with a muttered curse and physically pushing my own hands into the open air, the ship finally shifted. It sailed over the trees of the forest, leaving the Villa safe from a direct impact. The force of the crash would probably still cause some damage to the houses, but some pictures falling off the wall was much more preferable than an airship landing on someone's roof.

"Nice job," Ace said.

Havoc squinted at the ship. "You did that, too?"

"Uh…" Logically, I knew we hadn't had much choice but to use magic in front of people. The consequences of doing so, however, hadn't quite sunk in, yet.

Mom was going to be furious with me.

"It's not later yet," Ace said, neatly dodging the conversation.

"But there will be questions," Wilde said behind me.

I flinched and turned to face him. "Thank you for saving us."

"It was an honor to be of service," he replied politely. His eyes cut across to Ace. "Who is your…friend?"

I glanced at Ace, raising an eyebrow.

Ace crossed his arms and nodded.

I grinned. "This is my brother, Prince Alex. He goes by Ace." I was grateful to whatever made Ace finally accept what I'd been trying to tell him all along. More than that, I was downright giddy to officially claim him as my brother.

Wilde's calm demeanor gave way to surprise and incredulity. "Prince…you mean…"

I nod. "Congratulations, Captain Wilde. You saved both missing princes today."

The tips of his ears reddened, and he cleared his throat. "Right, well. The job isn't over until you're both back at the palace."

"We would very much appreciate an official escort," I said. We could walk home from here, but after this last week, I didn't want to take any chances.

"That goes without saying," Wilde said. "Collins, find a place to land. Fuery, keep an eye on that ship and report any movement."

"Yes, sir!" both men echo.

I could have cried with relief at Wilde's promise to see this through to the end. We were practically there already. The palace lay ahead of us, peaceful in the late morning.

When Ryan's ship crashed in the forest, we heard it even up

254

here.

We also heard the demonic shrieks.

Ace and I froze.

That wasn't one demon. That had been multiple. And they were way too close to the Villa and the palace for my liking.

"What in the world was that?" the woman asked.

Fuery, a short man with glasses, paled at his position on the rail. "Sir? There are…creatures…attacking the ship."

We all lined up at the rail to look. Ryan's remaining crewmen were putting up a good fight, but they didn't know they needed copper. They didn't stand a chance against the five demons converging on the ship.

"We have to get down there," I said. There weren't many crewmen left to save, but I couldn't abandon them. And I couldn't let the demons roam free either. Not this close to so many people. There was another barrier around the Villa, but I didn't know if it was strong enough to keep demons out. I didn't want to find out.

"Absolutely not," Wilde said.

"We know what these creatures are, we know how to fight them," I argued.

"Then tell me," Wilde said. "But neither of you are going on the front lines again."

"Um, sir?" Fuery started. "One of the creatures can fly, and it's coming right at us."

I whirled back around. This one wasn't like the other flying one Ace and I faced. This one slithered through the air.

Ace swore loudly and backed up from the rail.

"Copper," I said, my mouth dry. "We need copper!"

"Why?" Havoc asked, already trying to shoot it.

"It's the only thing they're weak to." Once again, I reached for a watch that was no longer there. It was probably gone forever at this point.

"We don't just have copper lying around," the woman argued.

"We'd better find some," Havoc said.

"Your rifles are made with it," I told them. "You can use them as sabers." Well, they were made with bronze, but that was close enough.

The woman pulled her rifle around in surprise to look at it.

"That means we're going to have to let that thing get close." Wilde put a hand to his chin.

"It'll tear the ship apart," the woman agreed.

"You don't have a choice," Ace said.

Wilde frowned. "Collins, make an emergency landing. I'll pay off whoever's lawn we ruin."

"Yes, sir!" Collins replied, pushing a lever beside the wheel. Another man called out course directions so the ship wouldn't land on a tree or anyone's fence.

The demon streaked past us, hovering for a moment before diving at the deck.

"Scatter!" Wilde yelled.

His men leaped out of the way, giving the demon room. They fired at it immediately, but stopped when they realized bullets were useless.

"Eggert, try the rifle like they mentioned," Wilde ordered, finding his own rifle to test the theory with.

Eggert, the blonde woman, nodded and jumped into the fray. The demon was focused on officers at the bow of the ship, giving her and Wilde the chance to sneak up on it and slash their rifles on its tail.

Black flesh hissed and oozed. The demon screamed and whipped around to snap at them, fangs scraping the air inches away from them.

256

"I'll be damned," Havoc mumbled. "That's how we do this, huh?"

The rest of the crew picked up on the trick and started attacking, rushing the demon from behind and then dancing out of the way.

Ace and I were kept on the top deck with the helmsmen, out of the demon's range. Every now and then it would turn towards us and slither a little closer, but Wilde and his men kept it at bay.

By the time the ship landed in someone's backyard, the demon melted into a pile of goop.

"Alright, then," Havoc said, looking a little queasy.

"What about the others?" I asked, looking towards the woods.

"We'll handle them," Wilde said. "Havoc, get the boys to the palace. Collins, Fuery, stay with the ship. The rest of you, grab a rifle and follow me!"

It was the best option. I knew that, and I repeated that to myself multiple times as we climbed down a rope ladder and apologized to the butler of the household who came out to see what we were doing there.

I continued to repeat it, like some kind of mantra, when Wilde led most of his men towards the woods and Havoc led me and Ace to the street.

I decided I didn't care when I saw a demon lurking in the tree line, just on the other side of the barrier.

Brushing Ace's wrist, I made another copper saber and sprinted for the trees.

"Hey!" Ace yelled.

"Your Highness!" Havoc called.

They were both only a few steps behind me. If I hadn't surprised them and gotten a head start, they would have caught me long before I reached the tree line.

I had just enough of a lead that I crossed the barrier first, and the second I did, the demon lunged at me.

257

This one was twice my height, with long, spindly legs holding up a massive body. Antlers sprouted out from its head, and sharp fangs protruded from its muzzle. I dived forward between its front legs. The bush I dived into scratched up my face.

Hooves stamped the ground a foot from my head. I slashed at them with the copper sword, rolling out of the way when its back legs gave out. Pushing myself onto my knees, I plunged the sword into the demon's stomach.

It continued to thrash, and a stray hoof kicked my calf. I stabbed it again, and an antler nearly took my eye out.

"Slash the throat!" Havoc shouted.

I followed his instructions, and with a gurgling bleat, it dissolved into black goop.

We all let out a sigh of relief. That was two demons down. Three remained, still swarming Ryan's ship.

Ace held out a hand to help me up. "I thought we agreed I was the reckless one," he said.

I laughed and accepted his hand. "Guess you're rubbing off on me."

"Well stop doing that," Havoc said. "We're going to the palace."

I narrowed my eyes, tightening my grip around the hilt. There wasn't any leather wrapping to make it a comfortable grip; I hadn't thought of one when conjuring it on the fly.

Havoc pointed back to the street. "Go on."

"No," I said. "I'm not running from this. I won't be that kind of leader."

He scratched the back of his head. "Come on, don't make me carry you out of here."

I brandished my sword. "Try it."

"Jack, maybe we should listen to him," Ace said. "The trained fighters will be fine."

"Then checking on them won't be dangerous, will it?" I asked.

"I hate when you get like this," Ace muttered.

Havoc shook his head. "No. We are not doing this. No."

"Then you can stay here," I said, leveling the tip of my sword at his chest and stepping around him in the direction of the ship.

We could hear the shouting and the demons shrieking from here, and the occasional gunshot. Had anyone discovered they could shoot inside the creature's mouth, yet? I'd forgotten to mention it.

Groaning, Havoc turned to follow us. "The captain is going to court martial me for this."

"Not if I tell him not to," I picked up the pace. The underbrush wasn't that thick yet, which made it easy to navigate through. And the sounds of the fight were easy to follow.

We were there in less than a minute, watching on the fringes for now. Ryan's ship had listed on its side when it crashed, and not many of the crew were still on their feet.

There was one pile of black goop, which meant Wilde and his men had successfully beaten one of the demons. The remaining two, however, were barely even scratched. Dark blue uniforms dotted the forest, many of them unmoving.

One demon jumped around on its two back legs, five eyes able to keep track of everyone at once. It gnawed on someone's arm, simultaneously searching for its next victim.

The second one charged through a group of Wilde's men. It had a horn protruding from its nose, spikes along its back, and had legs as thick as tree trunks.

"I don't suppose you could make more of these copper swords?" Havoc asked. "Or maybe copper bullets?"

"Bullets would be good." I nodded. "Let me see one of yours?" He pulled out a cloth bag he kept his ammo in, and I scrutinized the shape of the bullet. "It's just going to be a solid thing of metal, is that okay?"

"Better than trying to get close to these things," Havoc said.

I couldn't disagree with that.

Ace wordlessly held out his hand, letting me draw magic through him again. I made a handful of bullets for Havoc, and then another handful for Ace. He still had the pistol he'd snatched earlier tucked in his waistband.

Havoc loaded his pistol. "Please, for my sanity, *stay here.*" He leaned around a tree to aim and fire.

Ace struggled to load his pistol, not as familiar with the mechanics as Havoc was, and we couldn't exactly ask him right now. His hands trembled, and his fingers slipped pushing the bullet into the proper hole. He swore and rubbed at his eyes.

"It's okay," I said, taking over and loading the gun for him. By all rights, I should be just as terrified as he was. But my hands were steady, like I'd surpassed the amount of terror I could feel in one day and circled back around to calm and rational.

"What happens when you overuse magic?" he asked.

The random question threw me. Now didn't really seem like a good time for a magic lesson. Except his shaking hands might not be from fear. "Uh, I get dizzy and have to rest, usually. Sometimes I throw up. That's why I don't go beyond what my watch lets me."

"Definitely dizzy," he muttered.

"Ah, king's beard, I'm sorry." That was my fault. I kept drawing from him like he was some new limitless supply, but he wasn't. He was new to this, and he probably couldn't even handle as much as I could, anyway.

"You might want to shoot," Ace said. "I don't think I can aim."

Guilt sank in my stomach. I finished loading the gun and snapped the chamber shut, taking a deep breath to settle my rising nerves.

The two-legged demon shrieked and dropped the dismembered arm, clutching at its gushing eye.

"Ha! Take that," Havoc crowed.

"Take the sword," I told Ace, nudging it towards him with my foot. It wouldn't be incredibly helpful if he couldn't see straight, but it was better than nothing.

I'd just have to destroy these last two demons before they could attack us. Then it wouldn't even matter.

Nodding to myself, I peeked out over the bushes we were hiding behind, took aim, and fired.

The shot missed terribly. I'd never claimed to be an excellent marksman, but I usually wasn't so awful. Nerves must have gotten to me.

Worse, both demons swiveled around to look at me like I was the only person here. Bypassing every person between us, the demons dashed in our direction.

"Oh, king's beard," I muttered, firing another round. I managed to hit the one with the horns, grazing its shoulder, but it didn't even slow down.

"Get out of here!" Havoc yelled, stepping in front of me and emptying his pistol into the demon. He shot out two eyes, and when it roared in pain, he got a lucky shot down its throat.

Still running, the demon broke down into black ooze, splashing the bushes in front of us.

One more demon down, one to go. And it was coming at us fast, bounding forward on its back legs, jumping straight over a man to get at us.

Havoc tossed aside his empty pistol. "Go!" he repeated.

I pushed my pistol into his hand. "We're not going to outrun it." Even if I wanted to run, it was too late at this point.

Gnashing his teeth, Havoc took my pistol and aimed.

The demon leaped over every shot, bounced off a tree, and crashed into Havoc from the side. He disappeared into the underbrush with a pained yell.

"Havoc!" I backed up, pushing Ace behind me.

The demon turned to us.

It wasn't our imagination, then. The demons really were targeting me and Ace. But why?

"Hey, ugly! Over here!" Wilde yelled, waving his arms to get the demon's attention. His crew followed his lead, making all kinds of noise to entice it.

The demon ignored all of them.

Ace put a hand on my shoulder. "Go find your watch," he said. "I'll keep it busy."

"You can barely stand," I argued.

"Then you'd better hurry," Ace said.

The demon lunged at us, teeth first.

We each dived to a different side. Ace rolled back onto his feet, only swaying a little when he put the sword in front of him. His grip was all wrong, his stance unsteady. There wasn't time to correct it.

"Let's do this," Ace said. He thrusted forward.

The demon batted the sword aside and then recoiled at the copper.

I hesitated behind the demon. Abandoning Ace didn't feel right, but I wasn't much use empty-handed, either.

"Go, Jack!" Ace yelled. He slashed the sword, movements clunky and child-like.

Amateur or not, the demon wasn't eager to touch the sword again. It growled and backed up.

"Find the stupid watch!" Ace yelled. He stumbled over the underbrush, barely staying on his feet.

"Hey, ugly!" Wilde yelled, racing up and slamming his rifle on the demon's head.

Eggert put herself in-between Ace and the demon, taking the sword from him before he hurt himself with it. She had a much better grip on it

Ace gave me another look.

I forced myself to nod and sprinted to Ryan's ship. Ryan had been on deck, so he should be easy to find...

"What are you doing?" one of Wilde's men asked.

"Where's the Captain?" I asked, scanning all the bodies.

"Uh...over here, I think, why?" He led me over towards the top deck. Ryan was on the ground several feet away, missing a few limbs now.

I didn't let myself think about what I was doing as I slammed onto my knees beside him and started digging through pockets.

Eggert cried out, and I whipped around to see her fall.

Wilde roared and jumped onto the demon's back, only to be torn off and thrown into a tree.

Ace retrieved the sword again just in time to fend off snapping teeth.

"Come on, come on," I muttered. My hands shook as I checked each pocket, finally closing around a familiar shape. "Yes!" I yanked it free and clicked open the cover, already back on my feet and running towards my brother.

The hand was at four. That wasn't a lot for a fight like this, so I'd have to be smart about what I did.

The demon bit down on Ace's sword and ripped it from his hands, tossing it aside and growling at him with yellow blood dripping from its mouth.

I created another sword as I ran and threw it as hard as I could, wrapping a levitation spell around it to control its landing.

It sank into the demon's throat, poking out the other side. The demon paused, coughing up more blood, and then sank into a puddle.

No one moved.

I let out a breath and dropped to my knees again. Ace backed up into a tree, leaning heavily against it.

263

"Is it over?" one of the crew asked.

"I think so," I said.

A man groaned, and Wilde pulled himself up on a low tree branch.

Energy rushed into me, and I scrambled to find Havoc. Blood leaked from a bad gash on his head, and his arm was twisted at an unnatural angle.

I gripped my watch and placed a hand on him. Mom hadn't been able to teach me a lot about healing, but I'd absorbed every word she had told me. Back then, I'd hoped to use the spells on Ace if I ever found him again, before I'd even known his name.

The gash on Havoc's head closed up, and his arm twisted back to something normal. He squeezed his eyes shut before opening them, still dazed and confused, but awake at least.

"Wha…"

"You're okay," I said.

He wasn't perfect, and he'd still need a professional doctor to look him over, but the worst of his injuries had been taken care of. I didn't want to use all of my magic on him, though.

There were more injured people, after all.

CHAPTER 39

Jack went around healing people until his watch was empty, which was long enough to get most men back on their feet.

The ones that could be saved, anyway.

There were no survivors from Ryan's crew. Between the fight in the sky, the crash, and then getting ambushed by multiple demons, every single one had been killed. The thought turned my stomach, and if I thought too long about it, I'd make myself sick.

At least Petra and Sammy hadn't been on this trip. They'd be heartbroken at the loss of Captain Ryan, but they'd be alive. I'd take what victories I could get, small as they were.

Of Wilde's crew, a handful had been killed by the demons. The surviving men carried them back to the *Tachsif*, lining them up on the ground beside the ship.

The owner of the mansion had some choice words to say about that, but in the face of Captain Wilde, bruised and bloody from his own injuries, and upset at the loss of his men, the owner backed down quickly and sent a maid to fetch extra sheets to cover the bodies.

Eggert was left in charge of the ship and the men, while Wilde and Havoc brought Jack and me to the palace.

We walked through the quiet streets of what Jack called the

Villa. Gigantic houses with even bigger lawns sat on either side of us, and I couldn't stop staring at how fancy they all looked. One of them had a marble statue in the front yard.

"We finally made it," Jack said, laughing a little bit. He ran his hands through his hair. He looked so different from the boy who'd first approached me in a rainy market. Greasy hair, dirt-smudged cheeks, torn and muddy clothes, and a certain look in his eyes that he didn't have before. More alert and watchful. Hungry.

"Don't say stuff like that," I said. "You're asking for something else to go wrong." I was more than ready for this little adventure to be over. I wanted a safe place to sleep for a few days, I wanted some solid meals, and I wanted to see my friends again. Not necessarily in that order.

He shook his head. "Nothing can get to us now that would delay us that long."

The lingering dizziness in my head begged to differ.

"Is now a good time to ask questions?" Havoc asked. "Because I have several."

"Agreed," Wilde said. "We'll start with those creatures we just fought."

Jack sighed. "They're called demons. I don't know how much I can tell you about them."

"And the…magic…you two were doing?" Havoc asked.

I could barely wrap my head around magic, let alone the idea of me using it. It was bizarre to hear someone else asking about the magic I'd used. It didn't sound real.

"That's a royal secret," Jack admitted. "So, um, you're now sworn to secrecy?"

Wilde snorted. "There's a little more to officially swearing secrecy than that," he said. "But we'll keep quiet."

"Thank you," Jack said. "I'll ask Mother how much we can tell you about all of this."

"So, your whole family has always been able to use magic?"

266

Havoc asked.

"Dad can't," Jack said.

"This is a new thing for me," I chimed in.

The addition did not seem to make Havoc feel better.

"And how did you two end up on that Chimer ship?" Wilde asked. "Are they the ones who kidnapped you?"

Jack and I both sighed. "It's a bit of a long story," Jack said. "Would you mind waiting until we meet with my-our-parents, so we only have to explain it once?"

I almost stopped walking.

Our parents.

I was going to have to think about that now. I had parents. Nice ones, presumably, who didn't just abandon me on the side of the road like I always thought.

Would they still be nice when they met me, though? I wasn't some perfect prince, like Jack. Would they try and turn me into that? Would they even let me see my friends again? Or would they claim they were beneath me now?

Or, in a worst-case scenario, would they deny that I was their son? I didn't want to be, but that was my choice. The thought of them rejecting me was so much worse. They probably had some idea of what their son would be like, and I doubt they pictured a thieving street rat when they wondered about Prince Alex.

A large wall loomed ahead of us, an iron gate barring our entrance to the palace beyond.

Jack perked up when he saw it and walked faster.

I slowed down, making Wilde bump into me.

"Come on, your Highness, no getting cold feet now."

Jack's title being used on me made my head spin. That was going to be a thing now. I was the Crown Prince's brother. I was a prince. That was…not possible. Even with all the evidence saying it was true, even though I was growing used to the idea of being Jack's brother, the idea of being a prince, of being royalty, was just too much.

"Hello!" Jack called at the gate.

A guardsman on the other side did a double take. "Y-your Highness?"

"Yeah, it's me," Jack said, beaming at him. "Could you open the gate for us?"

The guard dropped the keys in his haste to get the gate open, and continued staring open-mouthed as the four of us walked in.

"Thank you," Jack said.

"Your discretion is appreciated," Wilde added.

That startled the guard into closing his mouth and nodding, throwing us a quick salute when we moved on.

We were on a cobblestone path, neatly trimmed grass on either side. There was a stable on one side and a garage on the other.

In front of us, the palace reached for the sky. The walls were a creamy stone, dotted with large glass windows.

Jack had grown up here? He called a massive place like this home? It felt like all of Gallen could fit inside those walls with room to spare.

"Mom and Dad are probably both in separate meetings," Jack mumbled. "Should we clean up before we see them? Or just summon them to the dining room with lunch?"

My stomach growled at the mere thought of food, and Jack put a hand over his own.

"You're right, we'll have lunch first, and then we can bathe. And then I'm going to sleep for three days in a real bed."

This was actually happening. My mouth was dry, and my heart pounded in my chest.

"They're going to be so excited to see us," Jack said. "You especially. You don't even know how happy it will make them that you're alive."

If they even like me.

He led us inside the palace, hopping up the steps two at a time, and then waved down someone who's only job seemed to be standing near the door to greet people. "Would you mind having the cooks send a full lunch spread to the small dining room?"

The boy didn't look any older than us, and he had the same awestruck look on his face the guard at the gate had. Like they couldn't believe the missing prince was just going to waltz back into the palace like nothing had happened.

"And send someone to find the king and queen, let them know that's where I'll be."

The boy bowed. "Of course, right away, your Highness!"

"Thanks!" Jack said.

The boy rushed off to do as Jack said, pausing once at the start of a long hallway to look back. "Welcome back, sir."

Jack grinned and thanked him again. "It's good to be home. Come on, the dining room is this way."

I continued following him. It wasn't like I had any other choice at this point.

Nothing would ever be the same after this. My simple street rat life was probably over the moment I met Jack.

Now I was a prince, with a crazy revolutionist hunting me, and an actual family that might genuinely want me. Every one of those facts was crazier than the last, but somehow, that was my life.

I'd always been good at making do with what I had. This was the first time I'd ever felt that, maybe, just maybe, I'd been given too much.

Only one way to find out.

CHAPTER 40

I was downright giddy to be home again. In a few minutes I'd have real food, as much as I wanted, and I could hug my parents for hours.

And I could sleep in my own bed. And bathe. Gods, I'd never wanted a bath more. Against the pristine palace halls, I felt even grimier. The servants could probably smell us coming three rooms away.

I led Ace, Wilde, and Havoc to the small dining room and took my usual seat. "Have a seat wherever."

Ace chose to sit next to me, while the men sat across from us.

A servant rushed in with a tea cart loaded with fresh pastries, steaming tea, and pitchers of water. My mouth drooled. We hadn't had anything like a pastry all week, and my sweet tooth was screaming.

Even the water tasted amazing, cool and refreshing, nothing at all like the stagnant water from the barrel on Ryan's ship.

We devoured everything on the cart by the time another servant pushed in a cart full of sandwiches, fresh fruit, and bowls of nuts.

This, too, was eaten rather quickly. Ace and I had barely eaten in the last two days, and our meals before then had been spotty and unsatisfying. But this? Perfectly seasoned meats between fresh slices of bread slathered with sweet nutty spreads...I wasn't sure I'd ever loved a meal so much in my life.

Wilde and Havoc looked slightly concerned at the speed Ace and I were eating, but they chose not to say anything, sticking to their tea and waiting silently for my parents to finally arrive.

They burst in maybe twenty minutes later, pausing in the doorway to make eye contact with me. They looked as put together as ever, not a hair out of place, but there were dark circles under their eyes. Mom teared up right there.

This hadn't been an easy week for them, either.

"Mom, Dad!" I leapt from my chair, wiping the back of my hand across my mouth and meeting them halfway.

"Jack!" Two pairs of familiar, strong arms encircled me. These arms meant safety and home.

"Thank goodness you're alright," Dad said. "We've been worried sick about you."

Mom squeezed me a little tighter. "I thought I'd never see you again, oh Jack!"

"I missed you guys so much," I said. "I have so much to tell you."

"We want to hear everything," Dad said, pulling back and running a hand over my hair. He grimaced and rubbed his fingers together afterwards.

"I know, I'm a mess," I said. "I'll take a bath soon, but there are some people you need to meet."

They finally glanced at the other people in the room. "Yes, please introduce us to your...guests," Mom said, gaze lingering on Ace.

I stepped away from her and walked over to Ace.

He stood up, back stiff, and chin raised, with a hunted expression in his eyes. He looked ready to bolt at the slightest sign this could go wrong.

"Relax," I told him. "Mom, Dad, this is....actually, you might want to sit down first."

271

They glanced at me in surprise.

"I'm serious. It's going to be a shock, and it will be hard to believe, but I've already proven who he is."

Mom and Dad cautiously took seats at the other end of the table next to one another. "And who exactly is he?" Dad asked.

I couldn't quite hide my grin. "This is Alex, my brother."

They didn't react. The expressions on their faces slipped to their polite court masks.

I pressed on. "It's true, I promise you. He...well, it's hard to see right now under all the dirt, but he looks like Mom, and he can use magic!"

Mom's eyes sharpened immediately, cutting across to Wilde and Havoc. "Jackson!" she hissed.

"They already know," I said. "We had to use magic in front of them, it was the only way to save people. There were...so many demons, and there's another magician out there, he's actually leading the Chimers, and he promised them he'd bring magic back to the whole kingdom, and..." My head was spinning. There was so much to tell them, and I was trying to get it all out at once. I was only overwhelming myself, though, with each reminder of every horrible thing we'd had to face.

Dad scrutinized Ace. "Perhaps it would be best if you started at the beginning. What happened when you went to town a week ago?"

I sat down again, relaying everything from the last week in a much more linear order. Ace didn't contribute much, idly playing with a butter knife on the table.

I didn't leave any detail out, so it took a while to tell them everything. They processed in silence for several moments when I finally finished. And then they started asking questions.

And they didn't stop.

"You were really attacked by that many demons?" Dad asked.

"Where did this Lord Basil come from? How can he use magic?"

Mom asked.

"Are you boys alright now?" Dad pressed.

"If someone outside the family can use magic, then maybe this isn't actually Alex," Mom said.

Dad snorted. "Are we looking at the same kid? That's definitely your son. He has the same mouth as you."

The same shape, maybe, I thought to myself. But the similarities would end the second Ace started talking. He was far more foul-mouthed than my mother could even imagine.

Ace scowled. "Look, I'm not asking to be your kid. I'm here because some lunatic keeps trying to kidnap me. I don't know how I've used magic, since I don't have a fancy watch like Jack. So, we don't have to get all mushy over this. We deal with Basil, and then I'll be out of your hair, and everything will be the way it was."

I glanced at him, frowning, already trying to come up with ways to convince him to stay beyond that.

Mom and Dad didn't like his proclamation, either.

"Let's not be hasty," Dad said.

Someone knocked on the door, and then one of Dad's guards poked his head in. "Sorry to disturb you, your Majesty, but there's a disturbance at the gate. A man is demanding an audience with the entire royal family."

"Tell them to make an appointment like everyone else," Mom dismissed.

"They've tried, your Majesty," the guard said. "But he claims he has knowledge about Prince Alex."

All eyes snapped to Ace.

My mind started racing. There were very few people in the kingdom who knew Alex was still alive. Most of them were in this room.

The only one who wasn't was Lord Basil.

"I think I know who it is," I said. "And maybe we can finally get some answers."

Dad studied me for a long moment. "Very well, then. Bring the man into the audience chamber. And summon more guards, just to be safe."

"As you wish," the guard said, and ducked back into the hall.

We moved into the audience chamber. It was a large room with white marble floors and a glass ceiling to let in sunlight, with three thrones at the far end. My parents took two, and Ace and I couldn't agree who would take the last one so we ended up standing on either side of it. Wilde and Havoc stood nearby, and my parents' guards stood ready on both sides of the room.

Like Dad requested, more guards filed in to stand at attention against the walls.

It seemed overkill for one man, but when Lord Basil was escorted in, it didn't feel like enough.

"Your Majesties," Lord Basil said, inclining his head but refusing to bow. "I am known as Lord Basil."

"Welcome," Dad said. "My men say you claimed to have information about Prince Alex?"

"I do," Basil said. "As you're no doubt already aware, he is standing with his brother."

"And how do you know this?" Mom asked.

Basil grinned. There was nothing pleasant or charming about it. His smile sent shivers down my spine. "Because I can feel his magical energy from here. It's identical to the energy I felt fourteen years ago when I kidnapped him."

Mom and Dad were on their feet in an instant. The guards drew their sabers. Wilde and Havoc stepped in front of Ace and I.

Basil never flinched. Never stopped grinning.

"Why?" Mom demanded, her voice cracking on that one word. "Why would you kidnap an infant?"

"How dare you walk into this palace and brag about it," Dad added.

"I did it because I needed the blood of a magician to fertilize the mystical desert this kingdom has become. The list of people who fit that requirement is limited to four of us in this room."

King's beard, he really did have a way to bring magic back to the kingdom. It wasn't just some nonsense he'd told the Chimers to convince them to work for him.

"And I'm only here now because I still intend to revive this kingdom. But it would be better for all of you if you cooperated, so I'm offering you the chance to assist me willingly." His gaze lingered on me and Ace, like he'd already written off my parents.

"We will never cooperate with you," Mom stated. "You are a detestable man, and you will spend the rest of your pathetic life in jail before you are tried and executed for your crimes."

"Arrest him," Dad ordered.

The guards sprang forward.

Basil slipped into the shadows beneath his feet, reemerging in front of the doors. "Don't say I didn't warn you. You had your chance to do this peacefully."

The guards converged on him, but he vanished into the shadows again.

"Find him!" Dad yelled. "Do not let him leave this palace!"

Mom whirled on me and Ace, putting a hand on my shoulder and drawing Ace in for a hug. "Oh, Alex."

He squirmed out of her embrace. "I go by Ace, actually."

She blinked.

"We'll call you whatever you like," Dad said. "Just promise us not to disappear without a word."

Ace looked supremely uncomfortable, and did not actually make any promises.

275

Mom teared up and pulled him into another tight hug. "Oh, I can't believe you're really here!"

Ace's desperate eyes found mine, pleading for help.

"Uh, Mom? Maybe let him breathe?" I suggested.

She loosened her arms and then took a deep breath, and then she took an entire step back.

As bad as I smelled, Ace was worse. I had at least bathed before our whole adventure started. Who knew the last time Ace even touched soap?

"I think it's time you two cleaned up. I want four guards around you at all times until Basil is found."

"That's really unnecessary," Ace protested.

"Not negotiable," Mom said.

"It'll ease her peace of mind," I said. "It's not a big deal, I promise."

Ace glared at me, clearly disagreeing on many levels. But then we were shepherded out of the audience chamber. I went up to my rooms, and Ace was taken to a guest suite while servants started preparing a more permanent room for him across the hall from me.

Bathing had never felt more wonderful. Once all the dirt and grime was washed away and I smelled like a fresh flower field, I collapsed into my bed and slept all the way through dinner, nestled in my comfiest blankets.

By the time I woke up for breakfast the next morning, Basil hadn't been found. The whole palace had been searched top to bottom three times.

The question was, had Basil escaped the palace altogether, or was he lying in wait somewhere to use one of us like he'd threatened?

To Be Continued in Book 2:
A PRINCE'S GUIDE TO BROTHERS AND RITUALS

AUTHOR'S NOTE

Thank you so much for reading *The Street Rat's Guide to Spells and Royalty*. I hope you enjoyed it. If you have the time, I hope you're able to leave a review online and let others know what you thought of it. Reviews are important for Indie Authors. They help us promote our books and allow us to keep writing.

At the end of the day, we're happy as long as our readers are happy.

So, thank you again for reading this book, and I hope you'll stick around for the sequel!

Follow me on social media for updates!

Twitter: @bylrweltmann
Facebook: L.R. Weltmann
Lydiaweltmann.com

CPSIA information can be obtained
at www.ICGtesting.com
Printed in the USA
LVHW012116181022
731001LV00010B/259

9 798986 333649